# THE FIERCE AND BEAUTIFUL WORLD

## STORIES

Andrei Platonov

■

*Translated by*

JOSEPH BARNES

*Introduction by*

TATYANA TOLSTAYA

**NEW YORK REVIEW BOOKS**

*New York*

W0006328

THIS IS A NEW YORK REVIEW BOOK
PUBLISHED BY THE NEW YORK REVIEW OF BOOKS

THE FIERCE AND BEAUTIFUL WORLD

English translation copyright © 1970, 1969 by E. P. Dutton & Co., Inc.
Published by arrangement with Dutton Plume, a division of
Penguin Putnam, Inc.

Introduction copyright © 2000 by Tatyana Tolstaya
All rights reserved.

This edition published in 2000 in the United States of America by
The New York Review of Books
1755 Broadway
New York, NY 10019

1  3  5  7  9  10  8  6  4  2

Library of Congress Cataloging-in-Publication Data

Platonov, Andrei Platonovich, 1899–1951.
   [Short stories. English. Selections]
   The fierce and beautiful world / by Andrei Platonov ; introduction
by Tatyana Tolstoya.
      p.    cm.
   Translated by Joseph Barnes.
   Originally published: New York : E. P. Dutton, 1970.
   ISBN 0-94032-233-1 (pbk. : alk. paper)
   1. Platanov, Andreæ Platonovich, 1899-1951—Translations into
English. 2. Soviet Union—Social life and customs—Fiction. I. Title.
II. Tolstaia, Ta§iana, 1951–  III. Barnes, Joseph, 1907–1970.
PG3476.P543 A23 2000
891. 73'42 21—dc 21                                      99-046036

ISBN 0-940322-33-1

Printed in the United States of America on acid-free paper.
May 2000
www.nybooks.com

NEW YORK REVIEW BOOKS

CLASSICS

# THE FIERCE AND
# BEAUTIFUL WORLD

ANDREI PLATONOV (1899–1951), the son of a metalworker and the eldest of ten children, was born in a village near the Russian town of Voronezh. He began to publish poems and stories in the 1920s and worked as a land reclamation expert in central Russia, where he was a witness to the ravages of the Great Famine. In the 1930s Platonov fell into disfavor with the Soviet government, and his writing disappeared from sight. "Proletarian art," he wrote, "will be outrageous. We grow out of earth, out of all its dirt, and everything there is on earth is in us. . . . Out of our ugliness will grow the world's heart."

TATYANA TOLSTAYA is the author of two collections of short stories, *On the Golden Porch* and *Sleepwalker in a Fog*.

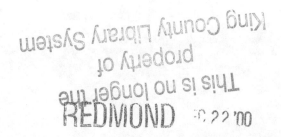

King County Library System
property of
This is no longer the
REDMOND

# CONTENTS

## INTRODUCTION

ANDREI PLATONOV IS an extraordinary writer, perhaps the most brilliant Russian writer of the twentieth century. In a sense he has no literary predecessors, and he is still little known to the Western reader, partly because of the extraordinary difficulty of translating his prose, and partly because he is not a "proper" writer, he is "different." Platonov never uses the formal elements of narrative—plot, character, denouement, conclusion—in a conventional way. He continually undermines the reader's expectations in the most bizarre manner. Reading a Platonov story, the reader encounters a range of sensations for which he has no sensory organ—and this organ may or may not develop in the process of reading.

"Woe to the people into whose language Andrei Platonov can be translated," Joseph Brodsky once said. What does this strange statement mean? The great difficulty of understanding Platonov arises from the fact that he created his own peculiar, unique language using only standard Russian, without resort to a single neologism.

In the story "Dzhan," for example, a poor young woman says to a man who has given her a great deal of money and many expensive gifts: "I will also soon give you presents. Wealth will soon arrive!" The translator renders the last sentence as "I'll be rich soon," but it means something entirely different. In Platonov's odd usage, wealth "will arrive," "will come," flowing out of the stream of time just as the future, the seasons and changes "will come," without human intervention, on their own. "Wealth," in Platonov's language and system of sensations, is just as much a part of Nature as the wind, spring, earthquakes, fate, time, and death. Even if one were to translate this sentence as "wealth will come," the English-language reader wouldn't sense the striking usage, wouldn't see it as a fragment of Platonov's unusual world.

Similar microdeviations from the norm, dislocations of meaning that suddenly reveal other ways of thinking and feeling, can be found in almost every paragraph of Platonov's prose, if not in every sentence. The linguistic shifts in the original are so distinctive and unique that it's possible that there is no adequate way to convey them in English (or French, or German). However, if these sorts of subtleties are lost in translation, other elements remain.

Platonov writes as though no one before him had ever written anything, as if he were the first person to take pen to paper. Things that are normally considered secondary often occupy a central place in his work, while "important" events are shunted off somewhere to the periphery. Characters who have no direct relationship to the narrative arise without evident necessity; on first (and even second) glance their role is unclear and they disappear without warning. Platonov's protagonist is energetically engaged in some important activity that consumes all his strength; then, a mistaken calculation, a blunder or a catastrophe destroys the fruits of his activity. He remains undeterred, however, and his life is not destroyed: like an ant, or a bee, he immediately begins to rebuild everything from the beginning, enriched by a new understanding of life, a new relationship to it.

At times it seems that Platonov's work was written by a creature from outer space forced to live among us. In his short novel *The Foundation Pit*, a story of collectivization and the impoverishment it brought, he wrote:

> From the age of twenty-five, Engineer Prushevsky had felt the restraint on his consciousness and the end to any further concept of life, as though a dark wall had arisen right up against his sensate mind. And since then he had been in anguish, moving about right next to that wall, and he comforted himself, thinking that in essence they had achieved the very median, true structure of the substance from which the world and people were combined. All essential science was located in front of the wall of his consciousness, and beyond the wall was only a boring place that there was no point in striving to reach. But still, he was curious—had anyone made it onward beyond the wall?
>
> In the distance, suspended and without salvation, shone a dim star, and it would never be any closer. Prushevsky gazed at it through the murky air, time was passing, and he couldn't decide: "Or should I perish?" Prushevsky couldn't see who would need him enough to definitely keep him going until his still far-off death. Instead of hope he had only patience left, and somewhere beyond the sequence of nights, beyond the gardens that withered, blossomed and perished anew, beyond encountered and passing people, there existed his time, when he'd have to lie down on his bed, turn his face to the wall and pass away, without having been able to cry.

Perhaps this is how a mythical beast would write if he were to assume human form—some nocturnal creature who hears with his legs, sees with closed eyes, and can smell a creature of the opposite sex a dozen miles away. He uses words awkwardly, incorrectly, he puts them in the wrong place in the sentence, where they don't go. Most important, he tries to convey some other kind or quality of soul with these words, another sense beyond the five familiar senses.

Andrei Platonov was born in 1899 in a small village not far from the town of Voronezh, into a large, poor, working-class family. He was the oldest son and he went to work at an early age in order to help his ten-member family survive. His parents died while he was still young. He worked as a train mechanic, an assistant foreman in a foundry, and as a journalist at a provincial newspaper. At the same time he began writing poetry, then prose. His youth coincided with the revolution of 1917 and the civil war that followed. The world as he had known it was destroyed in an overwhelming social cataclysm. The "destruction of the old world" and the "construction of the new world" with one's own hands were popular slogans of the era. If the first part of the agenda—destruction, the creation of chaos—was successful, the second part—construction —was a slow, tortured process.

New people rushed onto the scene, new classes that spoke in new voices. The new ideology basically negated the whole foundation of the known world—economics, psychology, law, education, even the laws of nature. The Bolsheviks promised that the new world built by the hands of the formerly oppressed classes would be one of complete and continuous happiness, an earthly paradise. Moreover, it was supposed that the Bolshevik party—the priestly caste—had some mystical knowledge of how to achieve this happiness. It is easy to see the influence of these ideas in Platonov's stories. The writer's interpretation of them, however, turned out to be so peculiar and unacceptable that Platonov was quickly pushed to the literary margins, and one can only speculate why he did not share the sad fate of many of his colleagues and was not arrested in the 1930s.

Platonov was hardly alone in his enthusiasm for construction, and his ideas did not spring solely from the new Communist ideology. In Russian circles in those years a certain kind of dreamer was common: a person obsessed with grandiose plans for reshaping life on earth and the world itself. Whether envisaging social changes (the creation of paradise on earth, a society of equality and abundance) or mastery of Nature's secrets—the Russian dreamer always thinks big. It won't do to make yourself and your family happy, you inevitably have to do it for all humanity. It's not enough to harness a stream or a horse to work for the common good, one must bridle the sun, the stars, the entire universe.

Characteristic of the Russian dreamer's mentality are impatience, a very particular sort of impracticality, a disdain for exactitude, and dismissal of details. How can you worry about details when humanity is faced with an urgent task— for instance, how to achieve instant immortality for all! A Westerner might choose to invent some modest, marvelously conceived gadget that actually works, and then organize mass production of a multitude of identical, marvelous, working gadgets. A Russian, on the other hand, consumed by a fever of grandiose, poorly thought out plans, will build something huge, ambitious, and unprecedented—which fails to work. The light bulb that Edison lit is still burning, but in Siberia, one "project of the century" after another lies in ruins. Thousands of miles of railroad lie rusty and overgrown with weeds: they built the railway, and only later realized it had nowhere to go and nothing to transport. The greatness of Russian thought lies not in its precision but in its scale, not in the details but in the strength, not in the realization but in the idea.

It is no accident that many of Platonov's early stories are about the construction of some giant electrical machine that is entirely inconceivable from the point of view of known physics and technology. With the aid of this device, which works off the energy of human will or thought, for example, one can turn the globe upside down, harness the energy of distant stars, knock a small planet into the sea and sink a ship, raise a huge wave in the ocean, or simply grow cucumbers year-round. This isn't "science fiction"—it's an entirely different genre. Platonov's leading characters take charge of such natural forces to their own detriment, and you'll find no normal plot and no moral in these strange texts, only the seething of words and dreams.

In the story "Fro," one of Platonov's best, the subject is, as always, the search for happiness, and here's what the married lovers talk about:

> ... Fedor listened to Fro, and then he explained to her in detail his own ideas and projects—about the transmission of electric energy without wires, by means of ionized air, about increasing the strength of all metals by processing their ultrasonic waves, about the stratosphere one hundred kilometers up in the sky where there exist special light, heat and electric conditions capable of guaranteeing eternal life to a man—this is why the dreams of the ancient world about heaven may now actually come true—and Fedor promised to think out and to accomplish many other things for Frosya's sake and at the same time for the sake of all the other people in the world.

Needless to say, Platonov does not put this "scientific" nonsense in Fedor's mouth in order to laugh at him. Apparently he himself believes in the possibility of such discoveries—well, if not precisely these, then similar ones. He believes in the power of human thought, which sooner or later will invent something unprecedented—and then happiness will reign, in the form of liberation from the torment of everyday labor. But at the same time he recognizes another kind of happiness as well:

> Frosya listened blissfully to her husband, half opening her already tired mouth. When they finished talking, they threw their arms around each other—they wanted to be happy right away, now, sooner than their future and zealous work would bring results in personal and in general happiness. The heart brooks no delay, it sickens, as if believing in nothing.

The mind believes but the heart doesn't; the mind can be directed toward the future, toward the submission of the universe, but the heart isn't interested; the Communists' plans are grandiose, but what does that matter to the simple human heart?

The central theme running through Platonov's work is the happiness of the mind and the happiness of the heart in their complex interaction; he studies what happiness really is, why and how it appears, where it goes, how to find and hold on to it. Even this theme the writer investigates as though he were not quite a human being but some other kind of creature. As he writes in *The Foundation Pit*:

> The disquieting sounds of sudden music gave feeling to conscience, they offered to preserve the span of life, to pass through the distances of hope to the very end and arrive at it, in order to find there the source of this

disturbing song and before death not to cry from the anguish of futility.

And:

He was more comfortable feeling bereavement on this terrestrial, extinguished star; alien and distant happiness provoked shame and alarm in him.

In 1922 Platonov wrote about himself in a letter to a publisher:

Besides the fields, the countryside, my mother, and the sound of bells ringing, I also loved—and the longer I live the more I love—steam engines, machines, shrill whistles, and sweaty work. I believed then that everything is man-made and nothing comes by itself; for a long time I thought they made children somewhere at the factory....
    ... There is some kind of link, some kinship, among burdocks and beggars, singing in the fields, electricity, a locomotive and its whistle, and earthquakes—there is the same birthmark on all of them and on some other things too.... Growing grass and working steam engines take the same kind of mechanics....

The world of Platonov's characters is a cosmic world, the world before (or simultaneous with) the appearance of God the Creator; the world of the soul, which seems to exist parallel with the Creator; the world of the spirit, which in some sense (for example in stubbornness and willpower) is equal to the Creator. The universe, as we know it, with its gravitation, molecules, hellish radiation, planets forming from lumps of star dust, and the blinding flash of suns burning at millions of degrees—this universe, according to Platonov, is in a state of constant becoming within each human soul. This is a universe where beast, grass, stone, electricity, and human beings—that is, all things animate and inanimate—are equal and indistinguishable in their foundation: they all exist. They are. They are incarnate. Moreover, incarnation continuously and incomprehensibly torments them. "Torment" is a key word for Platonov. Life, existence, being HERE is torment, anguish, albeit a creative, fruitful torment, a heroic anguish. Another key concept is "patience" or "endurance." One must live and be, one must endure. According to Platonov, one must not only endure grief, sorrow, need, and other forms of unpleasantness. One must endure happiness, love, and pleasure.

This is an entirely unique view of being, not merely a unique way of describing it. This is the way an angel of the upper heavenly circle might feel, if by some tragic accident or mistake he had been born among humans and had not yet forgotten the expanses of the otherworldly universe where he once flew in an increate whirl of magnetic fields, particles, and quarks. Life is the joy and torment of incarnation.

Platonov was published little during his lifetime, and the few stories that made it into print provoked invective from official critics. He was known only to a narrow circle of readers. Perhaps this is what saved him from arrest; his novels, *The Foundation Pit* and *Chevengur*, were considered shockingly anti-Soviet and were not published in the USSR until the very beginning of the 1990s. In the account of collectivization in *The Foundation Pit*, people are digging a foundation pit for a huge building in which all the inhabitants of a small town will live. They don't till the fields or sow their crops, they have nothing to eat; but they give themselves over entirely to heady dreams of the bright future that will soon arrive. And since only the poor are deserving of this bright future, everyone who owns anything at all is put on a raft and sent off down the river to the cold winter sea. Those people remaining gradually die of starvation. The theme is the same in *Chevengur*: people destroy everything in the name of an idea, in the name of the future.

The writer achieved fame only posthumously. He died in poverty, from tuberculosis, in 1951. In the last years of his life he lived in a janitor's room, ironically enough in the building of the Literary Institute. They say that he cleaned the courtyard, sweeping the yellow autumn leaves to one side. Hurrying to their classes in the morning, the students grew accustomed to seeing him and paid no attention to the coughing, middle-aged man. Some of them said that this eccentric also wrote stories.

In his youth Platonov wrote, "I know that I am one of the most insignificant of people. You have no doubt noticed this, but I also know another thing: the more insignificant a creature is, the more glad it is for life, because it is least deserving of it."

And further on, the mysterious words: "For you being a man is just a habit—for me it is joy, a holiday. . . ."

Whoever he may have been—let us be grateful that such creatures sometimes visit our world.

—TATYANA TOLSTAYA
*Translated from the Russian
by Jamey Gambrell*

THE FIERCE
AND BEAUTIFUL
WORLD

# DZHAN*

1

NAZAR CHAGATAYEV, a young man, not a Russian,
walked into the courtyard of the Moscow Institute of Economics. He looked wonderingly around him. He had been
walking through this courtyard for several years, it was here
his youth had gone, but he did not regret it. He had climbed
high now, high up the mountain of his own mind from which
could be seen all this summer world warmed by the setting
evening sun.

Patches of grass grew in the courtyard, a rubbish can stood
in one corner, farther back there was a dilapidated wooden shed,
and next to this lived a single old apple tree uncared for by anyone. Near this tree lay a stone weighing, probably, a half a ton,
brought from nobody knew where; still farther back the iron

---

*A *dzhan* is a soul looking for happiness, according to popular belief in Turkmenistan.

3

wheel of a nineteenth-century locomotive was half-buried in the ground.

The courtyard was empty. The young man sat down on the threshold of the shed, and pondered. In the office of the institute he had received confirmation of the acceptance of his thesis, and the diploma itself would be sent to him later by mail. He would not be coming back here any longer. He walked around all the useless things in the courtyard and touched them with his hand; for some reason, he wished that these things would remember him, and love him. But he didn't believe they would. From childhood memories he knew how strange and sad it is after a long absence to see a familiar place again, for these unmoving objects have no memory and do not recognize the stirrings of a stranger's heart.

An old garden grew behind the shed. They had set up tables, strung temporary lights, and arranged various decorations. The director of the institute had picked this date for an evening celebration of the graduation of Soviet economists and engineers. Nazar Chagatayev walked out of the courtyard of his institute to his dormitory, to rest and to change for the evening. He lay on his bed and unexpectedly fell asleep, with that sensation of sudden physical happiness which comes only to the young.

Later, in the evening, Chagatayev went back to the garden of the Institute of Economics. He had put on his good gray suit, saved through long years of study, and had shaved himself in front of a hand mirror. Everything he owned was either under his pillow or in the nightstand next to his bed. As he went out for the evening, Chagatayev looked with regret into the darkness of his cupboard; soon it would forget him, and the smell of Chagatayev's clothes and of his body would disappear forever from this wooden box.

The dormitory was lived in by students of other institutes, so Chagatayev went back to the institute alone. An orchestra invited from the movie theater was playing in the garden, the tables had been arranged in one long row, and above them were the bright lights that the electricians had wired between the trees. The summer night stood like a dome over the heads of those who had gathered for the celebration, to see each other for the last time, and all the fascination of this night was in the open, warm spaciousness, in the silence of the sky and of the garden.

The music played. The young people who were finishing at the institute sat at the tables, ready to go out into the land around them, to build their own happiness. The musician's violin died away like a voice fading away in the distance.

It seemed to Chagatayev that this was some person crying beyond the horizon—maybe in that country known to no one where he had once upon a time been born and where right now his mother either was living or had died.

"Gulchatai!" he said out loud.

"What's that?" his neighbor asked, a technologist.

"It doesn't mean anything," Chagatayev explained. "Gulchatai is my mother, and the word means a mountain flower. My people give themselves nicknames, when they're young and good. . . ."

The violin played again, its voice was not only complaining but also calling—to go away and not come back, because music always plays for victory, even when it is sad.

Soon the dancing started, with games and the usual festivities of young people. Chagatayev looked at the people, and into the world of night around them; he wished he could stay for a long time, working, and being happy.

A young woman Chagatayev did not know sat opposite him, her eyes shining with black light. She wore a blue dress cut high under her chin, like an old woman's dress, which gave her an awkward, sweet appearance. She was not dancing, either shy or not knowing how, and she looked at Chagatayev passionately. She was delighted by his round face, and its narrow,

5

black eyes which looked steadily back at her with kindness and reserve, by his broad chest which hid his heart with all its secret feelings, and by his soft mouth, capable of both crying and laughing. She did not hide her interest, and smiled at Chagatayev; he did not respond. The general gaiety grew steadily. The students—economists, planners, and engineers—took the flowers from the tables and picked plants from the garden, making presents out of them for their girl friends or just strewing the greenery on their thick hair. The woman who had been sitting across from Chagatayev was now happily dancing on the garden path which was littered with little pieces of different-colored paper.

Other women sitting at the tables were also made happy by the attentions of their friends, by nature all around them, and by this foretaste of their future, which seemed long and filled with hope of immortality. Only one woman was without either flowers or confetti on her head; no one leaned over her with joking words, and she was smiling wistfully to make it appear that she was taking part in the general celebration and that she belonged. Her eyes were sad and patient, like those of a big child whose feelings have been hurt. Sometimes she glanced shyly to one side, and then, convinced that no one wanted her, quickly swept up the flowers and colored paper from the chairs of her neighbors, and hid them furtively. Occasionally Chagatayev noticed this but couldn't understand it; he was already growing bored by the long celebration and was getting ready to leave. The woman who had been picking up the flowers dropped by other people also went off somewhere—the evening was running out, the stars had grown big, night was beginning. Chagatayev got up from his place and bowed to the comrades near him—he would not soon be seeing them again.

Chagatayev walked through the trees and he noticed the woman with the sad face hiding in the shadows; she did not see him, and she put the flowers and the ribbons on her hair and then walked back out of the trees to the lighted table. Chagatayev wanted to go back there: he wanted suddenly to topple over the tables, cut down the trees, and stop this enjoyment over which pitiful tears were being shed, but the woman was happy now, laughing, with a rose stuck in her dark hair, although her eyes were still red from crying. Chagatayev stayed in the garden; he walked up to her and introduced himself. She turned out to be a graduate student in the Chemistry Institute. He asked her to dance although he did not know how, but she danced excellently and led him in time to the music. Her eyes dried quickly, her face grew prettier, and her body, used to a shy fearfulness, pressed against him now with trust, filled with innocence, smelling good and warm like bread. With her Chagatayev forgot himself, ease and happiness poured out of this strange woman whom he would probably never meet again; this is how bliss often exists unnoticed right next to us.

The party and the gaiety went on until light began in the sky; then the garden emptied, only the plates and glasses were left, everyone departed. Chagatayev and his new friend Vera walked around Moscow, lighted up by dawn. The foreigner Chagatayev loved this city as his fatherland, and he was grateful that it was here that he had lived a long time, learned his science, and been fed and taken care of at no cost to him. He looked at his companion—her face had grown beautiful in the light from the sun rising far away.

The moment came when the sky was high and clean, the sun was strenuously and steadily sending its goodness—light —down to the earth. Vera walked in silence. Chagatayev glanced at her from time to time and was amazed that she could seem unattractive to everyone when even her modest quiet reminded him of the hush of grass, the loyalty of a familiar friend. He could see closely now the wrinkles of fatigue on her cheeks, her eyes deep under their eyelids, her full lips—all the mysterious arousing of this woman, all that was good and strong, hidden in this living human being. And he was timid with tenderness toward her and could not have done a thing against her, and he felt ashamed even to wonder if she was beautiful or not.

"I'm dead tired, for we haven't slept at all," Vera said; "let's say good-bye."

"Don't worry," Chagatayev answered. "I'm going away soon; let's be together a little longer."

They walked on farther, covering long streets, and at one spot they stopped.

"Here's where I live," Vera said and she pointed to a big building.

"Let's go to your place. You can lie down and rest, and I'll sit with you and then I'll go."

Vera stood still in embarrassment.

"Well, all right," she said, and she invited him in.

She had a big room with the usual furniture, but the room looked somehow sad, with its blinds pulled down, boring, and almost empty.

Vera took off her summer raincoat and Chagatayev noticed that she was heavier than she had seemed. Then Vera began to rummage around for something to feed her guest, while Chagatayev inspected an ancient double picture hanging over this woman's bed. It was the picture of a dream, when the earth was thought to be flat, and heaven close to it. A large man stood on the earth, punched a hole with his head in the dome of heaven and leaned out with his shoulders on the other side, into the strange infinity of that age, and looked into it. And he had looked for so long a time into that unknown, alien space that he had forgotten about the rest of his body, left below the ordinary sky. The same scene was painted in the other half of the picture, but with the rest of his body. The man's body was worn out, he had grown thin and, probably, died, and his withered head was rolling down in that other world—on the outside surface of the sky, which looked like a tin basin— the head of a seeker after a new infinity where there really is no end and from where there is no returning to the poor, flat place, the earth.

But all this now seemed to Chagatayev hateful and uninteresting. With a frightened heart, he put his arm around Vera as she stooped down near him to get something, and he drew her to himself strongly and carefully, as if he wanted to nestle as closely to her as he could, to warm himself and to grow calm again. Vera understood him right away, and did not push him off. She straightened up, held his head below her own, and began to caress his black, stiff hair, while she looked off to one side, turning her face away. Her tears dropped on to Chagatayev's head and dried there. Vera was crying quietly, trying not to change the expression on her face, so that she wouldn't sob.

"You see, I'm pregnant," she said.

"That's all right!" Chagatayev answered, forgiving her everything, as brave as a man condemned to death.

"No!" Vera said sadly, covering her face with the end of her sleeve to dry her eyes and hide her crying. "No. I can't do anything."

Chagatayev released her. It was enough for him just to be near her, to hold her hand, and ask her why she was crying— from grief or from outrage.

"My husband has just died," Vera said. "And it's so hard, you know, to forget the dead. The child, when he's born, will never see his father, and having only a mother will not be much for him. . . . Isn't that true, not much at all?"

"Not much," Chagatayev agreed. "Now I will be his father."

He embraced her, and they went to sleep while it was light, and the noise of building Moscow, of drilling into its depths, of citizens quarreling as they rode along the streets—all of this died away in their ears; they held each other in their arms, and each of them heard through sleep the toneless, gentle breathing of the other.

Toward evening, not long before the end of the working day in government institutions, they registered their marriage in the nearest marriage bureau. They stood between two large bouquets of flowers; the clerk in charge of the bureau congratulated them in a short speech, suggested that they kiss each other as a pledge of lifelong fidelity, and advised them to have many children so that the revolutionary generation might be extended into times eternal. Chagatayev kissed Vera twice, and said good-bye to the clerk in a friendly way while he thought to himself that it would have been good if the clerk had kissed Vera, too, and not limited himself to his professional duties.

Every evening after that day Chagatayev went to visit Vera, and she waited for him and was glad when he arrived. First, they embraced each other, Chagatayev holding Vera very carefully, protecting the child of the dead father. Then they would go out for a walk, arm in arm, along the streets, looking attentively at the store windows as if they were preparing to buy a great deal, studying the sky, and not overlooking any of the little things which took place around them, as if things were so hard for the heart in a time of loving that it had to be diverted constantly with trifles so it would not feel its heavy work.

But Chagatayev was not yet Vera's real husband; with tenderness and with terror she kept turning him away so as neither to offend him nor to surrender to him. It was as if she was afraid of destroying in passion her poor consolation, which had come so unexpectedly and strangely; or else she was simply being cunning, in a prudent, intelligent way, wanting to keep the heat from cooling in her husband so that she could warm herself from it for a long time and safely. But Chagatayev could not maintain his feeling for Vera on a spiritual attachment alone, and he sometimes wept over her when she was lying on the bed, appearing so helpless but smiling and unconquerable.

2

The summer ran on. The peat bogs around Moscow began to smolder in the heat, and in the evenings there was a smell of burning in the air mixed with the warm, steamy smell of distant collective farms and fields, as if everywhere in nature people were getting food ready for supper. Chagatayev passed his last days with Vera: he had received his work assignment; he was to go back to his birthplace, in the middle of the wilderness of Asia, where his mother was either living or long dead. Chagatayev had gone away as a small boy, fifteen years ago. His old mother, a Turkmen woman named Gulchatai, had placed a little hat on his head, put a piece of old, flat bread in his knapsack, added a biscuit baked of the ground-up roots of Asian reeds, and then put a thin reed cane in his hand so that a plant might walk along with him like his oldest friend, and ordered him to go.

"Be off, Nazar," she said, not wanting to see him dead by her side. "If you recognize your father, don't go near him. You'll see bazaars and riches in Kunya-Urgench, in Tashaouz, in Khiva—but don't you go there, keep going right on past, go far away to strangers. May your father be an unknown man."

The little Nazar did not want to leave his mother. He told her he was used to the idea of dying and he was no longer afraid he would have little to eat. But his mother drove him away.

"No," she said. "I'm already so weak that I can't love you. You live by yourself now. I will forget you."

Nazar, beside his mother, began to cry. He hugged her thin, cold leg, and stood there for a long time, clutching her weakened, familiar body; his small heart failed him then, it suddenly tired, and started to pound. The little boy sat down in the dust on the ground, and told his mother:

"I'll forget you, too. I don't love you either. You can't feed a little boy, and when you die you won't have anybody."

He lay face down and fell asleep in the dampness of his tears and his breathing. Nazar woke up in an empty place. His mother had gone. An insignificant, strange breeze was blowing out of the wilderness, without any fragrance and without any living sound. The little boy sat there quietly for some time, he ate his mother's piece of flat bread, looked around him, and thought some thought which now with age he had forgotten. In front of him was the land where he had been born, and where he wanted to live. That childhood country stood in the black shadow where the desert ended; there the desert drops away into a deep valley, as if preparing its own burial, and the flat hills, eroded by the dry wind, fence in the low place from the sky which covers Chagatayev's fatherland with darkness and quiet. Only the last light of the day breaks in there and throws a sad twilight on the sparse grass growing in the pale, salty ground, as if tears had dried on it but its grief had not gone away.

Nazar stood on the edge of the dark ground falling away below him; behind him began the sandy desert which was happier and lighter, and among the quiet little sand dunes, even in the stillness of that vanished day of childhood, a little wind was huddling, whining and wandering, driven there from far away. The boy listened to this wind and followed it with his eyes, trying to see it and to be joined with it, but he couldn't see anything, and then he started to yell. The wind fell away from him, and nothing answered. Night was falling in the distance; shadow had already dropped on the dark, low land which his mother had ordered him out of, and only a white smoke curled up from the nomad tents and the mud huts where the boy used to live. Nazar mistrustfully tried out his legs and his body: was he really still alive and on the earth, once no one remembered or loved him any longer? He had nothing even to think about now, as if he had been living on the strength and the desires of other people close to him, and now they no longer existed, they had driven him away.... A rough wandering bush called tumbleweed was rolling along the sand which stretched away before him. The plant was dusty, tired, hardly stirring after the hard labor of its life and its movement; it had nothing at all—no relatives, no close friends, and it was always traveling along. Nazar touched it with the flat of his hand, and he told it: "I'll go with you, I'm bored by myself. You think about me, and I'll do the same for you. I don't want to live with the others, they don't want me, let them all die!" And he shook the reed which was his walking stick threateningly at someone, probably at his mother who had abandoned him.

Nazar followed the tumbleweed and walked into the darkness. He lay down in the dark and fell asleep from weakness, touching the plant with his hand, so that it would stay with him. When he woke in the morning, he was suddenly frightened that the bush was no longer there: it had gone off alone during the night. Nazar wanted to cry, but then he saw the weed balanced on the top of a nearby sand dune, and the little boy caught up with it.

His fatherland and his mother had long since disappeared—let his heart forget them while it was growing up. On that day the wandering tumbleweed led Nazar to a shepherd, and the shepherd gave the little boy something to eat and to drink, and he tied the tumbleweed to a stick so that it could rest, too. For a long time Nazar followed the shepherd and lived with him, until snow fell; then his master let the shepherd go on some errand to Chardzhoui, because the shepherd was going blind, and the shepherd set off with the little boy, and in the city he turned him over to the Soviet authorities as someone not needed by anybody.

Many years went by, but nothing was forgotten, and

memories of his lost mother warmed his heart, as if childhood had never ended. Chagatayev had never known his father. A Russian soldier in the Khiva expeditionary force, Ivan Chagatayev was killed before Gulchatai had given birth to Nazar. She was then the young wife of Kochmat, by whom she had already had two children, but these children by Kochmat died while Nazar was still very young, and his mother told him about them only later, saying only that once upon a time they had been alive. Kochmat was poor, and much older than his wife. He lived by going to work on the Bey's lands in Kunya-Urgench and in Tashaouz, working in the fields so that at least in summertime he could give his family bread. And in wintertime he slept almost all the time in his mud hut, dug into one of the foothills of the Ust-Urt. He was saving up his failing strength, and Gulchatai lay there with him under the same cover; she also slept and dreamed through the long winters in order to eat less, and their children lay between them while they were still alive. Gulchatai went out occasionally, to get some plants to eat or to work as a farm girl in Khiva. One time she couldn't find any work in Khiva; it was winter and the rich people were drinking tea and eating mutton while the poor were waiting for the warmth to come, and for plants to start to grow. Gulchatai was huddling in a bazaar where she ate what she could find on the ground, left there by the traders, but she was ashamed to beg. It was at this Khiva bazaar that the soldier Ivan Chagatayev noticed her, and began to bring her every day a little of the soldiers' food in a pot. Gulchatai ate the soldiers' soup with beef in it in the evenings when the bazaar was deserted, and the soldier talked to her a little and then hugged her. It was against her woman's conscience to reject the man after the food he had given her, so she was silent and did not protest. She had been thinking: with what could she thank the Russian, and she had nothing except what nature had given her.

"Why do you have tears in your eyes?" Vera asked Chagatayev on the day of his departure for his own country.

"I was thinking of my mother, and how she used to smile at me when I was little."

"Well, how was that?"

Chagatayev was flustered.

"I don't remember. . . . She was happy for me and she was mourning me—people don't smile like that now. With her, tears ran down her happy face."

His mother had told Nazar that her husband, Kochmat, had not beaten her when he learned that Nazar was not his son but the son of a Russian soldier, nor had he become bitter at her, but just withdrawn and hostile to everybody. He went off by himself a great distance to catch his breath there from his sorrow; then he had come back and he had loved Gulchatai just as he had before.

Nazar Chagatayev went for a walk with Vera for the last time. That evening a train would take him to Asia. Vera had already fixed everything for his long trip: she had darned his socks, sewed on all his buttons, she had ironed his linen herself, and she tried out and tested all his things several times, caressing them and envying them because they were going away with her husband.

On the street Vera asked Chagatayev to go with her to a friend's house. Maybe in a half hour's time he would stop loving her forever.

They walked into a big apartment. Vera introduced her husband to an old woman and asked her:

"What's Ksenya doing? Is she home, or somewhere else?"

"She's home, she's home. She just came in," the housekeeper said.

A black-haired girl between thirteen and fifteen was sitting in a big, disordered room. She was reading a book, and twisting the end of her braided hair in her hand.

"Mama!" the girl shouted in delight to her mother as she walked in.

"Hello, Ksenya," Vera said. "This is my daughter," and she introduced the girl to Chagatayev.

Chagatayev shook her strange hand, childlike and feminine; the hand was sticky and dirty, because children do not learn cleanliness right away.

Ksenya smiled. She did not look like her mother—she had the regular face of a young person, a little sad and pale from the fatigue of growing. Her eyes had different colors—one was black, the other blue—which gave her whole face a meek expression, as if Chagatayev were looking at some regrettable and delicate abnormality. Only her mouth spoiled Ksenya—it had already grown thick, the lips were full, as if they were always thirsty for drink, and it was as if some strong, destructive plant were bursting through the innocent silence of her skin.

All of them were silent in the ill-defined situation, although Ksenya had already guessed what it was all about.

"Do you live here?" Chagatayev asked the girl.

"Yes, with my papa's mother," Ksenya said.

"And where is your papa, is he dead?"

Vera was at one side, looking out of the window at Moscow. Ksenya laughed.

"No, what are you saying! My papa is young, he's living in the Far East, and he builds bridges. He has already built two."

"Big bridges?" Chagatayev asked.

"Big ones ... One of them is a suspension bridge, another with two supporting piers and with sunken caissons, they've disappeared forever, they're lost!" Ksenya said happily. "I've got photographs of it from the newspaper."

"And does your papa love you?"

"No, he loves some strangers, he doesn't want to love Mama and me."

They talked some more: Chagatayev felt a confused regret

inside his heart; he sat there with the light, sad feeling of being asleep, or traveling somewhere. Forgetting ordinary life, he took Ksenya's hand in his, and held it, not letting go.

Ksenya sat there in terror and amazement, her different-colored eyes looked out poignantly, like two people who are very close but do not know each other. Her mother, Vera, stood apart, quietly smiling at her daughter and her husband.

"Isn't it time for you to go to the station?" she asked.

"No, I'm not going today," Chagatayev said. He felt an attachment to Ksenya, a feeling of human kinship and of anxiety about what would be best for her. He wanted to be a protecting strength for her, a father, and an eternal memory in her heart.

Excusing himself, Chagatayev went out for a half hour, bought various things at Mostorg, and brought them back as presents for Ksenya. If he hadn't done this, he would have regretted it for a long time.

Ksenya was delighted by the presents, but not her mother.

"Ksenya has only two dresses, and her last shoes have gone to pieces," Vera said. "For her father doesn't send us a thing, and I have only just started to work. . . . Why did you buy all this nonsense? What need does a girl have for expensive perfume, or a suede bag, or some kind of gay-colored bedspread?"

"Now, Mama, never mind, let it go!" Ksenya said. "They'll give me a dress for free at the children's theater, I'm an activist there, and the Young Pioneers will be giving out mountain-climbing boots soon, so I won't need shoes. Let me keep the bag and the bedspread."

"It all makes no sense," Vera complained. "And he needs the money himself, he has a long way to go."

"I've got enough," Chagatayev said. He took out four hundred rubles more, and left them for Ksenya's board.

The girl walked up to him. She thanked Chagatayev, holding her hand out to him, and she said:

"I'll soon be able to give you presents. I'll be rich soon!"

Chagatayev kissed her, and said good-bye.

"Nazar, do you love me anymore?" Vera said when they were out on the street. "Let's go and get a divorce, before you've gone away.... You saw—Ksenya's my daughter, you're the third one for me, and I'm thirty-four years old."

Vera fell silent. Nazar Chagatayev was amazed.

"Why don't I love you? Didn't you love those other men?"

"I loved them. The second one died, and I still cry for him when I'm alone. The first one deserted me and the girl, I loved him, too, and I was faithful to him.... And I've had to live long times without a man, go out to happy evening parties, and put paper flowers on my own head."

"But why don't I love you?"

"You love Ksenya, I know.... She'll be eighteen, and you thirty, maybe a little more. You'll get married. Just don't lie to me, and don't get upset. I'm used to losing people."

Chagatayev stood in front of this woman, not understanding anything. What was strange to him was not her grief but the fact that she believed that she was doomed to loneliness although he had married her and shared her lot. She was clinging to her grief, and was in no hurry to squander it. It meant that in the deepest part of a person's reason or of his heart there exists an enemy force which darkens one's life even in the embrace of loving arms, even under the kisses of one's children.

"Is this why you wouldn't live with me?" Chagatayev asked.

"Yes, this is why. For you didn't know I had a daughter like that, you thought—that I was younger, and purer...."

"Well, and what of it? It all makes no difference to me."

They walked quietly back to Vera's room. She stood in the middle of her dwelling place, without taking off her raincoat, indifferent and alien to everything, to the people and the things around her. At this moment she would have given away all her belongings to her neighbors; such a good deed would have comforted her a little, and diminished her suffering.

"Well, and how can I go on living now?" Vera asked, talking to herself.

Chagatayev understood Vera. He put his arms around her, and held her for a long time, in order to soothe her if only with his own warmth, because suffering which has been invented is the most inconsolable of all and does not surrender to any words.

Little by little Vera began to come out of her grief.

"Ksenya loves you, too.... I'll bring her up, I'll nourish her memory of you, I'll make a hero out of you. You can count on it, Nazar—the years will go by quickly, and I'm used to separation."

"Why get used to what's bad?" Chagatayev said; he couldn't understand why happiness seemed so improbable to everybody, and why people tried to entice each other only with grief.

Grief had displeased Chagatayev since his childhood and now that he was educated, when people and books had taught him about the struggle of people for happiness, grief seemed to him something vulgar, and he was determined to build a happy world in his fatherland because otherwise he couldn't understand what to do with his life, or how to exist.

"Never mind," Chagatayev said, and he stroked Vera's big stomach where her child lived, the inhabitant of this future happiness. "Get him born quickly, he'll be glad."

"But maybe he won't be," Vera doubted. "Maybe he'll be an eternal sufferer."

"We're not going to allow unhappiness any longer," Chagatayev said.

"Who are we?"

"We," Chagatayev repeated quietly and vaguely. For some reason he was afraid to speak clearly, and he blushed a little, as if his secret thought was not a good one.

Vera hugged him when he left; she had been watching the clock and their parting was drawing near.

"I know—you'll be happy, you have a pure heart. So take my Ksenya for yourself."

She cried because of her love and her uncertainty about the future; her face at first became even more homely, then her tears washed it, and it took on an unfamiliar look, as if Vera were looking at him from a distance and with a stranger's eyes.

3

The train left Moscow far behind; several days of travel had already gone by. Chagatayev was standing by the window and he recognized the places where he had walked as a child, or maybe they were different places but they looked exactly the same. It was the same land, uninhabited and old, the same wind blew, stirring the ragged blades of grass, and the distance stretched out spacious and boring like a doleful, unknown soul. Sometimes Chagatayev wanted to get out and walk along on foot, like a child abandoned by everybody. But his childhood and the old times had long gone by. At the little stations in the steppes he saw portraits of the leaders; often they were made by hand and stuck up somewhere on a fence. The portraits were probably not like the persons they represented, but each had been drawn as if with a child's hand and feeling for truth: Lenin looked like an old man, like the good father of all the people on earth without kith or kin, but the artist, without thinking, had tried to make the face like his own, so that people could see that he was not living alone on the earth and that he had paternity and kindred—this is why art is more important than technique. And now at any of these stations different people could be seen digging in the ground, planting, or building something, preparing a place for life and shelter for the homeless. Chagatayev saw no empty stations, without any people, or where only exiles could have lived; men were working everywhere, drawing back with all their hearts from centuries-old despair, from fatherlessness, and from poverty.

Chagatayev remembered his mother's words: "Go far away, to strangers, may your father be an unknown man." He had gone a long way, and now he was returning, he had found his father in a stranger who had brought him up and made his heart grow inside him and now, having taught him to understand people, was sending him home again to find and rescue his mother if she was still living, and to bury her if she was lying abandoned and dead on the face of the earth.

The train stopped one night in the dark steppe. Chagatayev walked out onto the platform of the car. It was quiet, the engine was puffing in the distance, the passengers were sleeping peacefully. Suddenly a single bird cried in the darkness of the plain, something had frightened it. Chagatayev remembered this sound across many years, it was as if his childhood had cried a complaint out of the silent darkness. He listened carefully; some other kind of bird repeated something very quickly, and then was silent, he could remember this sound, too, but he had now forgotten the bird's name: maybe it was a desert sparrow, maybe a small hawk or a kestrel. Chagatayev got down from the car. He saw a bush not far away, and walking up to it, he took it by a branch and said to it: "Hello, bush!" The bush trembled a little at the man's touch and then stayed again as it had been—indifferent and asleep.

Chagatayev walked still farther away. In the steppe something stirred and then hushed, it seemed noiseless only to ears which had lost the habit of listening. The land began to fall away in front of him, and high, blue grass began. Remembering this with interest, Chagatayev walked into the grass; it trembled around him, rippling up from below, for lots of unseen creatures were running away from his approach—some on their stomachs, some on their legs, some in low flight, however they could. They had probably been sitting there quietly until then, only a few of them asleep, by no means all. Each of them had so much to worry about that the daytime, it was clear, was not long enough, or else they were sorry to waste their short lives in sleep and were just barely dozing, letting a film fall halfway across their eyes so they could see a sort of half life, listening to the darkness and not remembering the worries of the daytime.

Chagatayev soon sensed the smell of wetness; somewhere near there was a pond or a pumping well. He moved in that direction, and quickly came to a small, humid sort of grass, not unlike a little grove in Russia. Chagatayev's eyes were growing used to the darkness, and now he could see clearly. Here the marshland began; when Chagatayev walked into it all the creatures living in it started to cry, to fly, or to stir about where they were. It was warm in the marshland. Animals and birds had not all disappeared in terror of man; judging by their sounds, some of them had stayed where they were. Chagatayev knew these sounds from long ago, and now, listening to these agonized, weak voices coming out of the warm grass, he felt sympathy for all of this impoverished life.

The train went on unheard. Chagatayev could have caught up with it, but he did not hurry; only his bag with his clothes was going on with it, and he could get this back in Tashkent. But Chagatayev made up his mind not to try to get it back, so as not to be distracted by anything. He went to sleep in the grass, flattening himself against the ground as he had used to.

In seven days Chagatayev walked into Tashkent along a footpath which was not far away. He showed up at the Central Committee of the Communist party where he had been expected for some time. The secretary of the committee told Chagatayev that a fairly small nomad people made up of different nationalities was roaming around in extreme poverty somewhere in the district of Sari-Kamish, Ust-Urt and the delta of the Amu-Darya River. Among them there were Turkmen people, Kalpaks, some Uzbeks, Kazaks, Persians, Kurds, Beludzhis and others who had forgotten what they were. Before, these people had lived almost always in the Sari-Kamish valley, from which they had gone out to work on the irrigation canals and pumps of the Khiva oasis, in Tashaouz, in Khodzheim, Kunya-Urgench and other faraway places. The poverty and despair of this people had become so great that they thought of work in the ditches, which lasts for a few weeks in the year, as a blessing because for these days at least they were given flat loaves of bread and even rice to eat. On the pumps these people took the place of donkeys, using their bodies to turn the wooden wheel which lifts the water up to the sluices. A donkey has to be fed right through the year, but these people from Sari-Kamish ate only when they were working and then they went away. The tribe did not die out entirely, and always returned the next year, after languishing somewhere in the bottom of the wilderness.

"I know that people, that's where I was born," Chagatayev said.

"That's why you're being sent there," the secretary said. "What's the tribe called, do you remember?"

"It has no real name," Chagatayev answered. "But it gave itself a nickname."

"What's that?"

"Dzhan. That means a soul, or dear life. These people don't have anything except their souls, and the dear life their mothers gave them when they were born."

The secretary frowned, and looked sad.

"That means, all they've got is the hearts inside their bodies, and they have that only while the hearts on beating. . . ."

"Only their hearts," Chagatayev agreed, "nothing but life; except for their bodies, nothing belongs to them at all. But even their life isn't really theirs, it only seems that way."

"Did your mother ever tell you just who the Dzhan were?"

23

"She told me. Runaways and orphans from all over, and old exhausted slaves who had been driven out. Then there were women who had betrayed their husbands and come there out of fear, girls were always coming who had been in love with men who died suddenly and they didn't want anyone else. And then people also lived there who didn't recognize God, people who made jokes about the world, criminals . . . but I don't remember them all. I was very little."

"Go on back to them now. Find those lost people—the Sari-Kamish valley is empty now and they can go back."

"I'll go," Chagatayev agreed. "But what am I to make there? Socialism?"

"What else?" the secretary declared. "Your people have already been in hell, let them live in paradise awhile, and we'll help them with all our strength. . . . You'll be our agent. The district officials sent somebody there, but he's hardly done anything; it seems, he wasn't one of us. . . ."

Then the secretary gave Chagatayev detailed and complete instructions, with a letter of credentials, and Chagatayev took his leave. He planned to float down the Amu-Darya River to his homeland, taking a light canoe somewhere near Chardzhoui.

At the post office in Tashkent he found a letter from Vera. She wrote that her child was getting close to being born; he was already thinking something inside her body, because he stirred around often and was dissatisfied.

"But I pet him, I stroke my stomach," Vera wrote, "and I put my face as close to him as I can and I say: 'What do you want? You're warm and quiet there, I'm trying not to move much so you won't be disturbed—why do you want to get outside of me?' I've grown used to him, I live with him all the time as with a friend, the way I wanted to live with you, and I'm afraid of his birth—not because it will hurt, but because it will be the beginning of separation from him for good, and his little legs which he's kicking with now will hurry to go away from his mother, farther and farther—as long as he lives—until my son will be quite hidden from me, from my cried-out eyes. . . . Ksenya remembers you, but she misses you with you so far away, and not coming back soon, and not even hearing from you. Are you sure you haven't already died somewhere out there?"

Chagatayev wrote Vera a postcard, sending kisses to her, and to Ksenya on her different-colored eyes, and telling her a little time must still go by before he could come back; he would come as soon as he had made his people, the Dzhan, happy.

### 4

Four canoes were being got ready to go down the river with supplies from Chardzhoui to Nukus. Chagatayev did not try to use his status as an agent sent by the party, since the rights this gave him were not well recognized, and he took a job as a sailor. He agreed to go as far as the Khiva oasis, where he would go ashore.

Long days of floating down the river followed. In the mornings and the evenings the river was transformed into a torrent of gold, thanks to the light of the sun piercing the water through its living, never-drying silt. This yellow dirt, traveling down the river, sometimes looked like bread, like flowers, like cotton, and even like a man's body. Sometimes a strange, many-colored bird sat on a rise in the marshlands, twirling around from some emotion inside it, its feathers glistening in the living sunshine, and singing with its glittering thin voice as if a state of bliss had already dawned for all the creatures in the world. The bird reminded Chagatayev of Ksenya, a little woman with a bird's eyes who was thinking something about him at that moment.

After fourteen days, Chagatayev went ashore at the Khiva oasis, accepting his pay and thanks from the senior sailor in charge. He stayed for several days in Khiva, and then walked up the road of his childhood toward his homeland in Sari-Kamish. He remembered the road by signs which had grown blurred: the sand dunes now seemed lower, the canal smaller, the path to the nearest well shorter. The sun shone as it had before, but it was not as high as it had been when Chagatayev was small. The little hills, the nomad tents, the donkeys and camels met along the road, the trees along the irrigation ditches, the flying insects, all these were as in the old days and unchanged, but indifferent to Chagatayev, as if they had gone blind without him. Every small creature, object or plant, it seemed, was more proud and more independent of its old attachments than a man.

Coming up to the dry bed of the Kunya-Darya River, Chagatayev saw a camel which was sitting like a human being, resting its front legs on a drift in the sand. The camel was thin, its humps had sagged down, and it looked shyly out of black eyes like a thoughtful, grieving man. When Chagatayev came up, the camel paid no attention; it was following the movement of some dead grass being blown by the wind—would it come closer or would it blow past? One blade of grass fluttered across the sand close to its mouth, and the camel chewed it with its lips, and swallowed it. In the distance a round tumble-weed was being dragged along by the wind, and the camel watched this big living plant with eyes made gentle by hope, but the tumbleweed moved by on one side; then the camel closed its eyes because it did not know how to cry.

Chagatayev examined the camel carefully; the animal had long since grown thin from hunger and disease, almost all the hair had fallen out leaving only a few clumps, and as a result the beast was quivering with chills. It had probably been unloaded and abandoned here by some passing caravan as a result of its weakness—or else the master had himself died, and the animal was waiting for him, meanwhile hoarding the strength of life left in it. Having lost the ability to move, the camel had raised itself up on its front legs in order to see the blades of grass being driven past by the wind, and to eat them. When there was no wind it closed its eyes, not wishing to waste its vision to no good end, and stayed in somnolence. It did not want to sink back and lie down—since it was no longer able to stand up—and thus remained sitting all the time, now observing, now drowsing, until death should strike it down or until some insignificant desert animal should finish it with one blow of a little paw.

Chagatayev sat next to this camel for a long time, watching and understanding. Then he collected some armfuls of tumbleweed from quite a large area, and fed them to the camel. He couldn't water it, for he had only two canteens of water for himself, but he knew that there were fresh water ponds and small wells farther along the Kunya-Darya riverbed. But it would be hard for him to carry the camel across the sand.

Evening set in. Chagatayev fed the camel, bringing it grass from nearby patches, until the camel put its head down on the ground; it fell asleep with the heavy sleep of new life. Night fell, it began to grow cold. Chagatayev ate a flat cake from his knapsack, then drew close to the camel's body in order to get warm, and began to drowse. He smiled; everything was strange to him in this world, as if it had been contrived for a quick and amusing game. But this special game was being dragged out endlessly, to all eternity, and no one wanted to laugh any longer, or could laugh. The empty land of the desert, the camel, even the wandering, sparse grass—all of this ought to be serious, big, and exultant. Does a feeling exist inside poor people of some other, happy, assignment, essential and indispensable, and is this why they feel so burdened, waiting for something? Chagatayev curled himself up around the stomach of the camel and fell asleep, lost in the wonder of reality.

**5**

After six days of traveling along the Kunya-Darya, Chagatayev saw Sari-Kamish. All this time he took with him the revived camel, which could walk by itself although it could not yet carry a man.

Chagatayev sat down at the edge of the sands, at the place where they run out, where the land runs downwards into the valley leading toward the distant Ust-Urt. It was dark there, low-lying, nowhere could Chagatayev see either smoke or a nomad tent—only in the distance was the shining of a small lake. Chagatayev let the sand run through his hands—this had not changed: the wind had blown it back and forth through all the years that had gone by, and the sand had grown old from staying in this everlasting place.

It was here that his mother had once led him by the hand, and sent him out to live alone, and now he had returned. He walked farther with the camel, into the depths of his native land. Wild bushes stood like little old men; they had not grown at all since Chagatayev was a child.

He spent several days in roaming around the country of his childhood, trying to find his people. The camel walked independently after him, afraid to remain alone and become despondent; sometimes it looked at the man for a long time, tense and observant, ready to cry or to smile, and tormented by its lack of knowing.

Passing the nights in wild places, eating up the last of his food, Chagatayev still did not worry about his own well-being. He was making his way into the heart of the unpopulated valley, to the very bottom of this ancient sea, in a hurry, and unquiet in his mind. Just once he lay down in the middle of his day's walking, and hugged the ground. His heart had suddenly started to hurt, and he had lost the patience and the energy to struggle with it; he was crying for Ksenya, ashamed of his feeling, denying it. He could see her now close up in his mind and in his memory; she was smiling at him with the sorry smile of a little woman who can love only in her spirit but doesn't want to be hugged and is afraid of kisses as of some mutilation. Vera was sitting some distance away, sewing children's clothes, shortening her separation from her husband and already almost indifferent to him because another, more beloved and more helpless man was stirring inside her. She was waiting for him, eager to see his face and frightened of parting from him. But it comforted her to think of the long years she would kiss and hug him whenever she wanted to, until he would grow up and tell her: "You're bothering me, Mama, and I'm tired of you!"

Chagatayev raised his head. The camel was chewing some kind of thin, bonelike grass, a little tortoise was looking out of black, tender eyes at the man lying there. What was in its consciousness at that moment? Maybe a magical kind of curiosity about the enormous, mysterious man, maybe just the sadness of slumbering intelligence.

"We won't leave you alone!" Chagatayev said to the camel. He worried about whatever was real around him as if it were something sacred, and his heart was too hungry for him not to notice whatever could serve as consolation to it.

He and the camel walked on farther, to Ust-Urt, where one old, forgotten man was living at the very foot of the mountain. The old man passed his nights in a mud hut dug into the dry slope of the hill, and he lived on little animals and on the roots of plants which could be found in crevices in the plateau. His great age and his squalor made him look unlike a human being. He had long outlived the human century, all his feelings had been satisfied, and his mind had learned and memorized the world around him with the exactness of truth that has been proved. He knew even the stars, many thousands of them, by heart and by force of habit, and now they bored him.

His name was Sufyan. He was dressed in an old Russian soldier's greatcoat from the times of the Khiva war, wore a visored cap, and his feet were bound with rags. When he saw Chagatayev, he walked toward him out of his earthen dwelling, and stared into space with faded eyes. A man with a camel was walking up to him. Sufyan recognized the newcomer immediately; he was secretly aggrieved that there was nothing he did not know.

"I know you," he told Chagatayev. "You were the little boy Nazar."

"But I don't know you," Chagatayev answered.

"You don't know, because you live the way you eat; what goes into you comes out again. But in me everything lingers on."

The old man made a wry face somewhat resembling a smile of welcome, but his face even when relaxed was like the empty skin of a dead, dried-up snake. Amazed, Chagatayev touched Sufyan's hand and his forehead. He told the old man that he had come from far away, because of his mother and his people. Were they still on earth or had they died a long time ago?

The old man was silent.

"Did you meet your father somewhere?" he asked.

"No. Did you know him?"

"I don't know," Sufyan answered. "I heard that word 'father' once from someone going by, and he said it was something good. But I think not. If it is good, let it show up in Sari-Kamish, for this is the hellhole of the whole world, and I live here worse than any other man alive."

"So I have come to you," Chagatayev said.

The old man's face puckered in a distrustful smile.

"You'll soon be going away from me. I'll die here all alone. You're still young, your heart beats strongly, you'll get tired."

Chagatayev walked up to the old man and embraced him.

"You'll die here of regret, of memories. Here, the Persians said, was the hellhole of the entire earth...."

They went into the mud hut where Sufyan lived on a litter of rushes. He gave his guest a flat cake made out of the roots of grasses which grew on the tableland. Through the opening of the entrance the shadow of the evening could be seen, running into the pit of Sari-Kamish where the world's hellhole used to be in ancient times. Chagatayev had heard this legend in his childhood, and now he understood its full significance. In the far-distant Khorosan, beyond the Kopet-Daga mountains, surrounded by gardens and pashas, lived the clean god of happiness, fruits and women—Ormuzd, defender of agriculture and of human reproduction, lover of quiet in Iran. And to the north of Iran, beyond the slope of the mountains, lay the empty sands; they stretched in the direction of the middle of the night, where only rare grasses languished—and these broken away by the wind and blown to the dark places of Turan, in the middle of which the soul of man is forever grieving. The dark people, unable to endure despair and death of hunger, ran away to Iran. They dug themselves into the depths of the gardens, into the women's quarters, into the ancient cities, and they hurried to eat, to look, to forget themselves, until they were destroyed and those who were spared chased back into the depths of the sands. Then they hid themselves at the end of the wilderness, in the Sari-Kamish valley, and they pined away there for a long time until need and memories of the limpid gardens of Iran raised them again to their feet. . . . Once more the horsemen of the black Turan appeared in Khorosan, beyond Atrek, in Astrabad, among the properties of the hateful, fat, settled people, destroying and enjoying. . . . One of the old residents of Sari-Kamish was named Ariman, which was equivalent to the devil, and this poor wretch was driven to fury by his grief. He was not the most evil of them, but he was the most unhappy, and all his life he knocked his way across the mountains to Iran, to Ormuzd's paradise, wanting to eat and to enjoy himself, until he bowed his

31

weeping face over the barren land of Sari-Kamish and passed away.

Sufyan took Chagatayev in for the night. The economist was tired of sleeping: days and nights were going by in vain, he had to hurry to create happiness in the hellish valley of Sari-Kamish. He could not sleep for a long time because of his impatience as he considered how time was passing. The stars were shining in the sky like the light of conscience, the camel was puffing outside, the withered grass, broken loose by the daytime wind, scraped carefully over the sand as if it were trying to move independently, using its little blades as legs.

The next day Sufyan and Chagatayev went off together to try to find the missing people. The camel went with them, being afraid of solitude as any affectionate man fears it who is living separated from his own people.

At the very edge of Sari-Kamish, Chagatayev recognized a place he knew. Gray grass was growing here, but no higher than it had in Nazar's childhood. It was here his mother had once told him: "Don't be afraid, little boy, we're going out to die," and she had pulled him close to herself by the hand. All the people were gathered around, so that they made a crowd of perhaps a thousand men, together with women and children. The people were noisy and happy; they had decided to go to Khiva, to be killed there all together and at once . . . not to live any longer. The Khan of Khiva had tortured this shy, insignificant people with his power for a very long time. At first seldom, but then more and more frequently, he sent horsemen from his palace into Sari-Kamish, and each of them picked up several men from among this people, and these were either executed in Khiva or else thrown into darkness without hope of return. The Khan was looking for thieves, criminals, and godless men, but it was hard to sort these out. So he then ordered that all mysterious and obscure people be taken, so that the inhabitants of Khiva, watching their execution and their torture, should know terror, and the shivering of horror. At first the Dzhan people were afraid of Khiva, and many of them experienced nervous breakdowns in advance; they stopped worrying about themselves and their families and simply lay flat on their backs in uninterrupted weakness. Then all the people began to be afraid—they kept looking into the empty wilderness, waiting for their horsed enemies to appear. They stood stock-still with terror in any kind of breeze which blew the sand from the top of the dunes, thinking that the mounted men were tearing toward them. When one third or more of the people had been taken off to Khiva without any news of them, the rest became accustomed to waiting for their doom; they realized that life was not as dear as it had seemed in their hearts and in their hopes, and each one who stayed safe was a little bored because they had not taken him off to Khiva. But young Yakobdzhanov and his friend Oraz Babadzhan did not want to go to Khiva for no purpose, if it was possible to die in liberty. They threw themselves with knives on four of the Khan's mounted guards and left them where they found them, stripped of their glory and their lives. The little Nazar, seeing strange, armed men, ran to his mother to get a sharp piece of iron which he had hidden away for playing, but when he had run back again it was already late: the guards had died without his sharpened iron. After this Oraz and Yakobdzhanov disappeared, riding the horses of the murdered soldiers, and the rest of their people walked to Khiva in a crowd, happy and peaceful; the people were equally ready then to destroy the Khan's regime, or to give up their lives without regret, since to be alive seemed happy or good to none of them and to be dead not hard or painful. The melon growers walked in front, muttering their song, and Sufyan, then already an old man, was right beside them. Nazar looked at his mother; he was surprised that she was happy now although she was going to die, and all the other people walked along just as eagerly.

Ten or fifteen days later the Sari-Kamish people could see the Khan's towers. The road to Khiva had been hard and long, but the difficulty and the demands of stationary life also required strong hearts, so that people felt no irritation at the extra fatigue. When they got to Khiva itself, the people were surrounded by a small mounted detachment of the Khan's men, but then the people, seeing this, began to sing and to rejoice. Everybody sang, even the most silent and awkward; Uzbeks and Kazaks danced first of all, one unhappy old Russian played a mouth organ, Nazar's mother held up one arm as if she were getting ready for a mysterious dance, and Nazar waited full of interest for the soldiers to kill them all, and him too, immediately. Heavy-set guards were standing around the Khan's palace, to protect the Khan from everybody. They watched with amazement the approaching crowd which marched proudly past them and was not afraid of the power of bullets or of steel, as if it were both deserving and happy. These palace guards, together with the horsemen, were supposed gradually to surround the Sari-Kamish people and drive them into underground prisons, but it is hard to punish happy people because they do not understand what evil is.

One of the Khan's assistants went up close to the old people from Sari-Kamish and asked them:

"What do you want, and why do you feel so happy?"

Someone answered him, maybe it was Sufyan or some other old man:

"You've been teaching us to die for a long time, now we're used to it, and we've come all together and at the same time—give us our death quickly, before we've lost the idea, while the people are still rejoicing!"

The Khan's assistant went back, and never returned. The horsemen and the foot soldiers stayed around the palace, never touching the people: they could have killed only those to whom death was frightening, and once the whole people was march-

ing happily past them to its death, the Khan and his chief soldiers did not know what to make of this or what to do. They
did nothing, and all the people who had come out of the valley
walked on farther, and soon they saw the bazaar. Merchants
were trading there, food was lying in piles around them, and
the evening sun shining in the sky lit up green onions, melons,
watermelons, grapes in baskets, yellow grain for baking bread,
gray mules drowsy with tiredness and with indifference.

Then Nazar asked his mother:

"And when will it be death? I want it!"

But the mother herself did not know what would happen
then; she could see that everyone was still alive, and she was
afraid to go back to Sari-Kamish again and once more to live
on there.

The people started to pick up various fruits at the Khiva
bazaar and to eat them, having no money, and the merchants
just stood there silent and did not beat these thieving people.
Nazar ate slowly, he kept looking around, waiting for murder,
and he managed to eat only one melon. When they had eaten,
the people grew uneasy because their happiness had passed, and
there was no death. Gulchatai led Nazar back into the wilderness. All the people also went away, back to the old place
where they lived.

Nazar and his mother returned to Sari-Kamish. They
had rested then, on this same gray, harsh grass where Chagatayev was standing now with Sufyan, and the mother had told
her son:

"Let's live again, we haven't died!"

"We're both alive," Nazar had agreed. "You know what,
Mama, we'll live."

"Lucky the one who dies inside his mother," Gulchatai said.

Then she looked at her son; happiness and pity filled her
face.

35

Now Nazar just patted the ancient grass which had stayed there unchanging up to the present time because it had really died before Nazar's birth, but still held on, as if living, by its deep, dead roots. Sufyan understood that some kind of deep emotion was now working inside Chagatayev, but he was not interested in it: he knew that a man needs something to fill his soul, and that if there is nothing, then the heart will greedily squeeze out its own blood.

After four days, Sufyan and Chagatayev wanted to eat so badly that they began to see dreams even while their legs still moved and their eyes looked at the usual daylight. The camel did not leave them, but moved along some distance off, where it could find a little forage in the grass along the way. Sufyan watched his flowing dreams hopelessly, while Chagatayev smiled at them sometimes, and was sometimes tormented by them. When they got to the Daryalik channel at Mangir-chardar, the two walkers stopped for the night, and Sufyan mixed some water on the shore so it would be muddy, thicker, and more nourishing, and then, having drunk it, both men lay down in a cave, so the body might forget it was alive, and the night be over sooner. When he woke up in the morning, Chagatayev saw the camel dead; it was lying nearby with its eyes turned to stone, on its neck the blood stood still in a deep cut, and Sufyan was digging deep into its interior, as into a sack filled with goods, taking raw pieces out with clean blood on them and stuffing himself with them. Chagatayev too crept to the camel, a smell of warmth and satiety came from the open body, the blood was still flowing in droplets down the creases of the dead body, life was taking a long time to die. When they had eaten, Chagatayev and Sufyan blissfully fell asleep again, and they didn't wake up quickly.

Then they walked farther—into the flooded places at the estuary of the Amu-Darya. They took with them a reserve of camel meat, but Chagatayev ate it without appetite: it was hard for him to nourish himself with the sorrowful animal; it too had seemed to him a member of humanity.

## 6

The residents of the Sari-Kamish valley were scattered among the reeds and bushes along the estuary of the Amu-Darya River. About ten years had gone by since the Dzhan people had come here and settled in this wet-loving vegetation. At first the mosquitoes ate the people so badly that they tore the skin off their bones, but after a little time their blood became used to the mosquitoes' poison and began to develop an antidote from which the mosquitoes became helpless and fell to the ground. Because of this the mosquitoes were now afraid of people, and would not come near them at all.

Some of the people had settled apart from each other, in order not to suffer for others when there was nothing to eat, and in order not to have to weep when people close to them died. But some of the people lived in families; in these cases they had nothing but their love one for another, because they had neither good food, nor hope for the future, nor any other happiness to distract them, and their hearts grew so weak that they could hold only love for a wife or for a husband, which is the most helpless, poor and everlasting of all feelings.

At first Sufyan and Chagatayev wandered for a couple of days through the gloomy reeds on the sodden ground before they saw a single grass hut. A blind man, Molla Cherkezov, lived in it, fed and taken care of by his daughter Aidim, a girl of twelve. Molla recognized Sufyan by his voice, but he had nothing to say to him. They sat facing each other on the litter of reeds, and drank tea made out of the dried, ground-up roots of those same reeds, and then they said good-bye to each other.

"Do you have any news?" Sufyan asked as he took his leave.

"No. Life goes on just the same way," Cherkezov answered. "My wife, my dear Gyun, fell into the water and died."

"Why did your worthy Gyun fall in the water?"

"She couldn't stand living. Take my daughter Aidim, and bring me instead a young she-ass. I'll live with her at night, to avoid thinking, and sleeplessness."

"I'm a poor man," Sufyan said, "I haven't any she-asses. You should trade your daughter for an old woman. Live with an old woman; it's all the same to you."

"It's all the same," Molla Cherkezov agreed. "But old women die off quickly, and there aren't enough of them."

"You've heard, Nazar has come to us from Moscow. They've ordered him to help us live a good life."

"Four men have come before Nazar," Cherkezov reported. "The mosquitoes bit them, and they went away. I'm a blind man, my business is the dark, nothing will do me any good. But if I had a wife, life would go by without my knowing it."

The girl Aidim sat on the ground, with her legs apart, and rubbed a small stone against a large reed rhizome; she was the cook here and she was preparing food. Beside the girl, in addition to the reeds, were several bunches of marsh and desert grass and one clean bone of a donkey or a camel, picked up in the sand somewhere faraway, for cooking. A scrubbed kettle stood next to her and she threw into it from time to time what her hands were getting ready, for she was fixing a soup for dinner. The girl was not interested in her guests; her eyes were engrossed with her own thoughts—probably she was living some secret, independent dream and doing the housework almost unconsciously, distracted from all the world around her by her concentrated heart.

"Let your daughter come with me," Chagatayev asked the master of the hut.

"She's not yet grown up, what will you do with her?" Molla Cherkezov said.

"I'll bring you another one, an old one."

"Bring her quickly," Cherkezov agreed.

Chagatayev took Aidim by the hand; she looked at him out of black eyes, which had the shine of blind, unseeing eyes, and she was frightened and did not understand.

"Come with me," Chagatayev said to her.

Aidim rubbed her hands in the dirt, to clean them, stood up and walked away, leaving all her things where they were, not looking at anything, just as if she had only lived here for a moment and as if she were not now leaving her own father.

"Sufyan, it's all the same with you, whether you go on with me or not, isn't it?"

"All the same," Sufyan answered.

Chagatayev told him to stay with the blind man and to help Cherkezov eat and live until he came back.

Nazar walked off with the young girl along the narrow track of people who had moved before him through the forest of reeds. He wanted to see all the inhabitants of this overgrown land, the people hiding here from poverty. He had not asked Sufyan about his mother; he hoped that unexpectedly he might run into her, alive and remembering him, but if she was dead, he could always find out later where her bones were lying.

Aidim walked humbly behind Chagatayev the whole long way. In places the reeds ended. There Nazar and the girl would walk out into empty, sandy dunes, covered with silt, next to little ponds; they would walk around stiff bushes, and plunge again into the thicket of reeds where the little path ran. Aidim was silent; when she was dead tired, Chagatayev took her over his shoulder and carried her, holding on to her knees while she held on to his head. Then they would rest, and drink water from the clean sandy pools. The girl kept watching Chagatayev with a strange look which he tried to understand.

"Why is everything bad here," he thought, "when what I need is what is good?"

Chagatayev put Aidim down against his arm, and ran his fingers through her hair. She fell asleep right away in his arms, trusting and pitiful, born only to be happy and to be taken care of.

The evening came. It was too dark to go farther. Chagatayev gathered grass, made a warm bed of it to guard against the cold at night, placed the girl in this grassy softness, and lay down himself beside it, sheltering and warming the little person.

Chagatayev lay there sleepless; if he had gone to sleep, Aidim would have been uncovered and numb with cold. Huge black night filled the sky and the earth, from the foot of the grass to the edge of the world. The sun alone disappeared, but in return all the stars began to shine, and the vast, unquiet Milky Way, looking as if some march with no return had just taken place along it.

7

The first dawn light picked out the figures lying on the grass. One of Chagatayev's arms was under Aidim's head, to protect her sleep from the hard, damp ground, and the other was across his eyes, to guard them from the morning. A strange old woman was sitting next to the sleeping pair, looking at them with absorption. Barely touching him, she felt Chagatayev's hair, his mouth, and his hands, then she smelled his clothing, looking around her, afraid someone might stop her. Then she carefully took Nazar's hand out from under the girl's head, so that he would feel no one, and love no one, and be only with her. Her back had long since become permanently bent, and when the old woman looked at something her face almost crawled along the ground, as if she were shortsighted and looking for something she had lost. She examined all Nazar's clothes, tried with her hands the little straps and tapes of his trousers and shoes, rumpled the cloth of his jacket between her palms, and traced Chagatayev's black, dusty eyebrows with her finger, moistened in her mouth. Then she relaxed, and lay down with her head at Nazar's feet, happy and exhausted, as if she had now lived through to the end of life and there was nothing more for her to do, as if in these shoes, rotting inside from sweat and covered with the dust of the desert and with swamp mud, she had found her final consolation. The old woman either dozed or fell asleep, but then quickly got up again. Chagatayev and Aidim were sleeping as they had before: children sleep a long time, and even the sun, butterflies, and birds do not wake them.

"Wake up, quickly!" the old woman said, putting her arms around the sleeping Chagatayev.

He opened his eyes. The old woman started to kiss his neck and his chest, through his clothes; crawling with her face toward her son she tested and examined all his body very closely: were his members whole or not, had none of them sickened, or lost something, while he had been away?

"You don't have to do that; you're my mother," Chagatayev said.

He got to his feet in front of her, but his mother was so hunched over that now she couldn't see his face, and she pulled at his hand, so he stooped down and sat in front of her. Gulchatai was shaking with age, or with love for her son, and she could say nothing to him. She just passed her hands over his body, fearfully becoming aware of her happiness, and not believing in it, afraid that it would go away.

Chagatayev looked into his mother's eyes, which had now become pale, unused to him, no longer lighted by their former dark and shining strength. Her thin, small face had grown rapacious and wicked, either from unceasing grief or from the

41

effort of keeping herself alive when there was no reason to live, and no one to live for, when she even had to remember that her own heart was beating, and to force it to work. Otherwise she might die at any moment, forgetting or not noticing that she was alive, and that it is essential to try to want something and to keep on being aware of one's own self.

Nazar embraced his mother. She was as light as air now, or as a little girl; she would have to start to live again from scratch, like a child, because all her strength had gone in the patient struggle against unending hardship. No part of her heart was any longer free of grief, able to feel the goodness of her own existence; she had never been able to understand who she was and to feel easy with herself before the time had come for her to be an old woman, and to die.

"Where are you living?" Nazar asked her.

"There," Gulchatai pointed with her hand.

She led him through short grass and sparse reeds, and they quickly came to a little village set down in a clearing in the reeds. Chagatayev could see some reed huts and several tents, also fastened together with reeds. In all there were about twenty dwelling places, perhaps a few more. Chagatayev saw no dogs, no donkeys, no camels in this settlement, there were not even chickens walking around on the grass.

Beside the farthest hut a naked man was sitting, his skin hanging from him in folds like worn-out, tired clothing; he was sorting reed canes on his knees, weaving them into things for domestic use or for decorations. This man was not at all surprised by Chagatayev's arrival, and did not even answer his greeting; he mumbled to himself, imagining something visible to no one else, giving his soul its own secret comfort.

"Do all our people live here, or are there others?" Chagatayev asked his mother.

"I've already forgotten, Nazar, I don't know," Gulchatai said, following him with a great effort, holding her head down low like a heavy burden. "There were some more people, about ten of them, they live in the reeds down toward the sea—that is to say, they used to live there, now it's time for them to die, they must have died already, none of them comes back to us. . . ."

The little huts and tents ended. Beyond them the reeds began again. Chagatayev stopped. Here it all was—his mother and his native land, his childhood and his future. Early daylight lit up the place: the green, pale reeds, the gray-brown ramshackle huts in the clearing with the sparse grass underfoot, and the air above filled with sunshine, the humid steam of the swamp, the loess dust of the oases which were drying up, stirred by some high, inaudible wind, a dull, exhausted sky, as if nature itself were nothing but a mournful, hopeless force.

Looking around him, Chagatayev smiled at all these shadowy, uninteresting elements, not knowing what there was for him to do. Over the top of the dense reed thicket, on the silver horizon, he could see a kind of disappearing mirage—the sea, or a lake with moving ships, and the shining white columns of a faraway city on its shore.

The mother was standing silently next to her son, her body sagging down toward the ground. She lived in one of these huts, built on clay, without a husband, without relatives. Two reed mats lay on the ground inside her dwelling—with one she covered herself, while she slept on the other. She still had an iron pot for cooking and a clay jug, and on a crossbeam hung the little trousers of her girlhood and a single rag, in which she had wrapped Nazar when he was nursing at her breast. Kochmat had died six years before, nothing was left of him but one trouser leg (Gulchatai had used up the other in patches for her skirt) and a piece of base which Kochmat had used to wipe the sweat and dirt off his body when he had gone out to work on the pumps in the oases.

Nazar's mother lived here as a poor, landless peasant. She was amazed that Nazar was still alive but she was not surprised that he had come back. She did not know about any other life in the whole world except the one she lived herself; she thought everything on earth was all the same. Chagatayev went back for the little girl Aidim; he woke her and took her into his mother's hut. Gulchatai went out to dig up some grass roots, to catch little fish with a reed net dipped into water holes, to look for birdsnests in the underbrush and to collect eggs or little nestlings. She did not come back until evening, when she began to prepare food from the grass, the roots of reeds and some little fish. She was no longer interested that her son was now there, near her, she did not look at him at all and she spoke no word, just as if her thinking and her feeling were weighted down in some deep, uninterrupted meditation which took all her strength. The brief, human feeling of gladness about her living, grown-up son had either gone, or it had never been at all, and there was only a wonder about this strange meeting.

Gulchatai did not even ask if Nazar would like to eat, or what he was thinking of doing in his native land, in this settlement in the reeds.

Nazar looked at her; he watched her stir about at her usual tasks and it seemed to him that she was in fact asleep, not really moving around but in a dream. Her eyes were so pale and helpless that there was no strength left in them for seeing, they held no expression of any kind, like the eyes of the blind and the deaf. Her big, crusted feet showed that Gulchatai lived barefoot all the time; her clothing consisted of a single dark skirt pulled up to her neck like a cowl, patched up with different bits and pieces of cloth including pieces of a felt shoe which were stitched around its hem. Chagatayev felt his mother's dress; it had been put on over her naked body and she had on no undershirt—his mother had long grown used to freezing at night and in the winter and to suffering in the heat. She had got accustomed to everything.

Nazar called his mother. She answered him, and understood him. He began to help her make a fire on the hearth which was built like a little cave under the slanting wall of reeds. Aidim watched these strange people out of her clear black eyes which still held the shining strength of childhood and the shyness which was sorrow, because what a child really wants is to be happy, not to sit in the dark of a mud hut wondering if they would give her anything to eat. Chagatayev remembered where he had seen eyes like Aidim's, but still more lively, happy and loving—no, not here, and that woman was not a Turkmen nor a Khirgiz, she had forgotten him a long time ago, and he too could not remember her name, and she could not even imagine where Chagatayev was now or what he was doing: Moscow was far away, he was almost alone here, around him a wilderness flooded with water and dilapidated dwellings made of dead grass. He began to long for Moscow, for many comrades, for Vera and Ksenya, and he wanted to go out that evening somewhere on a streetcar, to visit friends. But Chagatayev quickly recovered himself; "No, Moscow's here, too!" he said out loud, and he smiled, looking into Aidim's eyes. She became frightened, and stopped looking at him.

The mother boiled a kind of stew for herself in the iron pot, ate it to the last drop and wiped the inside of the pot with her fingers and then sucked them, the better to get her fill. Aidim watched Gulchatai carefully while she ate, how the food slipped down past the sinews in her thin throat, but she watched this without greed or envy, only with amazement and with pity for the old woman who was gulping the grass in hot water. After eating, Gulchatai fell asleep on her spread-out carpet of reeds, because night had fallen all around them.

8

Chagatayev's first day in his native land had been lived through. At first the sun had been shining, and there was something to be hoped for, then the sky had grown dark, and already one indistinct, paltry star showed far away in the sky.

It had grown raw and dead quiet. The people in this country of reeds were silent, Chagatayev could not hear them at all. He gathered some grass and made a bed out of it in his mother's hut and laid Aidim down in the warm place so that she might sleep.

Then he went out alone, walked as far as an empty channel of the Amu-Darya, and then returned. A powerful night now stood over this land, the small, young reeds were rustling at the base of the older plants, like children in their sleep. People might think there was nothing in this wilderness, only an uninteresting wild place where a melancholy herdsman drowses in the darkness, with the dirty valley of Sari-Kamish lying at his feet, where once upon a time a human disaster took place —it is over, and its martyrs vanished. But in very fact here, on the Amu-Darya and in Sari-Kamish, there was an entire hard world busy with its destiny.

Chagatayev was listening: someone was talking near him, humorously and quickly, but getting no answer. Nazar approached one of the reed huts. He could hear the breathing of sleeping people inside it, and their uneasy tossing.

"Pick up the wool on the ground, and put it inside my shirt," the voice of a sleeping old man was saying. "Collect it quickly, while the camels are shedding. . . ."

Chagatayev listened next to the wall of reeds. Now the old man was whispering in delirium, what he was saying couldn't he heard. He was dreaming some kind of life in perpetual motion, and his murmuring grew lower and lower, as if he were moving away.

"Dudri, Dudri!" a woman's voice began to call; she was stirring, and the reed mat which covered her was rustling. "Dudri! Don't run away from me, I'm dead tired but I'll catch up with you. . . . Stop, don't torment me, I've got a sharp knife, I'll slash you to pieces, so you'd better give up."

But the old man and the woman soon grew silent and slept peacefully again.

"Dudri!" Chagatayev called quietly from outside the hut.

"What?" the voice of the muttering old man answered from inside.

"Are you asleep?" Chagatayev asked.

"I'm sleeping," Dudri answered.

Chagatayev remembered this Dudri from his earliest childhood. Then he had been a skinny man from the Iomud tribe who roamed from place to place with his wife, and ate tortoises. He would come to Sari-Kamish when he started to be bored, and he would sit silently in a group of people listening to them talk, and smiling, and he was content with the secret happiness of meeting them; then he would go out again into the sands to catch tortoises and to think about something in solitude. A lonely woman (to Nazar, then, she too seemed old) walked behind her husband, carrying all their worldly belongings on her back. The little Nazar would go with them for a long time until they disappeared in the shining light, transformed into flowing heads without a body, into a boat, a bird, a mirage.

Another reed hut, built like a tent, was right next to him. A little dog was sitting by it. Chagatayev was amazed, because he had not yet seen a single domestic animal. The black dog looked at him, opened and closed its mouth in a threatening way, and barked, but made no sound. At the same time it lifted first its right, and then its left paw, trying to build up enough fury to lunge at the stranger, but it could not. Chagatayev leaned down to the dog and it took his hand in its mouth and

47

pressed it between empty gums; the dog did not have a single tooth. He felt its body, and its cruel, pitiful heart was beating fast, and there were tears of despair in the dog's eyes.

Occasionally someone laughed inside the tent in a silly voice. Chagatayev lifted the lattice hanging from the pole and walked into the dwelling. It was quiet and stifling in the tent, and nothing could be seen. Chagatayev knelt down and crawled around, trying to find out who was there. The hot, woolen air was suffocating him. Chagatayev was groping for the unknown man with his exhausted hands when he felt someone's face. This face puckered up suddenly under Chagatayev's fingers, and out of its mouth came a warm flow of words each one of which could be understood although what they said made no sense at all. Chagatayev listened in amazement, holding the face in his hands and trying to understand what it was saying, but he couldn't. The inhabitant of the tent stopped talking for a moment, and laughed quite reasonably, then started to talk again. It seemed to Chagatayev that he was laughing at what he was saying, and at his own mind which was now thinking something, but what it thought had no meaning. Then Chagatayev guessed, and he smiled, too: the words could not be understood because they were only sounds—they held no interest, no feeling, no life, as if there were no heart inside the man.

"Take put go to Ust-Urt bring something and carry it to me put it in my breast," the man was saying, and then he laughed again.

The mind was still alive and perhaps a man was laughing inside it, afraid and not understanding that his heart was beating, his soul was breathing, entirely without interest or desire. The complete solitude, the night darkness inside the tent, a strange man—all this made no impression on him, producing neither fear nor curiosity. Chagatayev touched this man on his face and arms, felt his body, he could even have killed him, but the man just went on babbling as he had before, without any concern, as if he were already a bystander in his own life.

Outside the night was just as it had been. Walking on, Chagatayev wanted to turn back, to take the muttering man along with him, but where could he take him, once he was so worn out that he needed not help, but oblivion? He looked around; the silent dog was walking behind him, people were sleeping and dreaming in the reed huts, the slight trembling of a weak breeze stirred sometimes along the tops of the reed thickets, blowing from here all the way to the Aral Sea. Someone was talking in a low voice inside the hut next to the one where his mother and Aidim were sleeping. The dog walked up to it and then turned back, hurrying off home as if afraid of forgetting where its master and its safety were.

Chagatayev also went back to his mother's, and lay down, without undressing, next to Aidim. The girl breathed little and very quietly in her sleep; it was terrifying to think that she might forget to breathe, and then she would die. Lying on the clay, Chagatayev listened as he drowsed to the sleepy muttering of his people in this God-forsaken bottom of the earth, and to the tortured churning of the grasses in their stomachs. In the hut right next to a him a husband was talking to his wife; he wanted them to have a child, maybe now was the time to begin it.

But the wife answered:

"No, you and I have nothing but weakness, for ten years we've been starting one but it never grows inside me, I'm always empty, like the dead. . . ."

The husband was silent, then he said:

"Well, let's do something together, the two of us, we've got little enough to be happy about together."

"Of course," the woman answered. "I've got nothing to wear, nor have you, either; how are we going to live in the winter?"

"When we're sleeping, we'll get warm," the husband answered. "What more can we do, poor as we are?"

"There's nothing else," the woman agreed. "There's not another thing you and I have that's any good; I've thought and I've thought about it and I see only that I love you."

"I love you, too," the husband said, "otherwise there'd be no living. . . ."

"There's nothing cheaper than a wife," the woman answered. "When we're so poor, what do you own except my body?"

"We don't have enough of anything," the husband agreed. "Thank goodness a wife is born and raised all by herself; otherwise a man would never get one. You have breasts, and lips, a stomach, your eyes can see, and most of all I think about you and you think about me, and the time goes by. . . ."

They grew quiet. Chagatayev cleaned the wax out of his ears and tried hard to listen—would he hear something more from where the husband and wife were lying?

"You and I have plenty of what's bad," the woman began again. "You're thin, and without much strength, and my breasts have dried up, my bones hurt inside me. . . ."

"I'll love whatever's left of you," the husband said.

Then they grew silent for good; probably they were embracing each other, so as to hold in their hands their only happiness.

Chagatayev whispered something to himself, smiled, and fell asleep, content that happiness should exist between two people in his native land, even in a poor way.

9

In the morning Gulchatai paid no attention to her son or to the young girl he had brought with him. Her strength of spirit had been just strong enough to recognize him when he was sleeping on the grass by the trail next to Aidim; now she was living her own life alone again. There was nothing to be done inside the hut, but for a long time the mother evened up the stems of the reeds in the sloping walls, collected all the wisps of grass, cleaned the inside of the cooking pot, straightened out and rolled up the reed mat, and did all this with the utmost concentration and zeal, anxious that her household goods should be intact because she had no other links at all with life or with other people. Since a person needs something to be thinking about all the time, it was clear that she was imagining something while she worked at her small, almost useless, tasks; she didn't know how to think without working; the cooking and the hut, while she picked it up, gave her memories, filling her weak, empty heart with feeling.

She asked her son to give her something. She asked this timidly, without hope and without greed, just so she might have a few more things and increase, by having them, her involvement with the world—the time of her living would go better. Nazar understood his mother, and he gave her his raincoat, the holster of his revolver (he put the revolver in his trouser pocket), a notebook, and forty rubles in money, and he instructed her at the same time to provide food for Aidim. But the girl went off herself to collect grasses for soup, and Gulchatai stayed at the hut.

"Do you know Molla Cherkezov?" Nazar asked her.

"I know everybody," his mother told him.

"Well then, go over there, live with him, it will be better for you. He's blind, but he'll take care of you until he dies."

The bent-over old woman stared at the ground; she could not understand why Cherkezov needed her since her heart was already beating not with emotion but simply out of habit, and since life had become for her almost imperceptible. But she went, taking nothing with her from her home except the things her son had just given her, and these only because they happened to be in her hands. It looked as if she didn't like her

51

older belongings any longer because she didn't have enough strength of spirit to be greedy for them.

Chagatayev stayed behind to live with Aidim, hoping that his mother's heart would be warmed by living with Molla Cherkezov. Aidim began right away to run the place, collecting and boiling grasses, catching fish, cooking the food for dinner. One time she walked far beyond the channels of the river and the area it flooded, all the way to a grove of leafless trees growing in the desert, and brought back firewood as a reserve against the winter. Then Chagatayev, too, went to this grove a couple of times and brought back wood, and he forebade the girl to go—she was supposed just to kindle a little fire in the stove inside the hut and to fix a pot of soup every day. But soon he had to do the household work all alone, because Aidim fell ill and was hot, burning, soaked with perspiration. Nazar covered her with grass against chills, wiped her parched eyes, and poured into her thin soup made of the grasses, but the young girl could not cope with the disease, and grew thin, silent, headed straight for death. Her eyes looked at Chagatayev without consciousness, she had nothing to think about to console her. Chagatayev sat with her through long, empty days, and tried to protect the sick girl from grief and fear.

There were sick and helpless people lying in the other huts and tents. Chagatayev figured that there were forty-seven persons in the Dzhan people, and of these twenty were sick. There were eleven women, and only three children under twelve, including Aidim. The women, who were the hardest workers, died first of all, and those left alive gave birth to children very rarely.

While Aidim was sick, the commissioner of the district government, Nur-Mohammed, came to see Chagatayev. Chagatayev told him he had been sent here to help his people, whom he was to make happy, progressive, and more numerous. Nur-Mohammed answered him that the people's hearts had long ago sickened in their hunger, that their minds had gone deaf, and that there was therefore nothing left with which happiness might be felt. Better to leave these poor people in peace, forget them forever, or else lead them off somewhere in the wilderness, in the steppes and the mountains, so that they might get lost for good, and then be considered nonexistent.

Chagatayev looked at Nur-Mohammed for a little while: he was a big man, already old, his eyes looked out through tightly cut eyelids as if through constant pain. He wore an Uzbek robe, with a skullcap on his head, and his shoes were felt slippers—the only man among the whole people who had kept such clothing. This was explained by the fact that Nur-Mohammed was not himself a member of the Dzhan people but had been sent to them six months before, and he looked at the people with a stranger's eyes.

"What have you done in this half year?" Chagatayev asked him.

"Nothing," Nur-Mohammed reported. "I can't resurrect the dead."

"Then what are you hanging around for? Why are you here?"

"When I came, this people numbered a hundred and ten persons, now there are fewer. I dig graves for the dead—it's impossible to bury them in the swamp, it would cause an epidemic—so I carry the dead ones far away into the sandy desert. I'll go on burying them until they're all gone, then I'll go away myself, and I'll report: my mission is accomplished. . . ."

"The people can bury its own—you're not needed for that."

"No, they won't bury them, I know."

"Why won't they?"

"The dead should be buried by the living, and there are no living here, just those who haven't died yet, living out their time in sleep. You won't make happiness for them, they don't even know their own grief now, they don't worry any longer because they've been worried out."

"What are we to do with you?" Chagatayev asked.

"Not a thing," Nur-Mohammed answered. "It's impossible to torment a man too long, but the Khiva khans thought it was possible. You do it a long time, and the man dies; you must do it a little bit, and then give him a rest, so you can begin it again. . . ."

"I'm not going to dig their graves," Chagatayev said. "I don't know who you are; you're a stranger, you'd better go away from here and leave us alone."

Nur-Mohammed stroked the sleeping Aidim's forehead, and then stood up:

"My business is in my head, and yours in yours. I'll be putting this girl in the ground soon. Good-bye."

He walked back to his own dirt hut. Chagatayev wrapped Aidim up in grass and then in the reed mat and carried her quickly to his mother and Molla Cherkezov: he told them to give her liquids to drink from time to time, and to protect her from the night cold. And Chagatayev himself set off for Chimgai, a hundred or a hundred and fifty kilometers away. He walked through dry stream beds, and channels of the river, through reeds and thickets of mixed growth for the rest of that day, all night, and still another day, getting scratched and hungry on the way, losing his path and carrying all the weight of his impatience, his mind darkening, until he lay down somewhere with his face to the ground. Then he woke up, and he saw a large ruin not far away, and he walked up to its walls of clay. The sun, already high, was pouring intense heat down on the old walls; sleep and oblivion, the unconsciousness of sweltering air, seeped out from under the wall, where the dry clay was aging. Chagatayev walked inside the fort, through a broken place where freshets had torn a gap in the wall. Inside, it was even stuffier with quiet; the heat of the sky was all collected in one pocket, overgrown by enormous grasses with thick, greasy stalks because there was no one here to eat them.

Chagatayev looked at these fatty plants with disgust, searching under them for some kind of smaller, edible grass. He found some small, broken bones; they had been chopped up, to produce a thicker fat, or cut several times with a saber, if this had been a man. Farther on he found some more bones and a whole half of a human skeleton, with the skull; this man had died with his face down, and his rib cage had fallen apart, as if to ease his breathing after his death, and the point of one rib had punctured a rumpled Red Army cap, already rotting now and with pale grass growing through it. Chagatayev pulled it out from under the rib; the cap still held the shadow of its five-pointed star, and inside it, on the cloth protecting the forehead, there had been written with a chemical pencil: "Oraz Golomanov"—the name of the Red Army soldier who had fallen here. Chagatayev cleaned the cap and put it on his head, and he placed his own cap on Golomanov's skull. On the clay wall inside the fortress, Golomanov or some other soldier had cut, probably with a bayonet, the words: "Long live the soldier of the revolution!" and the bayonet had cut too deep into the clay for time, wind and rain to smooth out the words and wash away the trace of this hope of the dead and of the living. It must have been that in 1930 or 1931 a Red Army unit had found itself here, fighting against the *basmachi* bandits and against the troops of the Khiva and Turkmen slave-owners, and Golomanov with his comrades had just stayed here to rot in peace, as if convinced that his unlived life could be lived out by others just as well as by himself. Chagatayev scattered some flowers and earth on Golomanov's skeleton, so eagles or wandering animals should not pilfer his bones, and he walked on to Chimgai.

In Chimgai he bought a box of medical supplies packaged for collective farms, and through the district government office he procured several dozen quinine powders, although he knew that none of these would really help his people which stood in need most of all of another kind of life, which could be endured without dying of it. On the off chance, he went to the post office, to ask if there were not, perhaps, a letter for him from Moscow. Placards hung inside it with descriptions of distant air routes, and signs pasted onto columns in the building gave examples of correct postal addresses, in Moscow, Leningrad, and Tiflis, as if all the local people were writing letters only to those places, and were homesick only for those splendid cities.

Chagatayev walked up to the General Delivery window, and they handed him a plain letter from Moscow which had been sent on here from Tashkent by thoughtful workers in the office of the Communist party central committee of Uzbekistan. Ksenya wrote: "Nazar Ivanovich Chagatayev! Your wife, my mama Vera, died in the second clinical hospital in the city of Moscow from the birth of a daughter who when she was born was also dead and I saw her body. They put the daughter in the hospital in one coffin with my mama, Vera, your wife, and they buried it in the earth at Vagankovsky Cemetery, not far from the writer Batyushkov. I've gone to the grave twice, stood there, and gone away. When you come, I'll show you where the grave is. Mama told me to remember you and love you, and I remember you. With Pioneer's greetings, Ksenya."

A Turkmen girl looked out of the window, and said:

"Wait a minute, there's a telegram for you, too. It's been here for six days."

And she handed Chagatayev a telegram from Tashkent: "Letter about wifes death read here because of difficulty communication with you excuse us you have permission go moscow for one month then return greetings organization department isfendiarov in case of nondelivery after twenty days return to tashkent sender."

Chagatayev put away the letter and the telegram, picked up his box of collective farm medicine, and walked out of the post office. Chimgai was nothing much—a few mud huts almost unnoticeable in the middle of the open space of the empty world around it. Chagatayev bought himself a loaf of barley bread and in five minutes was out of the town with his face into the breeze. The sun was shining high and hot, but all its light was not enough to warm a human heart. Chagatayev stopped thinking; he looked at some of the things along the road—at the blades of dead grass which had fallen from some wagon, at the clumps of digested food dropped by donkeys, at a decrepit Russian bast sandal left by some unknown wanderer; these remains and leftovers from strangers' lives or activities distracted Chagatayev from his own thoughts. Finally he saw a little tortoise: it was lying with its swollen neck stuck out, its feet helplessly extended, no longer defending itself inside its shell; it had died here, on the road. Chagatayev picked it up and looked at it. Then he took it to one side and buried it in the sand. This tortoise was now closer to his dead wife Vera than he was himself, and Chagatayev stood there in wonderment. He sat down on the ground, confused but still understanding that he was alive and acting with an established goal; the usual phenomena of nature in front of him were foreign to him and boring; he felt no need any longer for something to look at or to enjoy. He threw away with revulsion the barley loaf which was getting hot in his hand. Then he started to cry out as he had in childhood when his mother took him out of Sari-Kamish, and he began to look around in this unfamiliar place trying to see if someone were not listening to him—as if behind every man there walked his tireless helper just waiting until the final moment of despair before coming forward. . . . In the distance, in the silence, as if behind a dead curtain, in some close-by but different world, a noise kept on repeating itself. The sound had no meaning or precision. Chagatayev listened; he remembered that he had known these sounds before but he had never understood them and he let them slip through his attention. The sounds were repeated again, they came slowly, with dead pauses, as if wetness were falling in enormous, congealing drops, as if a small horn were being carried deeper and deeper into a blue forest and was being blown briefly from time to time. Or maybe these sounds came from much closer, inside Chagatayev's own body, coming from the slow throbbing of his own soul, reminding him of that other life which was now forgotten by him, smothered by the sorrow in his contracting heart.

Chagatayev got up and went quickly back to his people's village. Toward evening he was so exhausted that he fell asleep, without having taken refuge in a warm crevice in the ground. All night long he heard a confused murmuring, many kinds of agitation all around him, the uneasy stirrings of nature, believing in what it was doing and what it meant.

On the second night he was already inside the limits of the reed forest, close to all his relatives. He thought that the Dzhan people were asleep at that moment, and hoped the night might be a long one, a night when they were not hungry and not in torment, so that in the morning they would have, so as not to die, at least some weak sense of reality, something no bigger than a dream. This was why Chagatayev usually worried less at night; he realized that it was easier for sleeping people to live, and that right then his mother remembered neither him nor herself, while the little Aidim was lying alone, keeping herself warm, like a happy person who needs no one else.

He walked slowly, as if resting, past low, leafless desert trees, and he crossed a little channel; the late, yellow moon shone on the flowing water. A shimmering dust hung in the moonlight over the ancient caravan road running from Khiva to Afghanistan. Chagatayev could not understand this. The road had been abandoned for whole centuries; it ran on hard, packed sand; only in one place did it cross a crust of loess where just then, probably, it was dry, and a thick walker's dust was rising. Camels and donkeys don't make a dust like that, their dust rises higher and thickens over the rear end of the caravan. Chagatayev left his path, and walked diagonally across the wilderness in a southerly direction, to see what was moving there where there should have been nobody. For a long time he walked across the bowl of the reed forest, away from the marshes, parting the prickly, sweet-smelling bushes with his hands, before he came out on a dry, clean burial mound, swept by the winds, beneath which some forgotten prehistoric town was lying in its grave.

The old road bent itself around this mound at its base and then disappeared into the southeast, toward China and Afghanistan, into the darkness. The unknown walkers had not yet got this far, they were moving quietly, you couldn't hear them at all—perhaps they had turned off the road, or gone back, or laid down to sleep on the ground. Chagatayev went out to meet them; he did not expect to find anything happy or joyful, and he knew the dust might be rising in the moonlight from wild beasts coming from deep in the delta of the Amu-Darya and headed for the distant oases, for the collective farms, where there were sheep to be eaten.

People were walking toward him. Chagatayev lay down by the side of the road and watched them. The district commissioner Nur-Mohammed was leading the blind man, Molla Cherkezov, by the hand; behind them Chagatayev's mother was walking, and Aidim with her. Farther back were other people, among them the aged Sufyan, the muttering Nazar-Shakir, his wife whom he loved as the only gift in his life, then Durdi together with his wife, altogether fourteen persons, maybe eighteen. The rest of the people had probably not been able to wake up, or had lost all strength and desire to move.

Gulchatai was carrying some reed roots as a food reserve wrapped up in her son's raincoat; Aidim was dragging a sheaf of grasses along the road at the end of a stalk; Nazar-Shakir had a big bundle of blankets on his head; Molla Cherkezov was holding on to Mohammed with his left hand while his right hand was groping for something in the air—all of them had their eyes closed, they were walking in their sleep, some of them whispering or muttering, accustomed to living in their imagination. Only Nur-Mohammed had his eyes open, seeing the whole world clearly. He was smoking herbs wrapped in the dried leaf of a swamp bullrush, and he was silent.

Chagatayev went up to Mohammed and asked him: where was he taking the people?

Nur-Mohammed greeted Chagatayev, and answered him:

"What people? Their souls left them long ago, it's all the same to them whether they live or not."

He went on walking. Chagatayev walked beside him. Mohammed was smiling to himself and looking away; even in the darkness nature looked sorry and hateful to him, and behind him walked the almost nonexisting people.

The road wound around the little mound on which Chagatayev had just been. A new idea came to him as he looked at this hill of dirt mounded up over another small people which had mixed up its bones and lost its names and bodies in order no longer to attract the attention of those who would torment it. Slave labor, exhaustion, exploitation never take away just physical strength, just arms to work with—no, they take over the mind and the heart, too, and the soul is destroyed first of all, and next the body falls, and then man hides himself in death, sinks into the ground as if into a fortress and a refuge, not realizing that he has been already weaned from worldly interests, his brain already accustomed to just believing, seeing dreams, imagining what is not real. Was it possible that his Dzhan people would soon be lying somewhere nearby, the wind covering them with soil, and even the memory of his people vanishing simply because they had never succeeded in erecting something of stone or steel, had never dreamed up eternal beauty? They had dug the dirt out of irrigation canals, but the flowing of the water had filled them up again, and the people had dug out the silt and the extra soil, and then the muddy flow had brought new silt and covered up their labor, leaving no trace of it.

"Where are the others? Are they asleep?" Chagatayev asked Nur-Mohammed.

"No, they stayed behind, but they'll come after us; they'll catch up."

Aidim, who had been close to them among the ones in front, fell fast asleep, and lay down. Chagatayev noticed this, and looked around: two more sleeping people were lying behind them.

"Let them be!" Mohammed told him. "They'll recover in a while, and they'll come along."

But Chagatayev picked up Aidim in his arms and carried her. She was sleeping, no longer shivering with fever, her sickness had probably left her. In spite of the grass diet and her illness, her body was not thin, it had absorbed into itself all the goodness in even the dry stalks of the reeds, and she seemed now set to live for a long time and happily.

"Where are you taking them?" Chagatayev asked Nur-Mohammed.

"To Sari-Kamish, their birthplace and native land," Nur answered, "where they used to live."

"Why?"

"They've got to go somewhere. . . . I'm leading them by the long road, around the flooded areas. Anyone who walks always feels better for it."

"And the sick?" Chagatayev asked.

"They can walk a little, too. The road will make them well. We've left the swamps, and there'll be no more fever."

Chagatayev did not believe in Nur-Mohammed's good

intentions. He didn't know—would the sick be able even to feel good health once their minds had been distracted from their own interests for so long and their hearts had become so used to languishing? This was why they had stood disease and suffering so mute and unfeeling, as if it were none of their business. Chagatayev dropped back from Nur-Mohammed, in order to look at his mother. Aidim was sleeping quietly in his arms. Gulchatai opened her eyes when Nazar walked up to her but said nothing to him; the blind Molla Cherkezov, weak and childish, was holding on to her hand. The mother looked absentmindedly at her son, whom she recognized, but she could not remember if she had seen him up close. Nazar went on looking at his mother and she turned her eyes away from him because she was ashamed to be alive in front of him so weak and so unhappy; she would have liked to love him with all her earlier, forgotten strength, but now she couldn't, now she had heart enough only for her breathing, and she was pleased by her son's Red Army cap and she thought that she must get it from him as a present, to keep her head warm while she slept.

A little later the wandering people found dry, warm sand along their road and they lay down on it to sleep until morning. Chagatayev did not want to sleep; he put Aidim down between his mother and Molla Cherkezov and stayed by himself, not knowing what to do until morning. Sometimes bored, sometimes smiling, he mumbled something to himself, living out his useless life.

10

Those who had fallen by the roadside the day before or had stayed behind out of weakness arrived by morning, and once more they all moved on behind Nur-Mohammed. Aidim was walking now, and she even laughed with Chagatayev. He felt her forehead—there was no fever, she had become alive and frisky.

About noon the old Sufyan called Chagatayev to one side of the road. He told him that near the channel of the Amu-Darya River two or three old sheep might sometimes still be found, sheep which lived alone and had forgotten men except that, when they saw one, they remembered their shepherds of long ago, and ran up to him. These sheep had survived mysteriously, left behind from the enormous wild flocks which the Bey had wanted to drive into Afghanistan but had not been able to. The sheep had lived with their sheepdogs for some years; then the dogs began to eat them, or died, or ran away out of grief, and the sheep were left by themselves, gradually dying of old age or being killed by wild animals, wandering around the waterless sandy desert. But some of them still survived, and were still wandering, shivering, one next to another, afraid to stay alone. They walked in huge circles around the impoverished steppe, never deviating from their circular paths; it was to this intelligence they owed their lives, because the close-cropped grass which they had eaten grew up again while the sheep were covering the rest of their circular route before returning to the original spot. Sufyan knew four of these grassy circles around which the survivors of these dying wild flocks kept on moving until they died. One of them was not far away, and they were almost at its junction with the road along which the Dzhan people were now walking back to Sari-Kamish.

Sufyan and Chagatayev walked out to a small, damp depression in the sand, and stopped there. Sufyan dug a hole in the sand with his hands, and at the bottom it was wet. The old man explained that the sheep raked the ground with their front legs, and then chewed the damp sand, to slake their thirst. Here was the place to wait for them; he knew the time required for them to complete their whole circular route, and he figured it was time for them to show up here. The year before he had walked behind the flock and come as far as this place. Then the flock had numbered forty head, of these Sufyan had eaten six, seven had died along the road, and the rest had gone on farther.

Nur-Mohammed led the people, too, to where Chagatayev and Sufyan were waiting for the sheep, and they all lay down and drowsed beside the path where the year before the sheep had chewed the wet sand. All the people slept again, although it was still a long time before evening and only a little time had gone by since morning. Chagatayev walked alone among the sleepers, fearing that none of them would wake up again; he was bored and exhausted with his own thoughts and memories. He walked up to Aidim—she was sleeping with her eyelids closed sweetly over her eyes, and smiling in oblivion or in a dream. Having no happiness in her real life, she found it in feeling and in thinking, when she had her eyes closed. Molla Cherkezov had buried his head in Gulchatai's breasts, holding close to her, sleeping, not remembering that he was blind. Nur-Mohammed was lying off to one side; he was tossing on the ground, and whispering something.

"What are you whispering about here?" Chagatayev asked him.

"More than forty people are still left," Mohammed said. "That's still a lot."

He was counting the people, how many had died, how many were still alive.

Chagatayev talked a little with Sufyan; the old man was not asleep but just keeping his eyes shut as if he were saving his vision and didn't want to waste his spirit on impressions of the visible real world. Chagatayev told him that his wife had died in Moscow, but Sufyan did not share his grief and just muttered something, and then said that Chagatayev should go out to meet the sheep, or else they might find wet sand in some other place and pass to one side of the sleeping people.

Gulchatai had wakened. She was sitting up now, holding the head of the sleeping Molla Cherkezov on her knees. Chagatayev walked up to his mother to talk to her, but he didn't say anything. He realized that he was turning to the old man and to his mother just to get comfort from them, to be able to go on living. But was this all his existence was about, to secure for himself some spiritual peace, the consolation of people close to him? He had been wrong not to write a postcard to Ksenya —from that place where there had been a post office—telling her to go to the Communist party's central committee if it was hard for her to live without her mother, while he, her father, was far away and maybe not coming back at all to help her.

Chagatayev patted Gulchatai's bare head, and then put his Red Army cap on her, because the strong sun must be making his mother's head ache. She took it off, and hid it under her; she believed in property and saved it, this was why her blouse was now unbuttoned, inside it next to her naked body, hung the various things she owned, warming her breast. Close by his mother, a Kirgiz woman was lying face down in the sand. She was sleeping, and crying in her sleep in a child's voice, going off sometimes into a fit of childish weeping and then falling back into quiet, even breathing. Chagatayev raised her face a little by the temples, and he saw that she was an old woman and that her mouth did not open when she went off into her little baby cries. It seemed as if a child was crying inside her, a child so alone and so foreign to her that it did not wake her from her sleep. Or else this was the crying of her own child's soul.

Chagatayev laid the woman's head back on the ground and walked off to meet the wandering sheep. At first he walked slowly, but then when daylight began to be covered by the night he ran on faster, so as not to miss the sheep in the darkness. Sometimes he stopped and panted, then hurried on again. When it became quite dark, Chagatayev ran with his body bent far over, so he could see occasional little blades of grass and touch them with his hands—this was the direction in which the sheep might go. Otherwise he might wander off to one side, end up in the hungry sands, and not see the roving flock.

He ran for a long time along the empty sheep path. Midnight came, or perhaps it was later. From fatigue and grief, which he was not conscious of but which was smothering his heart, and from the cool, weak wind, Chagatayev lost his memory as he ran—he fell asleep, fell down, and could not stand up again. He slept hard, alone in the desert, in the thin silence, where nothing stirred. Four little blades of short grass, as lonely as orphans, stood around the sleeping man as if they were sorry that he would get up and go, and they would be there alone again.

Chagatayev opened his eyes at dawn, his consciousness lit up for a moment, and then went out, and he fell asleep again in warmth and oblivion. Two sheep were lying by Chagatayev's side, warming him with their body heat. Others stood around, waiting for the man to raise his face. There were forty of them, they had been missing their shepherd for a long time, and now they had found him. From time to time an old ram came up to Chagatayev and carefully licked his neck and the hair at the back of his head. The ram kept moving his body from side to side, trying to see the shepherd's dog, but no dog was there. He was tired of leading the sheep, of quieting them at the watering places, of guarding them at night from lonely animals. He could remember the good times of long ago when the shepherd and his dogs took care of all these worries. Now he had grown intelligent, thin, and unhappy, and the sheep hated him for his weakness and for his indifference to them, and they also could remember shepherds and dogs, even if the dogs, when they kept order among them at a watering hole, had sometimes bitten scraps out of their wool which they had a hard time growing back on the desert grass they ate.

When he woke up, Chagatayev drove the flock of sheep off toward his people, and he got there by nightfall. The people were drowsing as they had before, only Aidim was playing in the sand, making little streams and roads in it. Chagatayev woke the people and instructed them to collect firewood and some dead, dry grass, to light fires, and to cook the meat. Sufyan eagerly started to cut the throats of the sheep, and was the first to drink the blood from the neck veins but he then caught it in a basin and gave it to the others to drink.

Chagatayev ordered that not more than ten head should be butchered, with the rest kept for breeding and for eating later. The ram was left, he walked off and lay down in the distance, and all the sheep still living collected around him. Thin and hardened by their wild wandering life, from a distance they looked more like dogs.

The people started to cook the carcasses whole on the fire, without cutting them into pieces, and when they were browned they put them on the sand at one side. Then the eating started. The people ate the meat without greed or enjoyment, pulling the meat off in little pieces, and chewing it in weak, opened mouths. Only Nur-Mohammed ate a lot and quickly, he tore the meat off in layers and gulped it, then when he was full he gnawed the bones until they were clean and sucked the marrow out from inside them and at the end of eating licked his fingers and lay down on his left side to sleep. The married folk walked off to sleep at one side. Molla Cherkezov also led Nazar's mother away into the distance, the single people and the orphans stayed around the dying fires—they had grown so weak and they slept so hard that it was as if the food they had eaten had broken their strength and they were conquered by it.

During the night Chagatayev walked around the stopping place, counting the living sheep with the one ram, collecting the sheep-skins and the heads in one place, and he started to look into the darkness: what was Ksenya doing there now, far beyond this dark, under the electric lights of Moscow; and where was his dead Vera lying, what was there left on the earth of her big, shy body? Chagatayev walked among the sleeping people, they lay uncovered on the sand as if they had been slaughtered themselves and had left no gravediggers. But some of the husbands and wives were still stirring, making love to each other. Molla Cherkezov was lying with Gulchatai. Chagatayev saw this, and he wept. He did not know what to do here now, to teach this small people socialism. He could not leave them to die alone because he himself, abandoned by his mother in the wilderness, had been taken care of by a shepherd. Soviet power and an unknown man had fed him and nurtured him, for life and for growing.

The sick and the weak were dozing in their fever. Two of them had gone to sleep with sheep bones in their hands which they had been sucking before they slept, to build up strength. Chagatayev walked out to the wet hole dug in the sand, and fixed up a little well. When some water had collected in it, he went back to the sick, wakened them, gave each one a quinine powder, and then kept running back to the little well in the sand, bringing them water in which to drink the medicine.

It had already grown late. Chagatayev felt cold, he lay down next to one man who was feverishly ill, to get heat from his body, and fell asleep. By morning the ram and all the sheep had disappeared. Judging by their tracks, they had gone off into the open sands, abandoning their usual grazing path.

11

Sufyan figured it out in his head and then said that the sheep would inevitably come back to their grazing round or else wander over into another, larger circle which ran through Kara-Kum. But both these nomadic trails came out at the dirty

Sari-Kamish lakes, not far from which was the native land of the Dzhan people, so that sooner or later the sheep would show up at Sari-Kamish in the valley of eternal shadow and they would see the dark Ust-Urt hills where many of the persons now here had lived their whole lives. Nur-Mohammed agreed with Sufyan.

"We'll follow them," he said. "We'll drink their blood, and eat their meat. In seven or eight days, we'll come out at Sari-Kamish. . . . Did somebody die last night?" Nur-Mohammed asked.

They told him that one old woman had died, a Karakalpach, and Nur-Mohammed conscientiously marked it down in his little notebook. Chagatayev could not remember this old woman and he had not seen her—she had spent the night alone, going far away from the general camp, and had died there quietly.

The people moved in a long file along the tracks of the fleeing sheep. The sick and the weak walked behind, and sat down often to rest, drinking water out of their homemade wineskins. Chagatayev walked behind all of them, so that no one could fall down and die without being noticed. The animals had probably been running fast; this was Sufyan's guess from the tracks left by the sheep, and Chagatayev agreed with him. He walked up on a high sand hill and as far as the horizon stretched in front of him he could not see the smallest cloud of dust from the moving herd—the sheep had already gone too far.

An old woman serf from Khiva gave Chagatayev a rag which she tore from the hem of her skirt and he tied it around his head, which was hurting from the sun. The people moved patiently along; Aidim had recovered completely and she was cheerful—for her, since she knew nothing, there were enough things around to spark all the feelings and impressions she was capable of. When she grew tired, Chagatayev took her in his arms so she could sleep on his shoulder, making a little scream sometimes, and muttering in her strange dreams. But what dreams could nourish the consciousness of this wandering people, once it could accept its own fate? It could not live with the truth; it would perish of sadness at once if it knew the truth about itself. But men live because they're born, not by truth or by intelligence, and while the heart goes on beating it scatters and spreads their despair and finally destroys itself, losing its substance in patience and in work.

Late that night the people had not yet caught up with the sheep. By morning Nur-Mohammed was asking again: did someone die during the night, or were they all still living? Only one little boy had died, and Mohammed marked down the fallen soul with satisfaction in his little notebook. There were only two children left by now in the whole Dzhan people: Aidim and another little girl who had been born by accident three years before after some stranger had joined the people out of the sands and then, having lived with it for half a year, gone off again, leaving the child to be born to Guzel, who was the widow of a bandit from the Stari Urgench region.

On the second day the people found two sheep lying on the road; they had grown weak from running and from sickness and now they were dying. Their thinning wool was stuck together with fever sweat, their lean muzzles looked wild and wicked, they had begun to resemble jackals, there was no fat left in their tails. The people killed one sheep at once and ate him, without lighting a fire, and they divided up the bones and took them along for supper. In the next two days they found nothing edible at all except for a few stray blades of grass, and they found water twice in old holes.

The people moved now only in the evening and the morning; during the day they buried themselves in the sand from weakness and from the heat, and slept. Nur-Mohammed marked down the dead each day, and Chagatayev verified their deaths, listening carefully to the heart and examining the eyes because one time Sufyan and another old man, the slave Oraz Babayev from Ferghan, had pretended to be dead. But Chagatayev heard the hollow, distant heartbeat through their bones, lifted them to their feet, and ordered them to go on farther.

"Why did you want to die?" Chagatayev asked them.

"Our souls have fallen ill from living," Sufyan said. Their bones had dried out and grown twisted, their sinews had all tightened up, they wanted just to stretch out, let the rain wet them and the wind dry them and the worms chew them.

Oraz Babayev just stood there looking at Chagatayev and could say nothing: he probably considered himself already dead.

"We just can't live," he said out loud, "every day we've been trying to."

"Don't worry, we'll learn how together," Chagatayev told him.

"We'll stand it a little longer," Sufyan agreed, "and then suddenly we'll all die."

One old Russian, called Stari Vanka, walked up to Sufyan, felt his throat, lifted up his eyelids and looked carefully into each of his eyes, then felt his ribs, and told him:

"What's the matter with you? You're hardly weaned from your mother's breast, and you think you're dying! Hang on, we'll survive, we'll win, for sure, and we'll come to the land of honey yet."

The Russian walked away, smiling. His own life should have been finished almost every day for sixty years, but he hadn't yet died a single time so now he had lost his faith in the power of death and of all bad luck in general, living calmly and indifferently like some happy and immortal man. Chagatayev knew that Stari Vanka at one time—some thirty years before— had escaped from penal servitude in Siberia, had fastened on to this people which was not kin to him, and got along well with them all, having forgotten the road back to Russia.

A dark desert wind blew in the night and the sand started

wandering under this wind and gradually closed over forever the faint traces where the sheep had run. Early in the morning Chagatayev walked away from the sleeping, drowsy people when he realized that the herd of sheep was now gone for good and that to go after them made no sense, so that his enfeebled people found itself in the middle of the desert, without food or help, without the strength to go on to Sari-Kamish and at the same time unable to turn back to the floodlands of the Amu-Darya.

A queer morning wind was blowing into Chagatayev's face, sand swirled around his feet and groaned like a Russian blizzard outside the shutters of a peasant hut. Sometimes you could hear the plaintive sound of a musical cow's horn, sometimes a harmonica was playing, or a faraway trumpet, or most often of all a two-stringed instrument called a dutar. All this was really the sand singing, tortured by the wind, one grain of sand being reduced to powder by rubbing against another. Chagatayev lay down on the ground, to think about the future of his job: he hadn't been sent here for this, to die himself and to give his people nothing better than death.... He felt his face with his hand, it was covered with hair; lice had settled on his head; his unwashed, thin body was mourning from neglect. Chagatayev thought of himself now as a sorry, uninteresting person. Who even remembered him now, except for Ksenya? And probably even she had started to forget him; youth was too excited about its own happy problems. Chagatayev fell asleep in the unquiet sand, apart and fairly far from all the unsleeping people. Everything was standing stock-still inside him, deep down and for a long time, holding its breath inside his body, in order not to die completely. He woke up in darkness, half covered with sand; the wind was still blowing and it was already a new night. He had slept the whole day through. Chagatayev walked back to the camping place, but his people were not there. All of them had wakened long before and gone on farther and faster, away from death. Only Nazar-Shakir was lying there; he had died, his mouth was wide open and now the wind and the sand were saying something inside it. When Chagatayev found the dead man he felt him for a long time to be sure that he was really dead, and then he covered the man with sand so he would be invisible to anybody.

Chagatayev walked all night. Sometimes when he leaned over he could see the tracks of his people in front of him, and sometimes when the tracks had been wiped out by the wind, he went on by hunch.

In the morning Chagatayev noticed a place where there should be water, and he found an old well which had been filled in with sand. He dug with his hands into its damp bottom and began to chew the sand, but he had to lose more in spitting than he managed to swallow; then he started to gulp the wet sand itself, and the torment of his thirst left him. For the next four days Chagatayev tried to go forward across the desert but his weakness never let him go far and he would return to the wet sand so that, weak as he was from hunger, he should not die of thirst. On the fifth day he stayed where he was, determined to recover his strength in drowsing and unconsciousness and then to catch up to his people. He ate the two quinine powders he had left, and some crumbs from the lining of his pockets, and this made him feel better. He realized that his people must be close by, for they too had no strength to go far, but he didn't know the direction in which they had gone. Chagatayev pictured to himself the secret satisfaction with which Nur-Mohammed would mark down his death in his notebook. He smiled over one of his old ideas: why people counted so much on grief and destruction when happiness is just as inevitable and often easier to find than despair.... Chagatayev protected himself from the sun with wet sand and tried to sink into unconsciousness, to rest and save his strength, but he couldn't, and he kept right on thinking all the time, living a little, and watching the sky where a warm wind blew from the southeast through a weak haze, and where everything was so empty that there was no believing in the existence of a hard, real world, anywhere.

Still lying down, Chagatayev crawled to the nearest sand hill where he had noticed a tumbleweed bush half covered with sand. He crawled up to it, broke off several of its dried-out twigs, and chewed them, and then he pulled the rest of the bush out of the sand and set it off rolling with the wind. The bush bumped its way along and disappeared behind the dunes, headed off somewhere into distant places. Meanwhile Chagatayev, crawling around the vicinity, found some dried-out blades of grass growing in little sandy crevices, and he ate these, too, just as he found them. Sliding down the sand hill, he fell asleep at its base, and different memories flooded over him in his sleep, useless, forgotten impressions, the faces of uninteresting people he had seen at one time or another—all the life he had lived through turned back upon him. Chagatayev followed it helplessly and quietly, unable to forget for good the small unimportant things which had later been covered over by important happenings—and now he realized that everything had stayed intact, indestructible and safe. Here his friend Vera was leaning over him, hardly seen by him then, leaning over him and not going away, torturing the awareness of this man drowsing in the desert and not going away; and behind her, against a bank of clay were moving the shadows of silver branches which had grown at some time in the sunshine, perhaps at Chardzhoui, perhaps somewhere else; a Khiva donkey was looking at Chagatayev with familiar eyes and crying out plaintively, without interruption, as if reminding him that he should untie it and set it free; many more eternal little things like rotting trees, a village post office, unpopulated hills under the noonday sun, the sounds of a wasting wind, and tender embraces with Vera—all of this flooded into Chagatayev at the same time and stayed inside him, motionless and stubborn, even though in the past, in actuality, these happenings and people had been gentle ones, doing no harm to the conscience or the feelings of a man. But now these images, these thoughts, gnawed at Chagatayev's brain, and he wanted to scream but didn't have enough strength to do so. He started to listen hard—for infrequent, dripping, resonant sounds in the distance, from beyond the black, dead horizon, out of the dark, free night where the last shining of the sun was being swallowed whole, like a river falling down into the desert sands. Sometimes he heard the sounds of nature far away, not knowing the reason for them or their full meaning.

Chagatayev stood up on his feet, to get rid of sleep and this whole world sticking to the inside of his head like a prickly bush. Sleep flowed out of him, but all the strange thickness of memory and thought stayed alive in him even when he was awake. He saw something on a sand dune next to him, either an animal or a tent, but he couldn't understand what it was, and he fell backwards out of weakness. And whatever it was on the neighboring sand dune, an animal or a tent or a machine, moved now into Chagatayev's consciousness and boldly began to torment him, though he did not understand it or even have a name for it. This new phenomenon, tied in with all that had preceded it, overpowered Chagatayev, and he fell into unconsciousness again, to save his soul.

He woke early on the following day. The wind had disappeared without a trace, a shy silence stood all around him, so empty and so weak that a storm might suddenly have burst out inside it. The shadow of night moved up into the sky and lay there across the world, higher than the light of day. Chagatayev was well by now, his mind had cleared, and he thought about his problems as he had before; his weakness had not left him but it no longer tortured him. He foresaw that he would probably die here, and his people, too, would be lost as corpses in the desert. Chagatayev did not regret this for himself, his bigger nation would still be alive, and it would still bring general happiness to the unhappy, but it was hard that the Dzhan people, which stood in need of life and happiness more than all the other peoples of the Soviet Union, should be dead.

"It won't be," Chagatayev whispered.

He began to lift himself, pressing with all his body on his trembling hands placed flat against the sand, but immediately he fell back again: behind him, right behind the back of his neck, something was moving; Chagatayev could hear the quick, retreating steps of something alive.

Chagatayev closed his eyes and felt in his pocket for the handle of his revolver; now he was only afraid that he might not be able to cope with the heavy weapon because his hand had only a child's strength left in it. He lay there for a long time, not moving, pretending to be dead. He knew about a lot of animals and birds which eat dead people on the steppes. Probably wild animals were moving in a long, unseen procession behind his people, eating those who fell. Sheep, his people, wild animals—this triple train was moving in order across the desert. But the sheep, having lost their accustomed grazing round, began sometimes to follow the wandering tumbleweed being blown by the wind, so the wind became the true guiding force, of everything from grass to men. Probably they should be following the wind, in order to catch up with the sheep, but Nur-Mohammed didn't know anything, and Sufyan had become bored with living, and had stopped thinking.

Chagatayev wanted to jump up at once, shoot at the animal, kill it, and eat it, but he was afraid he might miss, out of weakness, and frighten the animal away for good. He decided to let the animal come right up to his body, and kill it at point-blank range.

Light, careful steps could be heard all this time behind Chagatayev's head, now coming closer, now going away. Nazar waited, holding his breath, for this slinking thing to hurl itself upon him, not yet sure that he was dead. He worried only that the animal might sink its fangs into his throat at its first pounce, or that, wounded, it might run far away. He could now hear the little steps right next to his head. Chagatayev pulled the revolver a little more out of his pocket, feeling inside him a real strength compounded out of all the little scraps of life left in him. But the steps moved past his body, and went beyond. Nazar half-opened his eyes: just beyond his feet two enormous birds were walking, moving away toward a sand dune opposite him. Chagatayev had never seen such birds; they looked like the eagle-carrion vultures of the steppes and at the same time like wild, dark swans. Their beaks were like vultures' beaks, but their thick, powerful necks were longer than those of eagles, and their solid legs carried high the delicate, airy bodies of true swans. The strong wings of one bird were a pure gray in color, while the other had blue, red, and gray feathers. This one was probably the female. Both birds seemed to have on trousers of snowy-white down. Even from one side, Chagatayev noticed little black spots on the female; these were fleas digging through the down into the stomach of the bird. Both birds looked like enormous nestlings which were not yet used to being alive, and were moving with extreme care.

The day had grown hot and dreary, little sandstorms were whirling across the surface of the sand, evening still stood high in the sky, above the light and the warmth. The two birds walked onto the sand dune opposite Chagatayev and looked at him with their thoughtful, farseeing eyes. Chagatayev watched the birds from under his half-closed eyelids, and he could see even the gray, thin color of their eyes as they looked at him full of thought and of attention. The female was cleaning the talons of its feet with its beak, and spitting out of its mouth some kind of old leavings, perhaps a remnant of the clawed-up Nazar-Shakir. The male rose into the air, but the female stayed where it was. The enormous bird flew low to one side, then soared upward with several flappings of its wings, and almost at once began to fall straight toward him. Chagatayev felt the wind in his face before the bird hit him. He could see its white, clean breast in front of his face, and its gray, clear eyes, not wicked but thoughtful, because the bird had now noticed that the man was alive, and watching it. Chagatayev lifted his revolver, held it with both hands, and fired straight at the head of the bird dropping down upon him. In the white down of the bird's breast, blown out by the speed of its downward flight, a dark spot appeared, and then the wind blew all the down and wisps of feathers around the spot of the direct hit, and for a moment the body of the eagle held itself motionless in the air above him.

The bird closed its gray eyes, and then they opened by themselves, but they no longer saw anything—the bird was dead. It lay across Chagatayev's body in the same position in which it had been falling, its breast against the man's breast, its head on his head, burying its beak in Chagatayev's thick hair, spreading wide its black, helpless wings on both sides of him, with its feathers and down strewed all over Chagatayev. Chagatayev himself fainted from the force of the blow, but he was not wounded; the bird had simply stunned him since the dangerous speed of its fall had been braked by the bullet. Chagatayev started up with sharp pain: the second bird, the female, had driven its beak into his right leg and having pulled out some of his flesh was flying off into the air. Chagatayev, holding the revolver with both hands again, fired twice but missed; the gigantic bird disappeared behind the sand dunes, and then he saw it flying away at a great height.

The dead eagle was no longer on top of Chagatayev, but lying on the sand at his feet. The female must have pushed it there in an effort to make sure that it was dead, and to say good-bye to it.

Chagatayev crawled over to the dead bird and began to eat at its throat, tearing the feathers away from it. The female eagle was still to be seen, but it had already climbed high up in the sky where the shadow of night, the dusk of dawn and sunset, stands even at full noon, and it seemed to Chagatayev that the bird would never come back, that there it had found the happy land in the air of all the birds that fly.

When he had eaten a little, Chagatayev tied one leg of the dead bird to his belt and he put the other end of the belt deep inside his trousers, so he would know it if some beast of prey tried to steal the eagle away from him. Then he treated the wound torn in his leg, wrapped it in cloth, and lay down quickly, in order to recover a little of his strength.

## 1 2

Gulchatai felt no sorrow over her son, she had forgotten him. She walked along behind the others, bent over, feeling the sand with her hands whenever it seemed to her that something desirable might be lying on it. Molla Cherkezov hung on to Gulchatai by her clothing, trying all the time to remember that he was still alive. Nur-Mohammed, with despair in his heart, held on to Aidim's hand; it was his plan to train this girl and fatten her so he could use her as a wife and then sell her to someone else. It worried him that there were too few women in the Dzhan tribe and that those who were still among the living had grown decrepit—there was hope only for Aidim because she was still a little girl. Women were priced higher than men because they could be used both for work and for love, although men could also be sold profitably in Afghanistan if they didn't die on the long trip.

On the morning when Chagatayev did not show up at the general stopping place, Nur-Mohammed smiled and made a detailed entry about the disappearance in his notebook. He was sure that Chagatayev had run away to save himself, as anyone would who had life and little courage, and Nur-Mohammed felt better without him. The people no longer kept on asking him if they would arrive soon at Sari-Kamish, and they never remembered now about eating. Nur-Mohammed himself might perish out of weakness, but he still had old reserves inside him because he had eaten a lot of rice and meat and fruit while he was living in the oases and when he had gone secretly into Afghanistan to see the Khan, Dzhunaid, who had run away a long time ago.

Sufyan started to walk on this day with the wind, with the broken-off spears of dead grass and the tumbleweed; he knew that this was the direction the sheep must now have taken, once the wind had blown away without a trace their grazing path along which, in spots around old oases, some stable grass could grow. The rest of the people would have followed Sufyan, but Nur-Mohammed ordered them to walk in the opposite direction—against the wind, toward the southeast. He pulled Aidim closer, trying to feel her breasts which were just starting to grow, but all he could feel was her thin ribs.

Nur-Mohammed looked at them all; the people were rocking in the wind, the sandy blast along the ground was beating against their legs, dead grass was flying in the faces of the walking people—the wind was ripping the grass out of the sandy wasteland by its roots with overpowering force. Some people fell down from the wind, others walked along in sleep, scattering in different directions, losing each other in the darkness of the blowing sand.

Nur-Mohammed stopped.

The wind was now blowing out of the southeast with the steady, oppressive strength of some great machine. The people were scattered by it and they no longer heard, or else they didn't recognize, Nur-Mohammed's voice calling each of them by name to follow him. He was panting himself, from impatience, from thirst and from hunger; his mind was already darkening under the shadow of indifference to his own fate. He had been planning until now to lead this insignificant, exhausted tribe into Afghanistan, and to sell it there in slavery to the old Khan, so that he might live out his happy life somewhere in an Afghan valley on the bank of a stream, in his own place filled with the good things of life. But now Mohammed saw, as he was all but swept off his feet by the wind and the sand, that the Dzhan people would either perish or be dispersed in unconsciousness: each person's body had grown empty, and his heart was gradually dying. They would not get as far as Afghanistan, or if they did they would not be able to serve even as the lowest kind of farmhands, because now they no longer had that small desire to live which is essential even for a slave.

Nur-Mohammed stood for a long time while the people were scattering in the darkness of the wind and lying where they had fallen in death or in sleep. Aidim wrapped herself around his neck, breathing quietly in her own oblivion. Mohammed held her carefully, and he watched the dying people with satisfaction, forgetting that he, too, wanted to drink and to eat. Sufyan sat down on the sand and collapsed. Gulchatai had been lying on the ground for a long time, with her blind husband, Cherkezov, folded against her on the side away from the wind as if he were trying to make himself comfortable with her in a bed. The Karakalpak nicknamed Tagan, who was thin but not very old, took off his clothes, his trousers and his robe, threw them into the wind, and buried himself naked in the sand so he could hardly be seen. Mohammed felt good, that the Soviet Union would now be diminished in numbers by an entire tribe. Even if nobody had known about this people, their potential usefulness to the government had now disappeared and these workers who once upon a time had dug whole rivers for the Beys and Khans would no longer be digging anything, even their own graves.

Nur-Mohammed not only felt satisfaction now, he even skipped a little in a kind of dance while he watched these people fall into their last sandy sleep. He held his own value dearer now: there would be more good things for him in the desert as on all the earth, because there were fewer people living. It's uncertain if he would have enjoyed selling this people into slavery more than now that he had lost it, now that nature had become more spacious, now that the mouths of all these greedy poor people had been closed forever. Mohammed made up his mind to go to Afghanistan for good, and to take Aidim with him so that he could sell her there, and recoup at least some of his losses from working in the Soviet Union.

The wind suddenly let up, and it grew lighter all around. Nur-Mohammed clutched the girl so tightly to himself that Aidim opened her eyes. Then he took her into a comfortable cave in the sand to fondle her, lonely for the pleasure to be had from another's body. Neither hunger nor long-felt grief could destroy in him the need for human love; it lived on imperishably in him, hungry and independent, breaking through all cruel misfortunes and not losing its strength in his weakness. He could have embraced a woman and made a child, in sickness, insane, a minute before his final death.

It was getting dark in the desert, night fell, and it went by in darkness. Some people who had fallen on the sand from the wind the night before stood up the next morning and began to look around them in the clean light and in the quiet of another day.

Not far away, from behind a desolate sand hill, a shot was heard. Sufyan, half asleep, sat up and began to listen. Aidim ran up to him, away from Mohammed who was sleeping some distance away and did not wake up.

The people were all alive although their lives were no

longer supported by their own will and were almost beyond their strength. They looked straight in front of them although they had no clear idea of what they should now do with themselves; eyes that had been dark started to grow bright with indifference, showing no attention to anything nor even that they still had vision, as if they were blinded or worn out. Aidim alone wanted to be alive, she had not yet used up her childhood nor her mother's reserve of energy, she looked at the sand with eyes that were still full of life.

Two more shots were fired behind the dune. Aidim walked out to see what it was but at first she could not find where the shots had come from. None of the other people moved; they feared no enemy and they expected no friend or helper.

Aidim walked over the fourth row of dunes and saw below her a man lying either asleep or dead next to a dark bird. The girl slid down the bank of sand, and recognized Chagatayev. She felt his face with her hands; it was warm, and breath was coming out of his mouth.

"Sleep!" Aidim said in a whisper, and she put her fingers on Chagatayev's eyelids which had started to open in his sleep.

Then Aidim untied the bird from the belt, took it by its leg and dragged it back across the sand to her people.

The whole tribe gathered around the bird and looked at it without greed, they had lost the habit of hoping for food. Then Aidim took a knife from the trousers Tagan had thrown away and started to pluck the bird and to cut it into little pieces. She gave each person who could still eat a little piece of the flesh of the bird, and she herself sucked the blood and the juice from each piece before giving it away. The people devoured their portions, sucked the bones and nibbled at the shredded feathers, but they were not satisfied and only wanted more.

Aidim went back to Chagatayev. The people, thinking there were more birds there, followed behind her. But the people walked too slowly now, some of them crawled, helping themselves with their hands. Chagatayev's mother was one of these, helping Molla Cherkezov to crawl too. Others stayed where they were because they no longer had the strength to move their skeletons. Aidim, moving away a little, stopped and waited for the people struggling after her. It was evening before they all reached the sand hill behind which Chagatayev was lying. All the time the tribe was moving, Aidim could hear the rubbing and the scraping of the bones inside them; probably all the fat had dried up in their joints, she thought, and their bones were now torturing them.

Nur-Mohammed watched this movement of the tribe from a distance but it did not interest him. He wanted first to look for some water in the neighborhood, even if it were salty, for without it he would not get to the Khiva oasis. He decided to come back for Aidim later, after he had found water, so he could give her some to drink and then go away with her forever to Afghanistan.

13

Pain made Chagatayev cry in his sleep, and he woke up; he thought he had dreamed the pain and it would quickly go away. Two dark birds—one the female of before, the other a new male—were walking away from him. They had pecked his body three times with their sucking beaks and had torn his flesh to the bone on his chest, his knee and his shoulder. When they had walked away a little, the birds stopped, turned their necks, and looked at Chagatayev—each bird out of one eye. Nazar pulled out his revolver and started to fire at the birds quickly, before a lot of blood had flowed out of his wounds and he had lost the strength that had been gathered while he slept. The birds rose into the air. He managed to fire at them twice, and one bird dropped its wings and floated down, folding its legs under itself; then it laid its head down on the sand and stretched out its throat as if in unbearable fatigue. Blood started to flow out of the bird's throat, soaking into its feathers and into the sand around it. Indifference showed in the bird's eyes as gray films were drawn over them. The other bird flew up into the sky where it gave a short, hollow cry, sounding as if it came from an empty underground cave, and disappeared into the mist of the sun's shining.

Aidim appeared from behind the sand hill. She walked up to the dead bird, and dragged it by its leg past Chagatayev.

"Aidim!" Nazar called to her.

The girl walked up to Chagatayev.

"Give me a drink," he begged.

Aidim pulled the dead bird to him and, kneeling down, placed its throat next to Chagatayev's lips while she began to squeeze the wet feathers so the blood would drop into Chagatayev's mouth.

"You go on lying there now, as if you're dead," Aidim told him. "The birds will fly down on you, and the jackals will come, you kill them all and we'll have something to eat...."

"Where are the other people?" Chagatayev asked.

"Here they come," Aidim told him.

Chagatayev asked her to bring some water, if there was any, and wash his wounds. Aidim examined them, pulled away from them the wool of his clothing, and then licked them with her tongue, since she knew that saliva can heal a wound.

"Don't worry, you won't die, your wounds are little ones," she said. "Now lie back quietly, or else the birds won't come back...."

Aidim dragged the dead bird behind the sand dune where her people had set up a new stopping place in the quiet of a deep depression in the sand. They ate the bird at once, and if people far away, who eat every day, could not have felt any slaking of their hunger from the tiny piece of shredded meat which Aidim gave to each person, this insignificant morsel of food almost filled up a person with this great hunger, and in any case it gave the body hope, and comfort.

It grew dark again. Sufyan dug down to a wet level in the sand with his hands, and started to chew it against his thirst. Some of the people saw what he was doing, walked up to him, and shared his supper of sand and water. Nur-Mohammed was afraid of the cold, and came back to the tribe in the night so he could lie down somewhere in their midst, and warm himself.

Early in the morning, Mohammed woke up Aidim, took her in his arms, and walked off with her toward Afghanistan.

Chagatayev was lying where he had been before, like a dead man, keeping watch for the birds. He had counted his bullets, there were only seven left. He was sure the birds would come back again, for it was the male he had killed, and the female with the colored feathers had flown away and would come back again, and not alone, to finish off the man who had murdered its first, and perhaps its favorite, mate.

Aidim jumped out of Nur-Mohammed's arms and ran to say good-bye to Chagatayev. He kissed her, stroked her face with his thin hand, and smiled. It was still not light. Nur-Mohammed was waiting for the girl a short distance away.

"Don't go away, Aidim," Nazar told the child. "We'll soon have some luck ourselves."

"I know," Aidim answered. "But he ordered me...."

"Call him," Chagatayev said.

Aidim beckoned to the tall Nur-Mohammed with her hand.

"You still dying?" Nur-Mohammed asked Chagatayev. "I thought the birds had eaten you up a long time ago."

"Why do you take the girl with you?" Chagatayev asked him.

"It's necessary, it must be," Nur-Mohammed said.

"Let her stay with us," Nazar said.

Aidim sat down on the sand next to Chagatayev. "I'm staying," she said, "I'm still a little girl, and I'm tired to death of walking. I don't have to go!"

Chagatayev leaned his elbows on the ground, and pulled the girl toward him. Dew had fallen, and Nazar quietly licked his tongue along Aidim's hair on which there were little drops of moisture.

"Go away by yourself!" he told Mohammed.

"It's high time for the dead to shut up!" Nur-Mohammed declared. "Lie back on the ground and sleep!" He kicked Chagatayev in the face with his foot in its canvas shoe.

Chagatayev fell backwards. He noticed that Mohammed's official briefcase was still hanging around his neck; Nur-Mohammed thought of his whole life as just temporary assignments to distant places, and perhaps the only pleasure he took in his own existence was in being able to leave one place and move to another: let those who were left behind perish by themselves!

Without thinking, Chagatayev got quickly to his feet. Now he felt empty and light, his body had become free, and he swayed like a weightless man. Aidim put her arms around his stomach, to keep him from falling. But Nur-Mohammed grabbed Aidim around her body, and walked away with her. Chagatayev started after them, but fell down, and then stood up again, trying to summon all his strength. His weakness made the whole world swing in front of his eyes: first it was there, then it wasn't. Nur-Mohammed went on walking away, without hurrying; he was not afraid of a man already half dead.

"Where are you going?" Chagatayev said with all the strength he had.

Aidim was crying in Nur-Mohammed's arms.

"Keep me here, Nazar Chagatayev. . . . I don't want to go to Afghanistan, there are bourgeois living there. . . ."

Where had she learned about bourgeois? . . . Chagatayev did not fall down again, some triumphal force of life came back to him, he raised his revolver in his stiffening arm and ordered Nur-Mohammed to stop. The latter saw the weapon, and started to run. Aidim had noticed a sore on Mohammed's neck, and she dug her long fingernails into it. Nur-Mohammed cried out in a terrible voice and struck the girl in the face, but there was no way for him to swing his arm, and his blows did not hurt her much. Aidim did not take her hand away from the sore and was swinging now around his neck, and he stopped holding her so that he could manage to hit her harder.

"Look, how it hurts you!" Aidim said. "We told you not to steal, that you mustn't. But you stole, you bandit! You suffer now, go on and suffer!"

Thick blood began to ooze out of Nur-Mohammed's sore. By now Aidim had pulled the dry scab completely off the sore.

Nur-Mohammed gave a loud groan, and finally managed to drop the girl. Having glanced at Chagatayev, he picked Aidim up and ran with her again; he didn't want to have worked for nothing. Chagatayev could not shoot straight at him for fear of killing Aidim whom Mohammed was now holding in front of his chest, so he fired at his legs. The bullet hit him. Nur-Mohammed was lifted off the ground like some strange and useless object, and he fell in a dive with his shoulder toward the sand, and he might well have crippled Aidim. But she managed to jump away as he fell, and she picked herself up and ran to Nazar. Chagatayev wanted to fire again, to destroy Mohammed, but he had too few bullets and he needed to save them, to hunt so he could feed his people.

Nur-Mohammed lay on the sand for a few seconds and then jumped up and ran away, scrambling up the steep slope of a sand dune like a strong and healthy man. He was crying with pain as he ran, because the movement had torn his wound open wider, but he did not hear his own crying. He vanished behind the sand hill and his voice was silenced forever for Chagatayev. Aidim stood there in amazement, looking after

Nur-Mohammed. She was wondering if he would die quickly or not.

Then she walked back with Chagatayev.

"Go quickly!" she said. "Lie down on the sand again, before the birds come back, or we'll have nothing to eat!"

Feeling weaker and weaker, Chagatayev walked back to the place where he had been lying, and fell back on the sand again. Aidim went back to the tribe at its stopping place. The day was still young, but all the people were already lying down, to hoard their lives in sleep, wrapped up in what was left of their clothing.

Chagatayev found himself alone in his sandy pass. He tried to think only about what was absolutely essential to the life of his people and their salvation. The eagle had flown away again, alive and unhappy. If he had killed its mate the first time, then what had he shot the second time? Probably a second mate . . . No, with birds it doesn't work like that; this meant it must have been a friend or relative of the first male, perhaps a brother summoned by the female to help in wreaking vengeance. Now that the brother was dead, too, where would the female turn for help? If no other bird could be found now, beyond the horizon or high in the sky, to help in the fight, then the female would come back alone. Chagatayev was convinced of this. From childhood he had known the feelings of wild animals and birds. They cannot cry, to find in tears and in exhaustion of the heart both comfort for themselves and forgiveness their enemy. Instead they must act, seeking to wear out their suffering in struggle, in the dead body of their enemy or else in their own destruction.

During his second life in the desert it had seemed to Chagatayev that he was always going somewhere, farther and farther away. He began to forget details about the city of Moscow; Ksenya's face stayed in his memory only in a general way, not as something living—he regretted this and strained his imagination to see her sometimes in his mind's eye as she really was; when he could fix her face in his memory, he always noticed that her lips were whispering something to him, but he didn't understand and couldn't hear her voice across the great distance. Her different-colored eyes watched him with surprise, and perhaps with sorrow that he was not coming back for a long time. But he felt this was only flattering himself. Actually, Ksenya had probably forgotten Chagatayev completely; she was still a child, and her heart was crowded with the fine life she was still creating for herself, and there was not room enough in it to keep all the impressions disappearing past her.

The day passed painfully, bringing no relief. Chagatayev knew that he couldn't feed his people just by killing one or two more birds, but he was not a great man and he couldn't think out what to do now that might be more realistic. Maybe his hunting the birds was an insignificant affair, but it was the only thing possible until his exhaustion had been overcome. With the strength he had had before, he would have scoured the desert for tens of kilometers around them, he would have found the wild sheep and driven them back here. With just one man in shape to walk fifty or a hundred kilometers to a telegraph station, he would have summoned help from Tashkent. Perhaps an airplane might appear in the sky above him! No, they didn't fly here ever, because so far no treasures had been found in the ground on which to waste a valuable machine. And this wretched, almost useless task, requiring chiefly patience in pretending to be a corpse, still comforted Chagatayev, but he made up his mind to go on the next day with his people to their homeland, to Sari-Kamish, no matter what happened.

He drowsed off. The world again alternated in front of him—now lively, full of light and noise, now fading away into dark oblivion.

In the evening Chagatayev heard confusing sounds. He got

ready, thrusting his right hand under his back, where his revolver was lying. He was wrong: this had not been the noise
of eagles flying. His mother had come up to him, carrying
her head low, touching his body with her hands and looking
hard with her eyes at all the sand around him, at the ground
where he was lying. She wasn't checking to see if her son was
alive or dead, she was searching with her all but blind eyes
for more dead birds. Strange creaking sounds came from his
mother's body; the dry bones of her skeleton moved only with
difficulty and with pain. Gulchatai went away slowly, helping
herself to move by holding the ground with her hands and
pulling at the sand.

Soon Chagatayev heard these same sounds of moving bones
again. He fought down sleep and concentrated on them. Something was moving beyond the sandy crossing of the hill where
he was lying. Old Vanka was looking at him from there, next
to him stood Sufyan who had obviously climbed up the hill
from the other side, then he saw someone else's indistinguishable face, and there, too, were Aidim and even Molla Cherkezov although he could not see the light. The human faces
gradually grew more numerous, and they were all looking at
Chagatayev. Chagatayev looked at them, too. Only the thought
of food had brought them here, but this thought was not clear
or sharp, as with ordinary men, but something guileless, capable of remaining unsatisfied without becoming bitter.

What did these people expect from Chagatayev? Could they
really eat their fill on one or even two more birds? No. But
their grief might turn into gladness if each one could receive a
shredded piece of the meat from a bird. It would serve not to
fill them up, but to unite them in a common life and with each
other, it would give them a feeling of reality, and they would
remember their own existence. Eating could serve at the same
time to nourish the human spirit and also to make sunken,
quiet eyes shine again, and see the light of the sun spread out

across the earth. It seemed to Chagatayev that all mankind, if it had been standing there in front of him, would have looked at him in the same way, ready and waiting to delude itself with false hopes, to carry on the delusion, once more to begin its various unavoidable ways of living.

Chagatayev smiled; he knew that grief and suffering are only ghosts and dreams, that even Aidim could destroy them with her child's strength; an unreleased happiness, not yet tested, goes on beating in the heart and in the world, as in a cage, and every man feels its power, and its drawing near. Soon now he would change the destiny of his people. Chagatayev waved his hand to them. Aidim understood, and told them all to go away, so as not to bother Chagatayev in his hunting.

At the start of night, when all the people had dozed off, Aidim went out alone into the desert to look for the wild sheep. First she told Sufyan and Stari Vanka to dig with their hands in a small depression between two long sand dunes. There she had found clay under the sand, and this ought to hold water, and she had already drunk a little of it from the hole. She remembered, too, that when there is nothing to eat, water can also nourish.

14

The night moved across the sand. Chagatayev was sleeping on his right side, filled with dreams which drove out his thirst, his hunger, his weakness, and all his suffering. He was dancing in a garden, lighted by electric lights, with a grown-up Ksenya, on a summer night smelling of the earth and of childhood, just before the dawn already burning on the very tops of the poplar trees like a faraway voice which could not yet be heard. Ksenya was tired in his careful arms, her eyes closed as if she were asleep. With the dawn a wind came through the trees out of the east to rustle the dresses of the dancing women. The music played, and the early light and the wind moved across the faces of the quiet, happy people. Then the music stopped, it grew quite light around them, and Chagatayev was carrying Ksenya in his arms. Suddenly he saw darkness where there had been light, his head ached, and, falling, he turned onto his back as he fell, so as not to hurt Ksenya whom he was holding in front of him like a little child: let her fall on top of him and not be injured. He grabbed at her, but she was no longer there. He cried out and jumped up from the ground into the darkness, and two sharp blows, on his head and on his chest, knocked him back again.

The big birds, falling onto him and then rising into the air, struck him with their beaks and tore his clothing and his body with their claws. Chagatayev tried to get on his feet, but he couldn't and he was losing strength from the pain and from new blows by the heavy birds falling onto him. He turned over and dug his hands hardened by despair into the sand surrounded by the desert night and soaked with his last blood. He wanted to scream, so as to pull up some desperate strength from what was left of his ebbing life deep inside him, but the stinging blows of the eagles' beaks and their claws ripping his tendons choked his cry before he could fill his lungs. The beating of their wings made a wind, and he couldn't breathe in this storm, and he was choking from the down and the feathers of the birds. Chagatayev realized that the first two blows of their beaks had hit him in the head near the back of his neck, where blood was now flowing down his neck, and one of the nipples on his chest, it seemed, had also been ripped and this wound hurt him with a tickling, aching pain.

Finally Chagatayev managed to get to his feet for a moment. He stretched out his arms, ready to grab the first bird which fell on him and to strangle it in his hands. The eagles were in the air, picking up momentum to dive on him. His foot stepped on his revolver, and he leaned down to pick it up, but couldn't lift it. The birds dove onto his back, but by now his head had cleared and he was able to figure, from the number of new beak wounds he got, that there were three eagles. Chagatayev, when he had picked up his revolver, threw himself backwards trying to shake off or to knock down the bird fastened to his back, but he threw his weight badly, and fell down awkwardly on his side, and the eagles flew off to one side. Chagatayev tried to raise himself for a better aim and all the exhausted bones in his body scraped against each other, just like the bones of the people in his tribe. He heard it, and he felt sorry for his body and its bones—once upon a time his mother had put them together out of the poverty of her own flesh, not from love or passion, not from delight or enjoyment, but from the most everyday kind of necessity. He felt himself to be some alien property, like the last possession of poor people which they want to squander to no good purpose, and this feeling drove him to a terrible fury. Chagatayev sat down firmly on the sand. The eagles, without even rising to any great height, rushed down on him again at great speed, their wings held tightly to their bodies. He let them come close, and then he pulled the trigger. Chagatayev could see the eagles clearly this time, there were three of them, and now he was firing accurately, cold-bloodedly, saving himself as if he were another person, a close friend who needed help. He fired five bullets almost point-blank at the birds rushing down at him. With a whistling of air the birds flew low over him, unable to check their momentum because they were either dead or fatally wounded. They fell some meters beyond Chagatayev on the dark night sand.

Chagatayev was shuddering with anxiety and exhaustion. He dug a little trench in the sand and lay down in it, squeezing his body in to get warm and to go to sleep, without worrying about how much blood would flow out of his wounds while he slept, not even thinking about them or whether he would live.

Aidim walked a long way that night, and then she grew tired, lay down, and fell asleep, without having heard Chagatayev's shots. But remembering that she must not sleep long, she soon woke up and anxiously walked on farther. A poor, late-rising moon came up out of the earth a great distance away, and threw its low light across the sand. Aidim looked around her with searching eyes. She knew it was impossible that nothing should exist on the earth around her. If one walks across the desert for a whole day, one will inevitably meet or find something; either water, or sheep, or one will see a lot of birds, somebody's lost donkey will turn up or various animals will run by. Older people had told her that there are just as many good things in the desert as in any country, no matter where, but there are few people, and this is why it seems as if nothing else exists. And Aidim didn't even know that there was any land richer or better than the desert sand or the reed thickets in the flood waters of the Amu-Darya River.

Aidim stood on the highest sand dune; the twinkling, glimmering moonlight drew her in one direction—everywhere else the light moved easily but in this one place something was blocking it. She walked to where the light was darker and soon she could make out a little baby lamb. The lamb was scratching with its legs on the very top of a small sand hill and throwing up the sand in such a way that from a distance, seen through the darkness and across the spectral hilly desert, it looked like something important and mysterious going on.

The lamb was probably digging up blades of grass which had been buried in the spring, and eating them. Aidim quietly climbed up the dune and grabbed the lamb. It did not struggle, for it knew nothing about men. Aidim threw it down and wanted to bite through its weak little throat, to drink its blood and then to eat it. But then she noticed, right under the hill, a lot of sheep breathing heavily like people and digging with their front feet into the sand, trying to get at wetness hidden

95

somewhere beneath them. Aidim let the lamb go and ran down from the dune to the flock of sheep. Before she got to them, a ram jumped up and stood stock-still in front of her, its head lowered for a fight. Aidim sat there for a while, facing the ram, and she thought in her small mind about what she should do now. She counted the flock; there were twenty-four of them including the lamb and two goats which were also living there. She crawled quietly up to the nearest sheep; the ram moved with her expectantly. With her hand Aidim felt the sand in the hole the sheep had been digging—it was dry, there was no wetness to be felt at all. A spume of tiredness was on the lips of the nearest sheep, sometimes they snapped at the sand with their mouths and then dropped it together with the last of their saliva. The sand was not watering them, but sopping up the last liquid in them. Aidim walked up to the ram; he was not very thin, but he was breathing heavily from thirst. Aidim took him by the horns, and pulled him along behind her. The ram went at first, then stopped to think about it, but Aidim tugged at him and the ram followed her. Some of the sheep lifted their heads and stopped working to follow the girl and the ram. The other sheep, and the goats, too, quickly caught up with them.

Aidim pulled the ram along in a hurry. Her memory for places was exact, but it was only at daybreak, with the moon extinguished in the sky, that she reached the deep depression where she had dug water for herself from the sand. She left the flock there, the sheep starting to paw the sand again with their front legs, and she went on to the sleeping place of her people. She was resentful that not a single water hole had been dug. Sufyan and Stari Vanka had either died or turned lazy, or perhaps they had drunk enough for themselves without worrying about the lives of the others.

At the stopping place Aidim felt all the sleeping, unconscious people: they were still used to living, they were breathing, not one of them had died. Aidim woke up Sufyan and Stari Vanka and told them to pasture and guard the sheep, and she went off herself to Chagatayev, to bring him back to the camp to eat.

For a long time Chagatayev did not waken when Aidim tried to rouse him; he was slowly dying because his blood had been trickling out of him while he slept and now it could be seen coming out of his wounds in infrequent little spurts and then drying in the sand. Aidim understood it all. She ran back to the place where her people had been sleeping, but they were all moving off to the flock of sheep in whatever way they could: some crawling, some barely getting to their feet, some managing only with the help of others. Aidim searched with her eyes to see which of them had a relatively whole or soft piece of clothing left, but she couldn't find what she wanted. All their clothing was either thin and bad, or there was very little of it. Molla Cherkezov had a pair of soft wide trousers but because of his blindness they were not clean. Aidim took off her own shirt and looked at it: never mind, she was still a little girl, she hadn't picked up the infections and the diseases of the older people, the shirt smelled only of sweat and of her body and there was no dirt on it—for the desert is a clean place. Aidim went back to Chagatayev, tore her shirt into strips, and bandaged all the wounds on his body and his head which were still bleeding. Chagatayev had wakened by now, and turned over, so it was easier for the girl to work. He opened his eyes, and he saw Aidim, and the dead birds, and the sand, as if through a heavy twilight, although the usual sunny morning had begun. He looked at the eagles again, and he saw that the biggest bird was the female, and the other two eagles were much smaller: they were its children. The female had flown back here with its husband's truest friends, its own children.

15

For four days the people ate, recovering from their grief and their misery. Aidim saw to it that no one ate too much, and she stopped those who were especially zealous over their food, or rapped them across the eyes: otherwise they would not have felt it. The wounds on Chagatayev's body began to heal over; he gave Aidim his underclothes and she sewed herself a skirt and a blouse, without which she would have been naked. Sufyan, who carried around with him all his life his own inventory of what was needed for day-to-day living—matches, a needle, thread, an awl, an ancient document attesting his identity, a small knife, and a few other things—asked Aidim to mend his clothes. She sewed up the large rips in the old man's robe, then at the same time she fixed up the decrepit clothing of all the people in those places where their bodies showed through; for many people she had to shorten their garments to save material which she could use for those who had too little. Out of such scraps she made a whole pair of trousers and a shirt for Tagan because he had thrown his clothes away somewhere in the sand when he had thought it was time for life to end, and since then he had gone naked.

This work took Aidim four more days—only Stari Vanka and Chagatayev helped her with the mending and the sewing. Besides this, she checked up on the general way of life of her people, on the distribution of food, on their sleep, and on the remaining sheep, seeing to it that they were pastured and watered and that they did not get thin, using up their bodies to no good purpose. At night Aidim tied each sheep to a person, while she placed the ram next to herself and tied a leash around his neck with its other end fastened with a strong knot around her stomach. Thanks to these precautions not a single sheep ran away, even though this meant that they stayed lying down all night without grazing and adding to their weight.

One morning nine days after Aidim had brought in the flock of sheep, the people took to the road again, walking toward their native land. By now there were only ten sheep left, plus the ram as the eleventh; the people had eaten thirteen sheep and three eagles. The people walked well now, and they felt that they really existed, without having to strain their memories for recollections of who they had once been.

There were only three full days of easy walking left between them and Sari-Kamish. On the second day they could already see the gray plateau of Ust-Urt and the darkness around its base, the valley of empty land with its few miserable streams. They were all glad and they hurried on, just as if this were a place where happiness was guaranteed, with tidy houses and doors standing open for them, waiting for their masters. Chagatayev led his mother by the hand, and he smiled, just as if he found himself once more, as in his childhood, face to face with a great future, ready for all its agonizing, patient labor, his heart filled with confused, shy feelings of inevitable triumph.

On the evening of the third day the people crossed the last shining sand—the frontier of the desert—and began to drop down into the shadows of the valley. Chagatayev looked at this land, its pale salt marshes, its loamy soil, the dark antiquity of its ground which still held, perhaps, the bones of that poor Ariman who had not been able to achieve the brilliant destiny of Ormuzd and had not conquered him. Why had he not been able to be happy? Maybe because the fate of Ormuzd and others who lived in distant countries filled with gardens was foreign and repulsive to him, their lot did not really appeal to him or attract his heart; otherwise he himself, patient and energetic, would have been able to create in Sari-Kamish all that there was in Khorosan, or to conquer Khorosan. . . .

Chagatayev liked to turn over in his mind this question of what people before him had not been able to accomplish, because this was precisely what it was now up to him to work on.

Two days later the tribe had passed through the valley and was approaching the foot of Ust-Urt. Chagatayev found a small reservoir of fresh water here, filled by the spring runoff from the high plateau, and the people stopped next to it, to rest and to pick their permanent dwelling places. There were only three sheep left, and the ram was a fourth. But this was not frightening for a people like the Dzhan, who knew how to use the good things of nature even in its most barren places. On the first day there, Aidim found some ravines filled with tumbleweed. This grass had been blown here from the desert by the southeasterly winds, and only those bushes of tumbleweed which bypassed these blind gullies were lifted over the slope to the higher table-land and blown farther on, into the steppes.

Sufyan went back to his cave, where he had been living before Chagatayev's arrival, and he advised the whole tribe to settle around it. It was a broad, spacious valley covered with grass, and a little stream which ran through it from Ust-Urt did not dry up until the middle of each summer. The people walked into this valley and on the way they found traces of their former stopping places, dating from the days of the Khans. Nothing much was left, just the usual wasteland, some hand-fuls of coal, some lumps of clay, the stake of a tent abandoned by everybody, worn by the heat and the wind. A child's skull-cap was half-buried in the ground; Aidim cleaned it and put it on her head.

The valley recommended by Sufyan was a good one to live in. Its grass cover stretched a long way, and even now, at the end of summer, not all the grass was dead; among the yellow stubble could be seen live, green blades of growing grass. The bed of the stream was empty, but in the heart of Sari-Kamish, a couple of kilometers away, you could see a mirror of water, a lake made by the mountain streams in spring and early summer; this was enough to exist on. When the people walked into the mouth of the valley a lot of tortoises had run out from under their feet and, at a safe distance, slowly stretched out their necks to look at the new arrivals, each tortoise with one black, vigilant, gentle eye. Chagatayev was delighted by it; now he could breathe deeply and collect himself; everything in life seemed possible to him now, as it had before, and the best part of it achievable right away.

He walked with Aidim far into the hills of Ust-Urt, up on to its high plains. He was looking for firewood, or at least the brushwood which grew sometimes in its ravines. Wood would be needed to make household tools and furniture. Along the way Chagatayev carried Aidim in his arms so that she would not get tired, and he kissed her cheeks, her eyes, her hair; this made him feel better in his heart. He loved to sense another's life, it seemed to him that something more mysterious and beautiful, more meaningful, was there than in himself, and both his health and his feelings were often made better just by the chance to hold someone by the hand. Aidim hugged Chagatayev, too, around his head, and she stroked with her fingers the two bald patches on his scalp which had been made by the eagles' wounds; she remembered that was the time when she had eaten an entire small eaglet all by herself.

Chagatayev had only a penknife, so it took him a long time to cut down and then cut up one not very big softwood tree growing all by itself in a stony gorge where nothing else was growing, as if some bird had once dropped the seed here from the air above.

For several days in the Ust-Urt valley which had been chosen to live in, only two people worked—Chagatayev and Aidim; the rest of the people drowsed in the caves which they dug out for night shelter along the slope of the valley, or they caught tortoises and fixed them for eating, but they ate little, and almost unwillingly, and they went once each day to the lake for drinking water. Chagatayev ordered that the three sheep and the ram were not to be touched, but kept in reserve against some extreme need. He counted the people, who was alive and who had died, and found one child missing, a three-year-old girl. No one could tell him, not her father nor her mother nor anyone else, where this little girl had disappeared or how she had died. No one could remember when she had slipped out of their arms and been blown away into the desert by the wind and the sand.

Chagatayev and Aidim started to collect the clay with which to make the first house, but no one helped them with the work. When Chagatayev ordered Sufyan and Stari Vanka, as the healthiest of them all, to help with the job, they carried clay twice, and then stopped. They sat down on the ground and thought, even though in all the years of their age they had long ago had time to think everything through and to arrive at truth.

Then Chagatayev summoned all the people, and he asked them: did they want to live? No one gave him any answer.

Many pale eyes were looking at Chagatayev with the strained attention needed to keep from closing, with fatigue and indifference. Chagatayev felt pain with his sadness; his people needed only oblivion, before the wind would first cool and then blow their bodies away into space. Chagatayev turned away from them all; his actions, his hopes now seemed to make no sense. He ought to take Aidim by the hand and go away from here forever. He walked off to one side and lay down with his face to the ground. He realized that no matter where he might go from here, he would come back again. For his people were the poorest in the whole world; they had squandered their bodies on the waterwheels and in the desert, they had been weaned from the goal of life and stripped of consciousness and of interest, because their desires had never been realized, in any degree, and the people had just lived mechanically. The skimpy daily food—of tortoises, and tortoise eggs and little fish caught in the same reservoir from which they drank their water—was not enough for them. Was there even a little spirit left in this people, enough for him, working with them, to create happiness for everybody? Or had it all been worn away long ago, with even imagination—which is the intelligence of poor people—now extinct? Chagatayev knew that any exploitation of a man starts with perverting him, adapting his spirit to death, to the master's ends, otherwise the slave would not be a slave. And this forced deformity of the spirit continues and grows stronger until the slave's intelligence has been transformed into insanity. The class struggle begins with the conquest of the "holy spirit" locked up inside the slave; then any insult to what the master himself believes in, his spirit or his god, is never forgiven, and the slave's spirit is ground down by lies and by the ravaging of hard labor.

Chagatayev recalled Stari Vanka's story about how once in Khiva, in the courtyard of a mosque, he had wanted to kill a peacock, so as to sell it later, as a stuffed bird to a Russian buyer. In a hurry, old Vanka had thrown a stone at the peacock, at the sacred bird itself, but had not hit it. In the distance, in the bushes, either the watchman or some other person had appeared. Stari Vanka picked up whatever was closest to his hand among the plants around him, and threw this object at the peacock. The bird immediately swallowed whatever it was that Vanka had thrown at it, and then uttered its mean, broken-throated cry, and Stari Vanka had run up to it to strangle it with his hands but had not managed to because some Moslems had appeared who grabbed Stari Vanka, carried him out to the street, and thrashed him until they thought he was dead, and then threw him into a disused irrigation ditch. While they were maiming him, Vanka held his face in his hands, and it was then that he realized, from the smell on his fingers, that the second missile he had thrown at the sacred peacock had been a piece of dried excrement. Vanka climbed out of the canal alive, but afterwards he loved to throw something unclean at all the flying or sitting birds he saw, especially if they were doves, until after many years he lost interest even in doing this.

Something alive was snuffling over Chagatayev's head, and he thought it was a sheep. But the animal took Chagatayev's ear in its mouth and began to rub it between its toothless jaws. This was the same ferocious but helpless dog Chagatayev had seen at the settlement where his people had lived on the Amu-Darya. It had not been with the people in the desert, it had fallen behind somehow, or perhaps it had stayed to be the solitary guardian of the abandoned settlement and then, having grown bored, come by a straight road to Sari-Kamish where it, too, had obviously lived in previous years. Chagatayev took the dog's head and pushed it to the ground, to make the dog lie down. The dog lay down quietly, it was trembling with exhaustion—grown old and wild, without the strength either to end or to change its wretched life but still convinced of the felicity of its existence.

The dog fell asleep next to Chagatayev. Aidim went on puddling the clay by herself with her bare feet, carrying the water two kilometers in wineskins. When Chagatayev woke up, several people were sitting around him, waiting for him to regain consciousness. Sufyan, the oldest man, told Chagatayev that it was natural that the people now had no spirit, and did not know any goal in life, were not tempted by better food, and warmed themselves by the weakest sort of heat from their own hearts, getting this warmth from the grass, the tortoises, the fish, and from their own bones when they had nothing to eat.

Sufyan leaned down to Chagatayev's ear, nudging the dog away. The dog looked at the people greedily and sadly. It had come all this way in pursuit of this tribe, separated from it, digging itself deep into the sand in the daytime so as not to be noticed by the eagles of the steppe and by other beasts of prey. Sufyan told Chagatayev:

"You figure this out the wrong way. The people must live, but they can't. When they want to eat rice, drink wine, have robes, and tents to live in, strangers will always come up and say: take what you want, wine, rice, camels, whatever in life will make you happy. . . ."

"Nobody gives things away," Chagatayev said.

"They used to give a little," Sufyan said. "A handful of rice, a flat loaf of bread, an old robe, songs in the evening, a few bribes, we had all these long ago, when we worked on the Bey's water-wheels. . . ."

"My mother ordered me to feed myself, when I was a little boy," Chagatayev told him. "We had little, we were dying."

"Very little," Sufyan agreed. "But we always wanted a great deal: sheep, and a wife, and water from the irrigation ditches. There is always an empty place inside a man's spirit where he can hide a little more of whatever he wants. And we worked for that little bit, for poor, infrequent food we worked until our bones dried out. We didn't know any other life," Sufyan went on. "I'm asking you: if we almost died from work and hunger, just for a little bit to eat, do you suppose even our death would be enough to earn real happiness for us on this earth?"

Chagatayev stood up.

"All you need is life! In the old days it was the slave's spirit that died first, then he stopped even feeling alive. A tumble-weed plant was freer than one of us."

"I've heard about that," Sufyan said indifferently. "We know that the rich are all dead now. But you listen to me." Sufyan was stroking Chagatayev's old Moscow shoe. "Your people are afraid to live, they've lost the habit, and don't believe in it. They're pretending to be dead; otherwise happier and stronger ones will come to torture them again. They've left themselves the least bit possible, what's not needed by anyone else, so no one will get greedy when he sees it."

Sufyan walked off with the people who had been with him.

Chagatayev went to Aidim and worked with her until evening. Then he put her to sleep in a dry cave and went on working himself, preparing adobe bricks out of clay mixed with old grass, for the building of the first house. There was no one near him or in the whole valley; everyone had gone off somewhere, perhaps to trap tortoises or to catch fish in the lake. Chagatayev worked more and more quickly and productively. It was not until late at night that he climbed up the slope to the plateau to see where all the people had gone. The clean, high moon made everything visible; moonlight stood over unpopulated Ust-Urt, covering the valley of Sari-Kamish with the shadow of the mountain, and then caught fire again far over the stinging deserts which stretched to the mountains of Iran. The three sheep and the ram were pastured in a nearby canyon, noisily turning over piles of tumbleweed as they looked for green grass that was still living. In the dark shadow of Ust-Urt, where Sari-Kamish began, a little bonfire was burning, and beyond the bonfire a thin cloud of mist hung over the lake. Chagatayev climbed down from the plateau and walked toward the bonfire. In a half hour he had come close enough to see that his whole people was sitting around the fire, on which desert underbrush was burning quietly. They were all singing a song, and did not notice Chagatayev. He listened to the song with delight; in his childhood he had heard a lot of songs from his mother, from various old men, and the songs were all beautiful but sad. This one had a meaning unfamiliar to him, there was a feeling in it which was not native to his tribe, but they all sang it as if carried away, still not noticing him. Chagatayev could make out even his mother's feeble, shy voice. The song said: we do not cry when tears come to us, but neither will we smile with joy when good times begin, and those times are near at hand. The song ended. Stari Vanka stirred the fire with a stick and pushed out of it some baked fish, testing them to see if they were cooked, and those that weren't ready he pushed back into the fire.

Chagatayev walked back, without having been seen by the people. He began to make bricks again, and he went on working until the moon went out in the sky and the sun began to shine. In the morning he noticed that the people were still sitting around the dead fire, while Stari Vanka was moving and shaking his whole body as if he were dancing. Chagatayev decided not to leave his work, since the night had gone by and there was no time to sleep. He shaped the bricks in the clay forms, putting all the strength of his heart into his labor. Aidim was still sleeping. Sometimes Chagatayev walked over to the hollow where she was lying, and covered her with grass to protect her from the flies and insects: let her refresh herself in sleep, for growing and for a long life. About midday Stari Vanka came up to Chagatayev; he took off the trousers which had been sewed for him out of various scraps by Aidim to replace those thrown away in the desert, climbed down into the trench where the clay was being mixed with water, and started to puddle it with his thin, hard feet.

### 1 6

Two months later, by autumn, four small houses had been built out of adobe bricks in the Ust-Urt valley. These houses, which had no windows because there was no glass, held all the Dzhan people who were finding real shelter for the first time from the wind, from cold, and from small flying, stinging creatures. For a long time some of the people could not get used to sleeping and living inside the blank walls—every once in a while they would go outside, breathe deeply, look at nature around them, and then walk back, sighing, inside the buildings.

At Chagatayev's suggestion the people elected its own soviet of workers, which included everyone, with Aidim as social and political worker, and Sufyan, as the oldest, became president.

The entire Dzhan people were now living as the majority of human beings in this world live, not conscious of their own death from day to day, producing their own sustenance from the desert, the lake, and the hills of Ust-Urt. Chagatayev even managed for them all to have dinner every day; he knew this was very important since only a minority of the world's people living on the land eat dinner, and most of them do not. Aidim took care of keeping them supplied, and made them all look for food and bring it back: grasses and fish, tortoises and small animals from the gullies in the hills around them. With Gulchatai she ground the roots of the edible plants, to make flour, and she reminded Sufyan in time to make the grass nets to catch the birds lighting on the shores of the lake to drink water. When someone forgot to do his job in helping feed them, Aidim would announce to him, in the presence of all the others, that the next day she and Nazar would dig a big trench for anyone to lie down in who didn't like living any longer.

"We don't need unhappy people," Aidim said.

But Chagatayev was not satisfied with the ordinary, skimpy kind of life which his people had now begun to live. He wanted to help make happiness, which had been dwindling away inside each unhappy man since birth, shoot out into the open and become an act and a force of destiny. Both science and common sense are concerned with the same single, essential thing: to help bring out into the light that spirit which is racing and beating inside a man's heart and which can be strangled there forever if it is not helped to free itself.

Pretty soon snow came, and it was harder for Chagatayev and all the others to get their food. The tortoises went into hiding and fell asleep; large flocks of birds flew from north to south over Ust-Urt without lighting to drink water at the little lake and without noticing the small people living down below them. The roots of the edible grasses froze and lost their taste, the fish in the reservoirs swam down to the bottom, toward the dark silence. Chagatayev understood all this and made up his mind to go off alone to Khiva where food reserves were kept and to bring back a whole winter's supplies for his people. Aidim mended his torn, old clothing, he fixed his own shoes with wooden nails he made himself and with narrow strips of leather cut from sheepskins. Then he said goodbye to each person, told them all to expect him back soon, and set off down the valley of Sari-Kamish. For the sake of speed he took no food with him, figuring that on an empty stomach he could make the trip in three days.

Chagatayev disappeared into the heavy fog covering the empty wilderness, and Aidim sat down on the slope of the hill and cried. Tears poured out of her shining black eyes, for she thought that Nazar would never come back again. But by the next day Aidim managed not to cry a single time over Chagatayev: she was absorbed in work, in her need and responsibility for people. She just sighed occasionally, like a poor old woman. The people were still working only weakly, they were not convinced that it was an advantage to be alive, the Beys had robbed them of this belief at their waterwheels, and they neither cherished their own existence nor understood what enjoyment was, even of food.

Most of the work now, after Chagatayev's departure, fell on Aidim. But it didn't hurt her, she had learned from Chagatayev that there are no rich people, and that she herself was poor but things would soon be all right for her, and then still better and better.

After three days of Chagatayev's absence, Aidim remembered him and she creased her face into a frown so that she could start to miss him and to weep for him. But it was already evening, and she had to look for the sheep and the ram, which had climbed up in the ravines some distance off, so she decided to postpone her grieving for Chagatayev until she went to sleep, when she would be alone. By the time she had driven the sheep back to the common hut, a mysterious light blinded her. Brighter lights than any Aidim had ever seen were shining next to the mud houses. She stopped, and she felt like running back with the sheep, to hide in a cave or in some ravine a long way off, and then come back the next day to see what might be there. She seized the ram by the horns but she kept on watching the lights next to the little houses; interest and amazement overpowered the terror in her and she led her small flock back to its home. She was thinking: the lights are either wild beasts, or else they're something good, from out there where the Bolsheviks live.

Aidim saw Chagatayev, walking past the lights. She ran up to him and, shuddering and screwing up her eyes, grabbed his leg. Chagatayev lifted her up in his arms and took her into one of the houses, laying her down to sleep on a bed made of grass, and then he went back outside to unload the trucks. He had met them on the second day of his trip, at the exit from Sari-Kamish into the desert. On orders from Tashkent the two trucks had left Khiva four days before. On one of them there was canned meat, rice, hardtack, flour, medicine, kerosene, lamps, shovels and axes, clothing, books and other goods, while on the other were two men, cans of gasoline, oil, and spare parts.

The Tashkent orders had been to search the Sari-Kamish district and between Ust-Urt and the Aral Sea for the nomadic Dzhan people, and to help it in all possible ways, and not to return until the people had been found, or traces of it which might prove that the entire tribe had perished.

By midnight the goods had been unloaded, and Chagatayev sat down to write a report to Tashkent about the condition of the Dzhan people while the drivers and the leader of the expedition were preparing the trucks for the return trip. Chagatayev wrote until dawn; he proposed at the end of his letter that his people be given the opportunity to recover from its poverty of many years (this chance had now been given, and the people could live through the winter with all it needed, thanks to the help sent by the government) and most important of all, that every person here needed to renew his exhausted body, lived out to its very bones, in which feeling and conscious thought were now too weak to function.

Chagatayev handed his letter to the expedition leader, and the trucks drove off toward the Khiva oasis. All the people were still asleep, it was early morning, snow was lying on Sari-Kamish. Chagatayev took an ax and a shovel, woke up Stari Vanka and Tagan, and went off with them to root out some desert trees. By midday they came back with firewood. Aidim lit the stove with dry grass and began to cook dinner out of the new food which almost no one had ever tasted before in all his life.

The people were so overwhelmed by the new food that they all fell asleep right after dinner. In the evening Chagatayev ordered that another dinner be prepared, and he began to make flat cakes himself out of the white flour, and then he prepared both tea and coffee. He knew that this kind of eating could be a little harmful, but he was in a hurry to feed the people so as to strengthen the bones inside them, so they might recover even a little bit of those feelings in which all other peoples except themselves were rich—feelings of egoism and of self-defense.

Chagatayev watched with pleasure as his people ate— without greed, chewing the food carefully in the mouth, with a consciousness of necessity, and with a brief thoughtfulness, as if they were conjuring up in their imaginations the faces and the spirits of the people who had worked so hard to make this food, and to give it to them.

Chagatayev went on living patiently, getting ready for the day when they could begin to achieve the real happiness of living together, without which there is nothing to work for and the heart is filled with shame. Occasionally he talked to his mother, who now asked him for nothing but only stroked his legs and his body on top of his clothes; he held her bowed head and wondered what he had to do to comfort and to recompense this almost completely destroyed creature inside whom he had begun his life. He did not know that his mother only remembered him at all because of Aidim's reproaches to her, and that she wiped her eyes in secret when she realized that she must love her son although she no longer knew him or remembered him in her own feelings; this was why she touched him as she would anything strange and good.

After a few days it grew very cold, and they had to heat the stove and cook their big dinner in one building, because the stove was used both for warmth and for cooking. No stoves had been built in the other houses. A strong wind was blowing from the top of Ust-Urt, carrying small, frozen snowflakes with it. Aidim took the sheep into the main room of the house where she slept, and left them there for the night. Chagatayev managed with difficulty to bring water from the lake in five wineskins loaded on a wheel-barrow he had made himself; he climbed up onto the plateau against the wind driving straight at him, and he pushed the wheel-barrow in front of him with great effort. And that wind, and the early winter fog lying over all the land around him, and the empty black valley of Sari-Kamish where the wind was trying to knock Chagatayev down and carry him away—all of this convinced him of the need for some different way of living.

People were stirring inside one of the houses, the light inside shone through its open door. There they had finished eating and were dozing off: Aidim was clattering the new dishes, washing away all the leftovers and the dirt, telling the people that they had better stay there for the night where the room had been heated: it would be crowded, but warm.

It was six o'clock, but all the people were already lying down in the one room, close to each other, sleeping in the closeness as if in paradise. Chagatayev ate his dinner standing up, for there was no place to sit down. Aidim went off to sleep in another house, where she had put the sheep, and then Chagatayev went there to sleep, too.

By morning a snowstorm was blowing, but it had grown warmer. There was not a sound in the main house, although day was breaking. Aidim was sleeping warm between two sheep. Chagatayev did not want to wake her, so he went out himself to the house where all the people were sleeping. He lit a lamp, and looked around him.

The people were lying in the same positions as the night before, just as if no one had moved through the long night. Many faces were lying there now in steady smiles. The blind Molla Cherkezov was sleeping with his eyes open, having placed his left arm under Gulchatai's back, so he could feel her constantly, and protect her. The old Persian who was nicknamed Allah was staring out of one half-closed eye, and Chagatayev couldn't guess what this man was seeing and thinking, what desire of the spirit was hidden inside him, whether it was the same as Chagatayev's or something different.

Chagatayev sat next to Aidim all the rest of the day, loving her face and her breathing, watching the flush of youth which more and more covered her cheeks. He let the sheep out into the snow; let them dig and roll in it as they pleased. Then Chagatayev took Aidim's hand in his, quietly rejoicing that Bolsheviks would stand around this poor, gentle being in a steel wall of defense, for this was the only reason why he himself was there.

Aidim woke up toward evening. She swore at Chagatayev —why hadn't he wakened her earlier? The whole day had been wasted. Chagatayev told her to go and wake the rest of the people—he would stay where he was, and not get up. Hearing this, Aidim gave a bitter little scream, and ran out to the neighboring house. She lifted the grass curtain hanging over the entrance, so the cold would pour over the people, and wake them up. But the sleepers only moved closer to each other, huddling together and sleeping like the dead.

A second night went by. In the morning Chagatayev looked at the sleepers again. Their faces had changed still more than the day before. Stari Vanka was pink with new life, and now he looked about forty years old. Even the ancient Sufyan had put on flesh, and Kara-Chorma, a sixty-year-old man, was lying there rose-colored and puffed up, gulping in air with the kind of deep feeling a man shows when he finds wetness at a time of great thirst. Leaning over his mother, Chagatayev could see no change in her face; Gulchatai, the mountain flower, might not have wakened at all, her eyes had fallen down and her cheeks had darkened, the print of the earth was on her. Molla Cherkezov's eyes were open as before, and a distant glimmer showed in them, as if sparking in the depths of his brain, and it seemed to Chagatayev as if vision was coming back to this man.

Nazar stoked up the stove for warmth, and went out for a walk with Aidim; this was the first time he had had a free hour for many months. The snowstorm had stopped during the night; now the last little flurries of snow were falling, and sunshine was already glittering on the highest slopes of Ust-Urt, happy, blinding, promising eternal triumph. Aidim laughed, and ran through the snow; she disappeared in the distance, diving into a gully, and then suddenly she threw her arms around his neck from behind him. Finally he caught her in his arms, and ran with her to the edge of the cliff on which they were standing. Aidim saw his intention.

"Throw me over, but I still won't die!" Aidim said.

While they were returning home, Aidim walked alone, beside him, and she asked Chagatayev:

"Nazar, when will they wake up?"

"Soon, soon . . . Maybe they're awake already."

Aidim was thoughtful.

The stove in the house had not quite gone out. Aidim filled it up again, and then he and Aidim cooked dinner for the whole people, just in case.

By evening some of the people were beginning to wake up. Sufyan woke first, then Stari Vanka and Molla Cherkezov, and by midnight they were all up except Gulchatai. She had died.

Chagatayev carried her into an empty, cold house, and laid her on a bed of dried grass. When they had come to their senses after this long sleep, the people sat down to dinner in the warm mud building, while Chagatayev went to sit next to his dead mother, and fell asleep.

Aidim fed all the people, and scolded them because they had slept through two nights in a row but still couldn't work out how to live. Stari Vanka burst out laughing at her:

"Now we can die!" he said. "Don't worry about us, daughter. . . ."

In the night Aidim went back to the house where Chagatayev was lying next to his dead mother. She lay down quietly in a corner and fell asleep at once. At dawn she got up, and went out to start the day's work. The heated house, where the people had stayed for the night, was empty, and there was no one to be found in the other two houses. Aidim looked at all the things and belongings, all the goods held in common by them, and counted them roughly, then she went into the building where the food supplies brought from Khiva had been stored; worried, she examined even the walls of the houses, but she saw nothing new or changed. The supplies were intact. The canned goods were exactly as they had been the night before when she had taken some of them to make dinner. The sacks of rice and flour stood untouched. Maybe something had been taken, but very little, perhaps some tobacco and matches, which were always taken without any accounting.

Aidim woke up Nazar. Chagatayev went off alone some kilometers; he climbed up to the highest ridge of the mountain, from where he could see the whole world far away, almost to its very ends. From there he could see ten or a dozen people walking one by one to all the countries of the world. Some of them were walking to the Caspian Sea, others to Turkmenistan and Iran, two of them, far apart from each other, were going towards Chardzhoui, and the Amu-Darya. He could not see those who had gone over Ust-Urt to the north and the east, or those who had traveled far during the night. . . .

Chagatayev sighed, and he smiled; he had wanted, out of his single, small heart, his compact mind, and his enthusiasm, to create for the first time a real life here, on the edge of Sari-Kamish, the hellhole of the ancient world. But the people could see better than he could how it was best for them to live. It was enough that he had helped them to stay alive, now let them find their own happiness beyond the horizon. . . .

**FRO**

HE HAD GONE far away, and for a long time, probably never to return. The locomotive of the express train sang its farewell into the empty distance as it disappeared; those who had seen it off walked back from the station platform into their settled lives, and a porter showed up with a mop and started to clean the platform like the deck of a ship stuck on a sandbank.

"Stand aside, citizen!" the porter said to two plump legs standing there by themselves.

The woman walked over to a mailbox on the wall and read the schedule printed on it: the mail was picked up often, you could write a letter every day. She touched the metal of the mailbox with her finger—it was solid, nobody's heart inside a letter would ever be lost out of it.

A new railroad town was just beyond the station; the shadows of leaves danced across the white walls of the houses, the evening sun of summer lit up the landscape and the buildings, as if through a clear emptiness where there was not enough air for breathing. On the edge of night everything in that world was seen too distinctly, blinding and unreal—this was why it seemed not to exist at all.

The young woman stood there in surprise at this strange light in front of her; in the twenty years of her life she could not remember such an emptied, shining, silent void, and she felt that her heart itself would grow weak inside her, from the lightness of the air and from hoping that the man she loved would come back again. She saw her reflection in the window of a barbershop: it was common-place enough, the hair fluffed up and then arranged in loops (this was a hairdo that people wore some time in the nineteenth century), her deep, gray eyes looked out with a strained, almost artificial, tenderness—she had grown used to loving the man who had gone away, she wanted to be loved by him steadily, without any interruption, so that a second beloved life might begin to grow inside her body, together with her own ordinary, uninteresting spirit. But she herself couldn't love as she wanted to—strongly and steadily; sometimes she grew tired, and then she cried from disappointment that her heart could not be indefatigable.

She lived in a new, three-room apartment; in one of the rooms her widowed father lived—a locomotive engineer, while the other two were occupied by her and her husband, who had now gone off to the Far East to build and to put in operation some kind of secret electrical devices. He was always busy with the secrets of machines, hoping by these mechanisms to transform the whole world for the good of mankind, or perhaps for something else: the wife did not know exactly.

The father did not go to work often, because of his age. He was classified as a reserve engineer, replacing men who were sick, breaking in machines that had been withdrawn for repairs, or driving lightweight trains on local runs. They had tried to retire him on a pension a year ago. The old man, who didn't know what a pension was, agreed at first, but after four days of freedom he walked back on the fifth day to the signal station, sat down on a little mound along the right of way, and stayed there until late in the night, weeping as he watched the engines pounding in front of the trains they were pulling. From then on he started to go to that little mound every day, to look at the engines, to live on his memories and his imagination, and then to go home in the evening as tired as if he had just come back from a long trip. At the apartment he would wash his hands, sigh, report that one engine had dropped a brakeshoe on the 9,000th gradient or that some such thing had happened, then he would shyly ask his daughter for some vaseline to rub into the palm of his left hand as if it had been chafed by the tight governor handle, have his supper, mumble something, and quickly sink into blessed sleep. The next morning the retired engineer would go back again to the right of way and pass another day in watching, through his tears, in dreaming, in remembering, in all the fury of his lonely enthusiasm. If he thought there was something wrong with an engine going by him or if the engineer was not driving it as he should, he would scream his judgment and his instructions from his little hill: "You've pumped too much water! Open the valve, you damn fool! Blow off!" "Tighten up your flanges, without losing steam: what do you think that is—a locomotive or a steam bath?" When a train was made up badly, with light, empty platform cars at the front or in the middle of the train where they could be damaged by heavy braking, from his little mound the engineer would shake his fist at the brakeman riding the last car. And when the engineer's own favorite locomotive went by him, driven by his former assistant Benjamin, the old man would always find something flagrantly wrong with it—even when there was nothing wrong at all—and he would advise the engineer to take immediate steps against his careless helper. "Benjamin, Benjamin, my boy, smash him in the teeth!" the old engineer would scream from his little mound next to the right of way.

He took an umbrella with him on bad days, and his only daughter brought his dinner out to him on his little hill, because she was sorry for her father when he came back in the evenings, thin, hungry and enraged by his unsatisfied longing for his work. But not long ago, when the old engineer was shouting and cursing as usual from his little elevation, the Communist party secretary of the station, Comrade Piskunov, walked out to him, took the old man by the arm, and led him back to the station. The office manager entered the old man's name again on the engineers' staff. The engineer climbed into the cabin of a cold engine, sat down at the controls, and began to dream, exhausted by his own happiness, holding the locomotive control with one hand as if it were the body of all laboring humanity to which he had once more been joined.

"Frosya," he said to his daughter when she came back from the station where she had accompanied her husband as he left on his long trip, "Frosya, give me something to chew on, so that if they call me to take the engine out during the night . . ."

From minute to minute he expected to be summoned to make a trip, but they seldom called on him—once every three or four days when some combined, lightweight freight shifting was scheduled or when there was some other easy task to be done. Still the father was afraid of going out to work unfed, unprepared, morose because he was always worried about his health, his spirits, and his digestion, since he considered himself an outstanding specialist.

"Citizen engineer!" the old man said sometimes, articulately and with dignity, addressing himself personally, and in reply he kept a highly significant silence, as if he were listening to a distant ovation.

Frosya took a pot out of the warming oven, and gave her father something to eat. The evening sun was lighting the apartment slantingly, the light percolated right through to Frosya's body where her heart was warm and where her blood and her feelings were moving in steady harmony. She walked into her own room. A photograph of her husband as a child stood on the table; he had never had his picture taken after he grew up, since he was not interested in himself and didn't believe his face had any significance. A little boy stood in the yellowing picture, with a big child's head, in a poor shirt, with cheap trousers, barefoot; behind him were growing some magical kind of trees and in the distance there was a fountain and a palace. The little boy was looking attentively at a world he still hardly knew, without even noticing the splendid life behind him in the rear of the picture. The splendid life was really in the little boy himself with his wide, enthusiastic shy face, holding a stalk of grass in his hands instead of a toy, and touching the earth with his trusting, naked feet.

Night was already falling. The settlement herdsman was driving the milk cows back from the fields for the night. The cows were mooing, asking the houses for rest, the women and houseworkers were leading them into the courtyards, the long day was cooling off into night. Frosya sat in the twilight, in the happiness of loving and remembering her man who had gone away. Pine trees were growing outside the window, marking a straight path into the heavenly, happy distance, the low voices of some kind of insignificant birds were singing their last, drowsy songs, and the grasshoppers, watchmen of the darkness, were making their gentle, peaceful noises—about how everything was all right and they would not sleep and would keep on watching.

The father asked Frosya if she was going to the club; there would be a new program there, with a tournament of flowers, and with the off-duty conductors as clowns.

"No," Frosya said, "I'm not going. I'm going to stay here and miss my husband."

"Fedka?" the engineer said. "He'll come back; a year will go by and then he'll be here.... What if you do miss him! I used to go away, for a day, or for two, and your mother used to miss me: she was an ordinary old woman!"

"Well, I'm not ordinary, but I'm lonely just the same," Frosya said, with surprise in her voice. "Or no, I probably am ordinary...."

Her father reassured her: "Well, just how are you like those old women? There aren't any of them left now, they died off a long time ago. You'd have to live a long time and study hard to become one: but there were good women, too...."

"Papa, go on into your own room," Frosya said. "I'll give you your supper soon, but right now I'd like to be alone."

"It's time for supper," her father agreed. "Or else a summons will come from the station: maybe someone's sick, or has got drunk, or had some kind of family row—anything could happen. Then I've got to show up right away; the trains must never stop. Ah, your Fedka is speeding along now on his express train—the lights are all shining green for him, the tracks are clear for forty kilometers ahead of him, the engineer is looking far ahead, the lights are on in his locomotive—everything's the way it ought to be!"

The old man was dawdling, loitering, and he went on mumbling his words. He loved to be with his daughter, or with anybody else, when his locomotive was not filling his heart and his mind.

"Papa, come on and eat your supper!" his daughter ordered him. She wanted to listen to the grasshoppers, to watch the pine trees in the night, and to think about her husband.

"Well, she's in a bad way...," her father said softly, and he walked away.

After she had fed her father, Frosya walked out of the house. The club was full of sounds of rejoicing. They were playing music, and she could hear the chorus of clowns singing: "Ah, the fir tree, what a fir tree! And what cones are hanging on it! 'Tu-tu-tu-tu' goes the engine, 'ru-ru-ru-ru' goes the airplane, 'pir-pir-pir-pir' goes the icebreaker. Bow down with us, stand up with us, sing 'tu-tu' and 'ru-ru,' more dancing, more culture, more production—that's our goal!"

The audience inside the club stirred, murmuring shyly and torturing itself with happiness, following the clowns.

Frosya walked on by; beyond the club everything was already empty, this was where the protective plantings began along the main line. Far away, an express train was coming from the east, the engine was working with its steam cut down, the locomotive was eating up distance with an effort and lighting everything in front of it with its shining searchlight. Somewhere this train had met the express train speeding to the Far East, these cars had seen him after Frosya had parted from her beloved man, and now she stared with careful attention at the express train which had been near her husband after she had been. She walked back to the station, but while she was walking there the train had stopped and gone on again; the last car disappeared into the dark forgetting all the people it had passed. Frosya did not see a single unfamiliar, new person on the platform or in the station—none of the passengers had left the express train, there was nobody to ask anything—about the train it had met or about her husband. Maybe someone had seen him, and knew something.

But only two old women were sitting in the station, waiting for a local train in the middle of the night, and the cleaning man again swept the dirt under her feet. They are always sweeping when someone just wants to stand and think; nothing satisfies them.

Frosya walked a little away from the man with the broom, but he caught up with her again.

"Do you happen to know," she asked him, "if the express train No. 2 is going along all right? It left here in the daytime. At the station, haven't they reported anything about it?"

"You are supposed to walk out to the platform only when a

train is approaching," the cleaning man said. "At present no trains are expected, so go back into the station, citizen.... All the time different types keep coming here—they should stay at home and read the papers. But no, they can't do that, they've got to go out and scatter more rubbish...."

Frosya walked along the track, next to the switches, away from the station. Here was the roundhouse of the freight engines, the coal feeder, the slag pits and the locomotive turntable. High lamps lighted the area over which clouds of smoke and steam were floating: some engines were accumulating steam in their boilers, ready to move out, others were releasing steam, cooling off for cleaning.

Four women with iron shovels walked past Frosya, and behind them was a man, either a foreman or a brigade leader.

"What have you lost, good-looking?" he asked Frosya. "If you've lost it, you won't find it again, whoever's gone away won't come back.... Come along with us and help the railroad out."

Frosya was thoughtful.

"Give me a shovel," she said.

"You can have mine," the brigade leader said, and he gave the woman his shovel. "Listen, you old ladies!" he said to the other women. "You start at the third slag pit, and I'll be at the first."

He led Frosya to a slag pit where the locomotives cleaned their fireboxes, told her to go to work, and then went away. Two other women were already working in the pit, shoveling out the hot slag. It was hard to breathe, because of the steam and the gas, and throwing the slag out was awkward because the pit was so narrow and hot. But Frosya felt in better spirits; here she could relax, be with people who were friendly, and see the big, free night lit up by the stars and the electric lights. Her love was sleeping quietly in her heart; the express train was disappearing far away, and in an upper berth of a hard carriage, surrounded by Siberia, her beloved husband was sleeping. Let him sleep, and worry about nothing. Let the engineer keep on looking far ahead, and not have any collision!

Soon Frosya and one of the other women climbed out of the pit. Now they had to shovel the slag they had thrown out onto a flat car. Throwing the hot coals up onto the flat car, the women looked at each other and from time to time talked, to rest a little, and to breathe in some fresh air.

Frosya's friend was about thirty. She was shivering for some reason, and she kept fussing with her poor clothing. She had been let out of jail today, where she had been held for four days on the denunciation of a bad man. Her husband was a watchman, his job was to walk all night long around the cooperative, with a rifle, and he was paid sixty rubles a month for this. When she was in jail, the watchman took pity on her, and went to the authorities to ask them to let her go, although she had been living until her arrest with a lover who had told her suddenly all about his swindling, and then, obviously, got frightened and wanted to destroy her so there would be no witness. But now he had got caught himself, let him suffer for a while, she was going to live in freedom with her husband: there was work to be had, they were selling bread now, and the two of them together would somehow manage to acquire some clothes.

Frosya told her that she had sorrows, too; her husband had gone far away.

"He's just gone away, he hasn't died, he'll come back!" her friend told Frosya comfortingly. "I got bored when I was arrested, locked up like that. I never was in jail before, I'm not used to it; if I had been, then it wouldn't have been so bad. But I've always been such an innocent, the authorities never touched me. When I got out of there, I went home, my husband was glad to see me, and he cried, but he was afraid to put his arms around me: he figured, I'm a criminal, an important person. But I'm just the same, I'm not hard to approach.

And in the evening he has to go to work, no matter how sad it makes us. He picks up his rifle—let's go, he says, I'll treat you to a drink of fruit juice; I've got twelve kopecks, which is enough for one glass, we'll drink it together. But I just feel sad, it won't work. I told him to go to the buffet by himself, let him drink the whole glass and when we get a little money and I've got over my prison sorrows, then we'll both go to the buffet and we'll drink a whole bottle.... That's what I said to him, and I came out to the tracks, to work here. They might be moving ballast, I thought, or shifting rails, or something else. Even at night, there's always work to be done. So, I thought, I'll be with people, it will calm my heart, I'll feel all right again. And it's true, here I've been talking with you as if I'd just found my own cousin. Well, let's finish this flat car; they're giving out the money in the office, in the morning I'll go out and buy some bread.... Frosya!" she yelled down into the slag pit; a namesake of Frosya's was working there. "Is there much left?"

"No," the Frosya in the pit answered. "There's just a little bit here, a few crumbs, that's all."

"Climb up here, then," the watchman's wife told her. "We'll finish up quickly and then we'll go and get paid together."

The brigade leader came up.

"Well, how's it going, old ladies? Have you finished the pit? Aha! Well, go into the office, I'll come right away. There you'll get your money, and there we'll see: who goes to the club to dance, and who goes home to take care of the kids!"

The women all signed for their money in the office: Yefrosinia Yevstafyeva, Natalya Bukova, and three letters a little like the word "Eva" with a hammer and sickle at the end instead of still another Yefrosinia—she was a relapsed literacy student. They each received three rubles and twenty kopecks, and they all went home. Frosya Yevstafyeva and Natalya, the watchman's wife, went together. Frosya had invited her new friend to her house, to wash and clean up.

The father was asleep on the chest in the kitchen, completely dressed to his winter coat and his hat with the locomotive badge on it. He was waiting for a sudden summons to some general breakdown where he would have to show up instantly in the center of the disaster.

The women tended to their business quietly, powdered their faces, smiled at each other, and went out again. It was already late; at the club they had probably started the dancing and the tournament of flowers. While Frosya's husband was sleeping in the train far away and his heart was not feeling anyway, not remembering her, not loving her, it was as if she were alone in the whole world, free from happiness and sorrow, and she wanted to dance a little, right away, to listen to music, to hold hands with other people. And in the morning, when he would be waking up alone and remembering her at once, then, maybe, she would cry.

The two women ran up to the club. The local train went by: midnight, not yet very late. An independent dance orchestra was playing in the club. An assistant engineer immediately asked Frosya to dance to "Rio Rita."

Frosya moved into the dance with a blissful face; she loved music, it seemed to her that sadness and happiness were inseparably linked in music as in real life, as in her own soul. When she danced, she hardly remembered herself, she felt herself in a light dream, with amazement, and her body found the right movements without trying, because Frosya's blood was warmed by the melody.

"Have they already had the tournament of flowers?" she asked her partner quietly, breathing quickly.

"It just finished a little while ago. Why were you so late?" the assistant engineer asked her meaningfully, just as if he had loved Frosya forever, and pined for her all the time.

"Ah, what a shame!" Frosya said.

"Do you like it here?" her partner asked her.

"Well, yes, of course," Frosya answered. "It's so lovely."

Natalya Bukova did not know how to dance, and she stood next to the wall, holding her friend's hat in her hands.

In the intermission, while the orchestra was resting, Frosya and Natalya drank lemonade, and they finished two bottles. Natalya had been in this club only once, a long time ago. She looked at the clean, decorated dance floor with a shy happiness.

"Fros, Fros!" she whispered. "When we have socialism, will all rooms look like this, or not?"

"How else? Of course, they'll look like this," Frosya said. "Well, maybe they'll be a little better!"

"That would be something!" Natalya Bukova agreed.

After the intermission, Frosya danced again. The dispatcher in charge of shunting asked her. They were playing a fox-trot, "My Baby." The dispatcher held his partner tightly, trying to press his cheek against her hair, but this hidden caress didn't affect Frosya, she loved a man who was far away, and her poor body was all tight and hollow.

"Tell me, what's your name?" her partner said into her ear while they were dancing. "I know your face, but I've forgotten who's your father."

"Fro!" Frosya answered.

"Fro? . . . You're not Russian?"

"Well, of course not."

The dispatcher thought about this.

"Why aren't you? . . . After all, your father's Russian: Yev-stafyev."

"That doesn't matter," Frosya whispered. "My name's Fro."

They danced on in silence. People stood along the walls and watched the dancers. Only three couples were dancing, the others were shy or didn't know how. Frosya leaned her head closer to the dispatcher's chest, he could see her fluffy hair in its old-fashioned hair-do right under his eyes, and this relaxed trustingness was dear and pleasant to him. He preened himself before those who were watching. He even wanted stealthily to stroke her head, but he was afraid people might notice it. Besides, his fiancée was there, who might pay him back later for his closeness to this Fro. So the dispatcher moved a little away from her, for appearance's sake, but Fro leaned on to his chest again, onto his necktie, and the tie shifted to one side under the weight of her head, showing a strip of his naked body in the middle of his shirt. The dispatcher continued to dance, in terror and awkwardness, waiting for the music to stop. But the music grew more agitated and energetic, and the woman did not move away from his arms. He could feel little drops of dampness on his chest, which was bare under his necktie, right where the hair grew on his man's chest.

"Are you crying?" the dispatcher asked, frightened.

"A little," Fro whispered. "Take me over toward the door. I don't want to dance any more."

Without stopping his dancing, her partner steered Frosya to the exit, and she went out into the corridor quickly, where there were few people and she could recover herself.

Natalya brought her friend's hat to her. Frosya went home, while Natalya went off to the cooperative warehouse where her husband was the watchman. Right next to the warehouse was a building materials yard, and a pleasant-looking woman was the watchman there. Natalya wanted to find out if her husband did not have a certain affection for this woman guard.

The next morning Frosya received a telegram from a station in Siberia, beyond the Urals. Her husband telegraphed her: "Dear Fro I love you and I see you in my dreams."

Her father wasn't home. He had gone to the station, to sit and talk in the Red Corner, to read the railroadmen's paper, to find out how the night had gone in the traction department, and then to go into the buffet where he could drink a beer with some friend he might find there and talk briefly about their spiritual concerns.

Frosya didn't even start to brush her teeth; she hardly washed, just throwing a little water on her face, and paid no more attention to what she looked like. She didn't want to waste time on anything except her feeling of love, and this now had no connection with her body. Through the ceiling of Frosya's room, on the third floor, the short notes of a mouth organ could be heard, then the music would stop, and start again. Frosya had wakened in the dark early morning and had then gone back to sleep, and this was when she had heard this modest melody above her, like the singing of some gray bird working in the fields without enough breath for real singing because all its strength was spent in work. A little boy lived above her, the son of a lathe operator at the depot. The father had probably gone out to work, and the mother was doing the laundry —it was pretty boring for him. Without eating her breakfast, Frosya went off to her classes—she was taking courses in railroad communication and signals.

Frosya had not been to class for four days, and her friends had probably missed her, but she was going off to join them now without any real desire. Frosya was excused a great deal in class because of her capacity to learn and her deep understanding of the subjects of technical science; but she herself never understood how this could be—in many things she lived only in imitation of her husband, a man who had finished two technical institutes and who felt the mechanisms of an engine as if they were part of his flesh.

At first, Frosya had been a bad student. Her heart was not attracted by Pupin's induction coils, relay gears, or figuring the resistance of metal wires. But her husband's lips had once pronounced these words and, what's more, he had showed her the vital functioning of these objects which were dead for her, and the mysterious quality of the delicate calculations thanks to which machines live. Frosya's husband had the capacity to feel the strength of an electric current like a personal passion. He could animate everything that engaged his hands or his mind, and so he had a real sense of the direction of forces in any mechanical construction, and he could feel directly the patient, suffering resistance of the metal structure of a machine.

Since then induction coils, Wheatstone bridges, contractors, and illumination units had become sacred objects for Frosya, as if they were spiritual parts of the man she loved; she began to understand them, and to cherish them in her mind as in her heart. In difficult times Frosya would come home and say humbly: "Fedor, that microfarad and those wandering currents, they bore me!" But embracing his wife after their daytime separation, Fedor would transform himself temporarily into a microfarad and a wandering current. Frosya almost saw with her own eyes what, until then, she had wanted to understand but could not. These were just the same simple, natural, attractive things as different-colored grasses growing in the fields. Frosya often grieved at night because she was only a woman and could not feel herself to be a microfarad or a locomotive, or electricity, while Fedor could—and she would carefully move her finger along his hot back; he slept, and didn't wake. Somehow he was always hot, strange, and he could sleep through loud noise, eat any kind of food—good or bad, he was never sick, he loved to spend money on trifles, he was getting ready to go to Soviet China and become a soldier there. . . .

Fro sat in class now with weak, wandering thoughts, mastering nothing of the assigned lesson. She despondently copied from the blackboard into her notebook a vector diagram of the resonance of electric currents and listened sorrowfully to the teacher's lecture on the influence of the saturation of steel on the appearance of higher harmonics. Fedor wasn't there, now communications and signals no longer attracted her, electricity had become something alien to her. Pupin's induction coils, Wheatstone bridges, microfarads, iron cores had all dried up in her heart, and she could not understand a thing of the higher harmonics of electric current; in her memory there sounded all the time the monotonous little song of a child's mouth organ: "The mother is washing clothes, the father's off at work, he won't come back soon, it's lonely and boring all alone."

Frosya's attention left the lesson altogether, and she wrote in her notebook: "I am a stupid, wretched girl, Fedya, come back quickly and I'll learn communications and signals, and then I'll die, you'll bury me, and go off to China."

At home her father was sitting with his boots on, his coat, and his engineer's cap. He was sure that he'd be summoned to take a trip today.

"You've come home?" he asked his daughter. He was always glad when someone came into the apartment; he listened to all the steps on the staircase, as if he were constantly expecting some extraordinary guest who would be bringing him happiness, carrying it in his hat.

"Can I warm some kasha with butter for you?" her father asked. "I'll do it right away."

The daughter refused.

"Well then, let me fry you some sausage."

"No," Frosya said.

The father was quiet for a minute, but then he asked again, but more timidly:

"Maybe you'd like some tea and crackers? I'll heat the water...."

The daughter remained silent.

"Or how about the macaroni from yesterday. It's still there, I left it all for you...."

"Will you please drop it?" Frosya said. "They should have sent you off to the Far East...."

"I volunteered, but they wouldn't take me—too old, they said, eyesight not good enough," the father explained.

He knew that children are our enemies, and he did not get angry at his enemies. But he was afraid, instead, that Frosya would go off into her own room, while he wanted her to stay with him and talk, and the old man was hunting for some reason to keep Frosya from going away.

"Why haven't you put any lipstick on your lips today?" he asked her. "Or have you run out of it? I'll be glad to buy you some, I can run down to the drugstore. . . ."

Tears started to well up in Frosya's gray eyes, and she walked into her room. The father stayed alone; he began to clean up the kitchen and to fuss with housework, then he squatted down on his heels, opened the door of the warming oven, put his head in it, and started to cry on top of the pan holding the macaroni.

Someone knocked on the door. Frosya did not come out to open it. The old man pulled his head out of the oven, wiped his face, and went to open the door.

A messenger had come from the station.

"Sign here, Nefed Stepanovich: you're to show up today at eight o'clock—you're to go with a cold locomotive being sent off for major repairs. They'll hitch it on to 309, take your grub and clothes with you, you'll be gone at least a week."

Nefed Stepanovich signed in the book and the messenger left. The old man opened his metal lunchbox: yesterday's bread and onion were still there, with a lump of sugar. The engineer added some millet porridge, two apples, thought for a minute, and then closed the box with its enormous padlock.

Then he knocked carefully on the door of Frosya's room.

"Daughter! Lock up after me, I'm going out on a job . . . for two weeks. . . . They've given me a 'Shcha' engine—it's cold, but never mind."

Frosya came out a little after her father had left, and closed the door to the apartment.

"Play! Why aren't you playing?" Frosya whispered at the floor above, where the little boy with the mouth organ lived. But he had probably gone out for a walk—it was summertime, the days were long, the breeze fluttered in the evening among the sleepy, happy pine trees. The musician was still a little boy, he had not yet chosen some single thing out of the whole world for eternal loving, his heart beat empty and free, stealing nothing just for itself out of the goodness of life.

Frosya opened the window, lay down on the big bed, and dozed off. She could hear the trunks of the pine trees moving slightly in the air blowing at their tops, and one far-off grasshopper sounded, not waiting for the time of darkness.

Frosya awoke; it was still light, she should get up and live. She looked at the sky, full of a ripening warmth, covered with the lively traces of the disappearing sun, as if happiness were to be found there, happiness made by nature out of all its pure strength, so that this happiness might flow from nature into a man.

Frosya found a short hair between two pillows, it could have belonged only to Fedor. She examined the hair in the light, it was gray: Fedor was already twenty-nine and he had some gray hairs, about twenty of them. Her father was also gray, but he never came even close to their bed. Frosya was used to the smell of the pillow on which Fedor slept—it still smelled of his body and his head, they had not washed the pillowcase since the last time her husband had put his head on it. Frosya buried her face in Fedor's pillow and grew calmer.

Upstairs on the third floor the little boy came back and started to play his mouth organ, the same tune he had been playing in the dark morning of that day. Frosya got up and hid her husband's hair in an empty box on her table. Then the little boy stopped playing—it was time for him to go to sleep because he had to get up early, or else he was playing with his father, who had come home from work, and sitting on his knees. The mother was breaking up sugar with a pair of sugar tongs, and saying they must buy some more linen, what they had was worn out, and tore when it was washed. The father was silent, he was thinking: we'll manage somehow.

All evening long Frosya walked along the tracks at the station, out to the nearest woods, and through the fields where rye was growing. She stood next to the slag pits where she had worked the day before—they were almost full again, but nobody was working. Nobody knew where Natasha Bukova lived, Frosya had not asked her yesterday; she did not want to go and see any friends or acquaintances for she felt somehow ashamed in front of everyone: she couldn't talk about her love with other people and all the rest of life had become uninteresting and dead for her. She walked past the cooperative warehouse where Natalya's husband was walking with his rifle. Frosya would have liked to give him some rubles so that he could drink fruit juice with his wife the next day, but she was embarrassed.

"Move on, citizen! You can't stand here—this is a warehouse, a government building," the watchman said to her when Frosya stopped and groped for the money somewhere in the pleats of her skirt.

Beyond the warehouse lay desolate, empty land, on which some small, coarse, wild grass was growing. Frosya walked up to it and stood there languishing in that small world of thin grass from which, it seemed, the stars were only a couple of kilometers away.

"Ah, Fro, Fro, if only someone put his arms around you!" she said to herself.

When she got home, Frosya lay down at once to sleep because the little boy who played the mouth organ had been asleep for a long time and even the grasshoppers had stopped chirping. But something kept her from falling asleep. Frosya stared into the darkness and sniffed: it was the pillow on which Fedor used to sleep that was bothering her. It still gave out the moldering, earthy smell of a warm, familiar body, and this smell started the grief in Frosya's heart all over again. She wrapped Fedor's pillow up in a sheet and hid it in the closet, and then she fell asleep alone, like an orphan.

Frosya did not go back to her classes—science had become incomprehensible for her anyway. She lived at home and waited for a letter or a telegram from Fedor, afraid the postman would take the letter back if he did not find anyone at home. But four days went by, and then six, and Fedor sent no word except for his first telegram.

The father came back from his trip in charge of the cold locomotive; he was happy that he had gone and taken the trouble, that he had seen a great many people and distant stations and different happenings; now he had enough to remember, think about, and talk about for a long time. But Frosya didn't ask him anything; so her father began to tell her on his own —how the cold locomotive had been moved and how he had not slept at night, to keep mechanics at stations along the way from stealing parts from the engine, where they were selling fruit cheap and where it had been ruined by late spring frost. Frosya made no comment, and even when Nefed Stepanovich told her about the voile and the artificial silk he had seen in Sverdlovsk, his words did not interest his daughter. "What is she, a Fascist?" her father thought. "How did I ever conceive her in my wife? I can't think."

Having received neither a letter nor a telegram from Fedor, Frosya went to work at the post office as a mail carrier. She thought that letters were probably being lost, and so she wanted to take them herself to all the addresses. And she wanted to get Fedor's letters sooner than some strange, unknown letter carrier would bring them to her, and in her own hands they would be safe. She got to the post office ahead of all the other carriers—the little boy on the third floor would not yet be playing his mouth organ—and took part as a volunteer in the sorting and distributing of the mail. She read the addresses on all the envelopes coming into the little town—Fedor wrote her nothing. All the envelopes were addressed to other people, and inside the envelopes were uninteresting letters of one sort or another. But just the same twice each day Frosya distributed them to the proper addresses, hoping there was some comfort in them for the people who got them. In the early morning light she would walk quickly along the street of the town with a heavy bag on her stomach, looking as if she were pregnant, knocking at the doors and handing the letters and packages to people in their underwear, to naked women, or to little children who had got up before the grownups. The dark blue sky was standing above the neighboring land but Frosya would already be working, hurrying to tire out her legs so her anxious heart would also grow tired. Many of the people getting letters became interested in her and when they received their mail would ask her questions about her life: "Do you work for ninety-two rubles a month?" "Yes," Frosya would answer, "but that's before deductions." "And do you work during your monthly periods, or do they give you time off?" "They give me time off," Frosya told them, "and they give out a government girdle, but I haven't received mine yet." "They'll give it to you," the addressee told her, "it's in the regulations." One subscriber to the magazine *Krasnaya Nov (Red Virgin Soil)* made Frosya an offer of marriage, as an experiment: whatever happens, maybe it will produce happiness, he said, and that's always useful. "What's your reaction?" the subscriber asked her. "I'll think about it," Frosya answered. "Don't think about it," the addressee told her. "Come and stay with me as a guest, try me out first: I'm a tender man, well read, cultured—you can see for yourself what I subscribe to! This magazine is produced by an editorial board, there are clever people there—see for yourself—and not just one man, and we'll be two! It's all quite solid, and just like a married woman your authority will be greater. A girl—what's she?—a single person, somehow an antisocial kind of person!"

Many people recognized Frosya standing with a letter or a package in front of a stranger's door. Sometimes they offered her a glass of wine, or snacks to eat, and they complained to her about their private fate. Life was nowhere empty or calm.

When he went away, Fedor had promised Frosya to let her know the address of his new job right away, for he didn't know exactly where he would find himself. But here fourteen days had gone by since his leaving, but there was no letter from him, and nowhere for her to write. Frosya endured the separation, she went on delivering the mail faster and faster, breathing all the time more quickly, in order to busy her heart with other work and to wear out its despair. But one day she suddenly started to scream in the middle of the street, during the second delivery of mail. Frosya had not noticed how the breathing had suddenly tightened in her chest, squeezing her heart, and she continued to scream in a high, shrill voice. People walking by noticed her. When she came to herself, Frosya ran into the field with her letter bag because it had become so hard for her to stand her wasting, empty breathing; she fell to the ground and went on screaming until her heart had got over it.

Frosya then sat up, straightened her dress, and smiled; she felt all right again, with no more need to cry. After she had delivered the mail, Frosya went to the telegraph department where they handed her a telegram from Fedor with his address and kisses. At home, without eating, she began immediately to write a letter to her husband. She did not see the day end, outside the window, nor did she hear the little boy who always played his mouth organ before he went to sleep. Her father knocked on her door and brought his daughter a glass of tea with a buttered roll, and he turned on the electric light so Frosya would not ruin her eyes in the dusk.

That night Nefed Stepanovich was dozing on his chest in the kitchen. For six days he had not been summoned by the railroad; he assumed they would need him this night and he was waiting for the footsteps of the messenger on the staircase.

At one o'clock in the night, Frosya walked into the kitchen with a folded piece of paper in her hand.

"Papa!"

"What do you want, daughter?" The old man slept lightly.

"Take this telegram to the post office for me, since I'm tired."

"But what if I go out, and then the messenger comes?" the father asked, frightened.

"He'll wait," Frosya told him. "You won't be gone long. But don't read the telegram, just hand it in at the window."

"I won't," the old man promised. "But you wrote a letter, too. Give it to me, and I'll mail it at the same time."

"It's none of your business what I wrote.... Have you got money?"

The father had money; he took the telegram and walked out. In the post and telegraph office, the old man read the telegram: why not, he decided, maybe his daughter was writing something wrong, he should look at it.

The telegram was addressed to Fedor in the Far East: "Come back by first train your wife my daughter Frosya is dying of fatal complications in respiratory organs father Nefed Yevstafyev."

"What a pair they are!" the old man thought, and he handed the telegram in at the window.

"But I saw Frosya today!" the telegraph clerk said. "Has she really got sick?"

"It must be," the engineer explained.

The next morning Frosya sent her father back to the post

office again to take a statement from her that she was voluntarily resigning from her job for reasons of bad health. The old man went, he had wanted to go to the station anyway.

Frosya set about washing linen, darning socks, scrubbing floors and cleaning up the apartment, and she went nowhere outside the house.

Two days later an answer came by telegraph: "Leaving am anxious terribly worried no burial without me Fedor."

Frosya figured precisely the time of her husband's arrival and on the seventh day after the telegram came she went down to the station platform, quivering with happiness. The Trans-Siberian express pulled in from the east right on time. Frosya's father was on the platform, too, but he stayed some distance away from his daughter in order not to destroy her mood.

The engineer brought the train into the station with splendid speed, and softly, tenderly braked it to a stop. Nefed Stepanovich, watching this, shed a few tears, forgetting even why he had come to the station.

Only one passenger got out of the train at this station. He wore a hat, and a long, blue raincoat, and his eyes were shining. The woman ran up to him.

"Fro!" the passenger said, and he dropped his bag onto the platform. The father picked it up and carried it behind his daughter and his son-in-law.

On the road, the daughter turned to her father.

"Papa, go over to the depot, and ask them to give you an assignment somewhere, it must be boring for you to have to sit at home all the time. . . ."

"It's boring," the old man said, "I'll go right away. You take the suitcase."

The son-in-law looked at the old engineer.

"Hello, Nefed Stepanovich!"

"Hello, Fedya. Welcome home."

"Thank you, Nefed Stepanovich. . . ."

The young man wanted to say something more, but the old man gave the bag to Frosya and was walking away, toward the depot.

"Darling, I've cleaned the whole apartment," Frosya said. "I wasn't dying."

"I guessed it on the train, that you weren't dying," her husband answered. "I didn't believe your telegram for long."

"Then why did you come back?" Frosya asked in surprise.

"I love you, and I was lonely," Fedor said sadly.

Frosya was suddenly grieved.

"I'm afraid you'll stop loving me some time, and then I really will die...."

Fedor kissed her cheek from the side.

"If you die, then you'll forget everything, including me," he said.

Frosya recovered from her grief.

"No, to die isn't interesting. It's passivity."

"Of course, it's passivity," Fedor said, smiling. He liked her high-flown, intelligent words. Fro had once asked him specially to teach her intelligent phrases, and he had written out for her a whole notebook full of intelligent, empty words: "Whoever says a must also say b," "If it's so, it's precisely so," and other similar phrases. But Fro guessed the fraud for herself. She asked him: "But why is it necessary to say b after saying a, if I don't have to and I don't want to?"

At home they lay down at once to rest and fell asleep. Three hours later the father knocked. Frosya opened the door for him and waited until the old man had put some food in his metal box and gone out again. They had probably sent him off somewhere on a job. Frosya closed the door, and went back to sleep again.

When they woke, it was already night. They talked for a little, then Fedor made love to Fro, and they fell silent until morning.

The next day Fro quickly fixed dinner, fed her husband

and ate something herself. She was doing everything now any old way, messy, not tasty, but it was all the same to both of them what they ate and what they drank, just so long as they didn't waste the time of their loving on any material, unimportant needs.

Frosya told Fedor that she would now begin to study well and diligently, she would learn a lot, and she would work hard, so that life could become better for everybody in the country.

Fedor listened to Fro, and then he explained to her in detail his own ideas and projects—about the transmission of electric energy without wires, by means of ionized air, about increasing the strength of all metals by processing their ultrasonic waves, about the stratosphere one hundred kilometers up in the sky where there exist special light, heat and electrical conditions capable of guaranteeing eternal life to a man— this is why the dreams of the ancient world about heaven may now actually come true—and Fedor promised to think out and to accomplish many other things for Frosya's sake and at the same time for the sake of all the other people in the world.

Frosya listened blissfully to her husband, half opening her already tired mouth. When they finished talking, they threw their arms around each other—they wanted to be happy right away, now, sooner than their future and zealous work would bring results in personal and in general happiness. The heart brooks no delay, it sickens, as if believing in nothing. Smothered with fatigue from thinking, from talking and from pleasure, they woke again fresh and ready for life to repeat itself. Frosya wanted to have children, she would bring them up, they would grow and share their father's work, the work of communism and science. In the passion of his imagination, Fedor whispered to Frosya words about the mysterious forces of nature which can bring wealth to humanity, about the root-and-branch transformation of the sorry spirit of man. Then they kissed and caressed each other, and their noble dream turned into delight, as if it had been accomplished all at once.

In the evening Frosya went out for a short while, to buy groceries for herself and her husband; all this time, their appetites were growing. They lived through four days and nights without leaving each other. The father had not come back from his trip: probably he had been sent again to take a cold locomotive a long way.

After two more days Frosya told Fedor that they could go on together like this a little longer but then they should get down to business and pick up life again.

"Tomorrow, or the day after tomorrow, you and I will start to live life the way we ought to," Fedor said, and he put his arms around her.

"The day after tomorrow!" Fro agreed in a whisper.

On the eighth day, Fedor woke up sad.

"Fro! Let's get to work, let's start living the way we should. . . . You've got to start going to class again."

"Tomorrow," Fro whispered and she took her husband's head between her two hands.

He smiled at her, and gave in.

"When do we start, Fro?" Fedor asked his wife the next day.

"Soon, soon," a sleepy, gentle Fro answered him; her hands were holding his hand, and he kissed her forehead.

One day Frosya woke up late, the day had been flaming a long time outside. She was alone in the room, it was probably the tenth or eleventh day of her inseparable reunion with her husband.

Frosya jumped quickly out of bed, threw the window wide open, and heard the mouth organ which she had completely forgotten. It was not being played upstairs. Frosya looked out of the window. Next to the shed in the courtyard a plank was lying and a barefoot little boy with a big child's head was sitting on it and playing music.

It was strangely quiet all through the apartment. Fedor had absented himself somewhere. Frosya walked out to the kitchen. There was her father, sitting on the stool and dozing, his head with his hat on resting on the kitchen table. Frosya woke him.

"When did you come?"

"What?" the old man stammered. "Today, early in the morning."

"But who let you in? Fedor?"

"Nobody," her father said. "The door was open.... Fedor found me at the station, I was sleeping there on the counter."

"And why were you sleeping at the station? What's the matter? Have you no home?" Frosya asked him angrily.

"What of it! I'm used to it," the old man said. "I thought— I'd be in your way...."

"Well, all right, you old hypocrite! But where's Fedor? When will he be back?"

The father was embarrassed.

"He won't be back," the old man said. "He's gone away...."

Fro was silent in front of her father. The old man was looking carefully at the kitchen dishrags, and he went on:

"In the morning the express went through. He got on, and went back to the Far East. Maybe, he says, he'll go on from there to China, he doesn't know yet."

"And what else did he say?" Frosya asked.

"Nothing," her father answered. "He told me to come home and take care of you. It depends on how things work out, he says, either he'll come back here, or he'll send for you."

"What kind of things?" Frosya asked.

"I don't know," the old man said. "He said that you'd know all about it: communism, I guess, or something else, too, whatever happens."

Fro left her father. She went back to her room, leaned on the windowsill and began to look at the little boy and how he was playing his mouth organ.

"Little boy!" she called out. "Come and call on me."

"Right away," the musician answered.

He stood up from the plank, wiped his instrument on the edge of his shirt, and walked to the building to call on her.

Fro stood alone in the middle of the big room, in her nightgown. She was smiling as she waited for her guest.

"Good-bye, Fedor!"

Maybe she was stupid, maybe her life was only worth two kopecks and there was no need to love her and take care of her, but still she alone understood how to change two kopecks into two rubles.

"Good-bye, Fedor! You'll come back to me, and I'll wait for you."

Her little guest was knocking shyly on the outside door. Frosya let him in, sat down on the floor beside him, took the child's hand in her hands and began to feast her eyes on the young musician: in this being, probably, was just that humanity about which Fedor had told her so lovingly.

## THE POTUDAN RIVER

GRASS WAS GROWING again on the packed dirt roads
of the civil war, for the fighting had stopped. With peace the
countryside grew quiet again, and almost empty of people:
some had died in the fighting, many were getting over their
wounds, resting with their families, forgetting the heavy work
of war in long sleep, while a few of the demobilized soldiers
had not yet managed to get home and were still walking in
their old overcoats, with packs on their backs and field helmets
or sheepskin hats on their heads—walking through the thick,
unfamiliar grass which they had not earlier had time to see, or
maybe it had been trampled down before by their marching,
and not growing. They walked with stunned, astonished hearts,
seeing again the fields and villages spread out along the roads;
their spirit had changed in the torment of war, in its sick-
nesses, and in the joy of victory. They were walking now as if
to some new life, only vaguely remembering what they had
been like three or four years before, for they had been transformed into different people. They had grown out of their age,

147

and become wiser, they had grown more patient, and they felt inside themselves the great worldwide hope which had now become the central idea of their still-small lives which had had no clear goal or purpose before the civil war.

The last of the demobilized Red Army soldiers returned to their homes late in the summer. They had been retained in labor armies where they were used at various unfamiliar jobs, and they were sad, and only now were they told to go home to their own lives and to living in general.

A former Red Army soldier, Nikita Firsov, had been walking for two days along the hills which stretch out above the Potudan River toward his home in a little-known district town. He was a man of twenty-five, with a modest face which seemed always sorrowing but perhaps this expression came not from grief but from some controlled goodness of character or from the usual concentration of youth. Light-colored hair, uncut for a long time, stuck out around his ears from under his cap, and his big gray eyes looked with a kind of sullen tension at the quiet, ordinary, monotonous countryside, as if he were not a local man.

About noon Nikita Firsov lay down next to a little stream which ran from a spring along the bottom of a gorge down to the Potudan. He dozed on the ground under the sun, in the September grass which had stopped growing here since spring. It was as if the warmth of life had grown dark in him, and Firsov fell asleep in the quiet of this deserted place. Insects flew over him, a spider web floated above him, a wandering beggar stepped across him and, without touching the sleeper, uninterested in him, went on about his business. The dust of summer and of the long drought stood high in the air, making the light in the sky weaker and more diffuse, but still the time of peace, as usual, moved far behind the sun. Suddenly Firsov awoke and sat up, heavily, panting in fright as if he had lost his wind in some invisible running and fighting. He had had a strange dream of being smothered by the hot fur of a small, well-fed beast, a kind of little animal of the fields fed on pure wheat. This animal, soaked in sweat from its efforts and from its greed, had squirmed through the sleeper's mouth into his throat, trying to burrow with its paws into the center of his soul, trying to stop his breathing. Choking in his sleep, Firsov wanted to scream and to run away, but the little animal pulled itself out of him by its own effort and disappeared—blind, wretched, frightened, and trembling itself—into the darkness of its night.

Firsov washed his face in the stream, and rinsed out his mouth, and then he went on quickly; his father's house was not far away, and he could get there by evening.

As soon as it started to get dark, Firsov saw his birthplace in the dim onset of night. It was a gradual sloping ridge which rose from the bank of the Potudan up to the high-lying fields of rye. On this ridge was the small town, almost invisible now in the darkness. Not a single light was burning.

Nikita Firsov's father was asleep: he went to bed as soon as he came home from work, before the sun had gone down. He lived alone, his wife had died a long time ago, two sons had been killed in the imperialist war and his last son, Nikita, was off at the civil war. Perhaps he would come back, the father thought, for the civil war was going on closer to where people lived and there was less shooting than in the imperialist war. The father slept a lot, from sunset right through until dawn; otherwise, if he didn't sleep, he'd start to think, imagining what had been long forgotten, and his heart would be torn with sorrow over his wasted sons, and with regret for the lonely life behind him. In the mornings he would go off quickly to the workshop making peasant furniture where he worked; he could endure this, and forget about himself. But by evening, his spirits would be low again and he would go back to the room where he lived, and sleep almost in terror until morning

came: he had no need for kerosene. At dawn the flies would begin to bite him on his bald spot, and the old man would wake
up and take a long time dressing, putting on his shoes, washing, sighing, stamping around, fixing up his room, muttering to
himself, stepping outside to look at the weather, then going
back in—all this just to waste the time that had to be filled before his work began in the furniture workshop.

On this particular night, Firsov's father was sleeping as he
always did, out of both habit and fatigue. A cricket had lived in
the wall of the house for nobody knew how many summers—
this might have been the same cricket as the summer before
last, or its grandson. Nikita walked up to the wall and knocked
on his father's window; the cricket was silent for a little, as if
he were listening—who was this strange man who came so
late? The father got up from the old wooden bed on which he
had slept with the mother of all his sons; Nikita himself had
been born on this same bed. The old man was in his underwear, which had shrunk from long wearing and from launder-
ing so that now it came only to his knees. The father leaned
close to the windowpane and looked through it at his son. He
had already seen and recognized him but he went on looking,
wanting to look his fill. Then little and skinny, like a boy, he
darted around through the hall and the courtyard to open the
gate which had been locked for the night.

Nikita walked into the old room with its stove that could
be slept on, its low ceiling, its one window onto the street. It
had the same smell as in his childhood and as three years before when he had gone off to war; he could catch even the
smell of his mother's skirt there—the only place in the world
where that smell was left. Nikita took off his pack and his cap,
slowly slipped off his coat, and sat down on the bed. His father
was standing in front of him all this time, barefoot and in his
underwear, not daring yet to greet him properly, or to start
talking.

"Well, how is it with the bourgeois and the Cadets?" he asked after a minute. "Did you kill them all, or are there some left?"

"We killed almost all of them, I guess," his son said.

"They're a flabby sort!" the old man said, talking about the bourgeois. "Whatever they might have done, they'd just got used to living free of charge."

Nikita stood up in front of his father, and now he was the taller, by a head and a half. The old man stood quietly next to his son in the humble bewilderment of his love for him. Nikita put his hand on the father's head and drew it to his chest. The old man leaned against his son and started to breathe deeply and fast, as if he had just reached his resting place.

On another street in this town, running straight out into the fields, stood a wooden house with green shutters. An elderly widow had once lived here, a teacher in the town school, with her two children, a boy of ten and a daughter of fifteen, a fair-haired girl named Lyuba.

Some years before, Nikita Firsov's father had wanted to marry the widow teacher, but he soon gave up the idea. He took Nikita, twice, when he was still a little boy, to call on the teacher, and Nikita saw the thoughtful girl Lyuba there, sitting, reading a book, paying no attention to the strange guests.

The old teacher served tea with crackers to the cabinet-maker and made some remarks about enlightening the people's minds and about repairing the stoves in the school. Nikita's father sat there silently, he was embarrassed, he quacked and coughed and smoked his little cigar, and then shyly drank his tea out of the saucer, not touching the little crackers because—he explained—he was already full.

There were chairs in the teacher's apartment, in both of its two rooms and in the kitchen, with curtains hung at the windows, and in the first room there were a little piano and a wardrobe, while the second, farther, room had beds, two arm-chairs upholstered in red velvet, and a great many books on shelves along the wall—probably a whole collected edition of some kind. This furniture seemed too luxurious to both the father and the son, and after having visited the widow twice, the father stopped going there. He never even managed to tell her that he had wanted to marry her. But Nikita would have liked to see the little piano again, and the pensive girl who had been reading, and he asked his father to marry the mother so they could call on her again.

"I can't, Nikita," the father told him then. "I've had too little education, so what would I talk to her about? And I'd be ashamed to invite them here; we haven't any china, and our food's not much good.... Did you see what armchairs they had? Antiques, from Moscow! And that wardrobe? With fret-work all over the front—I know what that is! And the daughter! She's probably going to go to the university."

And the father had not seen his old flame for several years, and had only occasionally missed her, perhaps, or thought about her at all.

The day after he came back from the civil war Nikita walked over to the military commissariat to register in the reserve. Then he walked around the whole familiar town where he had been born, and his heart ached at the sight of the rundown little houses, the broken walls and wattle fences, and the occasional apple trees in the courtyards, some of which had died and dried up for good. In his childhood these apple trees had still been green, and the one-storied houses had seemed big and rich, lived in by mysterious, intelligent people, and the streets then had been long, the burdocks high, and even the weeds growing in the empty lots and in the abandoned kitchen gardens had looked in the old times like sinister, dense forests. But now Nikita saw that the houses of the townspeople were miserable and tiny, they needed paint and repairs, even the weeds in the bare spots were poor things, lived on only by ancient, patient ants, and all the streets petered out in empty land or in the light-filled distance of the sky—the town had become a little one. Nikita realized this meant he had already lived a lot of his life, once large and mysterious objects had become small and boring to him.

He walked slowly by the house with green shutters where he had once gone to call with his father. He knew the paint on the shutters was green only from memory, for only traces of it were left now, it had been faded by the sun, and washed by storms and showers, right down to the wood itself, and the metal roof of the house had rusted badly, so that rain probably ran right through it now, and soaked the ceiling above the little piano. Nikita looked carefully into the window of this house; there were no curtains any longer, and a strange darkness could be seen on the other side of the window glass. Nikita sat down on a bench near the gate of this dilapidated but still familiar little house. He thought maybe someone would play the piano, and he would listen to the music. But everything inside was quiet, telling him nothing. After he had listened for a little, Nikita looked into the courtyard through a crack in the wall; old nettles were growing there, a little path wound through some bushes toward the shed, and three wooden steps led into the building. It must be that the old teacher and her daughter Lyuba had both died a long time ago, and the boy had probably gone off to the war as a volunteer. . . .

Nikita walked back to his home. The day was moving toward its evening, his father would soon be coming back for the night, he would have to talk over with him how he was going to live from now on and where he would go to work.

There were a few persons walking along the main street in town, because people were beginning to perk up after the war. Now there were office workers and students on the street, demobilized soldiers and those convalescing from wounds, young people, men who worked at home or in handicraft trades, and others like them; factory workers would come out to walk later, after it had grown quite dark. People were dressed in old clothes, poorly, or else in outworn military uniforms dating from imperialist times.

Practically all the walkers, even those going arm in arm and about to be married, were carrying some kind of household goods. Women were carrying potatoes in kitchen bags, or sometimes fish, men held their bread rations under their arms, or a half a cow's head, or they held tripe fixed for the kettle carefully in their hands. Almost no one seemed dejected except for an occasional tired old man. The younger ones were usually laughing, and looking closely at each other, in high spirits and confident, as if they were on the eve of eternal happiness.

"Hello!" a woman said shyly to Nikita from one side.

The voice both touched and warmed him at the same time, as if someone dear to him and in some trouble had called on him for help. But then it seemed to Nikita that it had been an error and that it was not he who was being greeted. Afraid of making a mistake, he looked slowly around at the people who were walking past him. There were only two of them, and both of these had gone by him. Nikita looked behind him—a big, grown-up Lyuba had stopped and was looking at him. She gave him a sad, embarrassed smile.

Nikita walked up to her and looked her over carefully, as if to see if she had kept herself in good shape, for even in his memory she was precious to him. Her Austrian boots, tied up with a string, were clearly worn-out, her pale muslin dress came only to her knees, probably because that was all the cloth there was; the dress filled Nikita with compassion for Lyuba right away, he had seen dresses like that on women in their coffins, while here the muslin was covering a living, grown-up, even if impoverished, body. She was wearing an old woman's jacket on top of the dress—probably Lyuba's mother had worn it when she was a girl, and there was nothing on Lyuba's head—just her hair twisted below her neck into a light-colored, firm braid.

"You don't remember me?" Lyuba asked him.

"No, I haven't forgotten you," Nikita answered.

"One should never forget," Lyuba said with a smile.

Her clear eyes, filled with some secret emotion, were looking tenderly at Nikita as if they were feasting on him. Nikita was looking at her face, too, and his heart was both glad and sorry at the sight of her eyes, which were sunk deep from hardships she had lived through and lighted up with confidence and hope.

Nikita walked back with Lyuba to her home—she still lived in the same house. Her mother had died not long before, and her young brother had been fed during the famine by a Red Army field kitchen and had grown used to it and gone off to the south with the Red Army to fight the enemy.

"He got used to eating porridge, and there wasn't any at home," Lyuba said.

Lyuba was living now in just one room—she didn't need any more. Nikita looked with a sinking feeling at this room where he had first seen Lyuba, the little piano, and the expensive furniture. Now there was no piano, and no wardrobe with fretwork on its front, there were just the two upholstered chairs, a table and a bed, and the whole room was no longer as interesting and as mysterious to him as it had been when he was younger—the paper on the walls was faded and torn, the floor was worn down, next to the big tiled stove stood a small iron one in which a handful of chips could be burned to make a little heat.

Lyuba pulled a notebook out of the top of her dress and took off her shoes, so that she was barefoot. She was studying medicine at the district academy; in those days there were universities and academics in all the districts because the people wanted to advance their knowledge as quickly as they could;

155

like hunger and want, the senselessness of life had tormented the human heart too long, and it was high time to find out what the existence of men was all about, was it something serious, or a joke?

"They hurt my feet," Lyuba said, pointing to her shoes. "You sit down for a while, and I'll get into bed, because I'm terribly hungry, and I don't want to think about it. . . ."

Without undressing, Lyuba climbed under the blanket on the bed and placed her braid on top of her eyes.

Nikita sat there silently for two or three hours, waiting for Lyuba to go to sleep. Then night fell, and Lyuba stood up in the darkness.

"My friend, probably, won't be coming today," Lyuba said sadly.

"What of it? Do you need her?" Nikita asked.

"Very badly," Lyuba said. "They have a big family, and the father is in the army, she brings me supper when there's something left over. . . . I eat, and then we study together. . . ."

"But do you have any kerosene?" Nikita asked.

"No, they gave me firewood. . . . We light the little stove, and then we sit on the floor and we can see by the flame."

Lyuba smiled helplessly, and ashamed, as if some cruel, unhappy thought had occurred to her.

"Probably her older brother didn't fall asleep," she said. "He doesn't like to have his sister feed me, he begrudges it. . . . But I'm not to blame! I'm not so fond of eating: it isn't me, but my head starts to ache, it starts to think about a piece of bread and keeps me from living and thinking about anything else. . . ."

"Lyuba!" a young voice said outside the window.

"Zhenya!" Lyuba called out.

Lyuba's friend walked in. She took four big baked potatoes out of the pocket of her jacket and put them on the iron stove.

"Did you get the histology book?" Lyuba asked her.

"And where would I get it?" Zhenya answered. "I signed up for it at the library. . . ."

"Never mind, we'll get along without it," Lyuba declared. "I memorized the first two chapters in the department. I'll recite it, and you take notes. Won't that work?"

"Even better!" Zhenya answered, laughing.

Nikita stoked up the little stove so its flames would light the notebook, and then got ready to go back to his father's for the night. "You won't forget me now?" Lyuba asked as she said good-bye to him.

"No," Nikita said. "I have nobody else to remember."

Firsov lay around the house for a couple of days and then went to work in the same furniture workshop where his father was employed. They listed him as a carpenter and assigned him to getting materials ready, and his pay was lower than his father's, hardly more than half as much. But Nikita knew this was temporary, while he got used to the trade, and then they would give him a rating as a cabinetmaker, and his pay would be better.

Nikita had never lost his habits of work. In the Red Army people were busy not just making war—in their long halts and when they were being held in reserve Red Army soldiers dug wells, repaired the huts of poor peasants in the villages, and planted bushes on the tops of ravines to keep the earth from washing away. For the war would be over and life would go on, and it was necessary to think about this in advance.

After a week Nikita went to call on Lyuba again; he took her some boiled fish and some bread as a present—it was the second course of his dinner at the workers' restaurant.

Lyuba was hurrying to finish a book by the window, profiting from the light still in the sky, so Nikita sat quietly for a while in her room, waiting for the darkness. But soon the twilight caught up with the quiet on the street outside, and Lyuba rubbed her eyes and closed her textbook.

"How are you?" Lyuba asked him in a low voice.

"My father and I get along, we're all right," Nikita said. "I brought you something to eat there, go on and eat it, please."

"I'll eat it, thank you," Lyuba said.

"Then you won't go to sleep?" Nikita asked.

"No, I won't," Lyuba answered. "I'll eat my supper now, and I'll be full!"

Nikita brought some kindling from the shed and lit the iron stove to make some light. He sat down on the floor, opened the door of the stove and fed chips and little twigs to the flames, trying to keep the heat at a minimum with as much light as possible. Lyuba sat down on the floor, too, when she had eaten the fish and the bread, facing Nikita and next to the light from the stove, and began to study her medical book.

She read silently, sometimes whispering something, smiling, and writing down some words on a pad in a small, quick handwriting, probably the more important points she read. Nikita just took care that the fire burned properly, and only from time to time—not often—looked at Lyuba's face, and then stared at the fire again for a long time because he was afraid of bothering Lyuba with his looking at her. So the time went, and Nikita thought sadly that it would soon go by completely and it would be time for him to go home.

At midnight, when the clock struck in the tower, Nikita asked Lyuba why her friend Zhenya had not come.

"She's got typhus, for the second time, she'll probably die of it," Lyuba answered, and she went back to reading her medicine.

"That's really too bad!" Nikita said, but Lyuba did not answer him.

Nikita pictured to himself a sick and fevered Zhenya, and it seemed to him he could have fallen really in love with her, if he had known her earlier and if she had encouraged him a little. For she was also pretty, it seemed: it was a shame he had not seen her clearly in the dark and could hardly remember what she looked like.

"Now I want to sleep," Lyuba said, sighing.

"Did you understand everything you read?" Nikita asked her.

"Absolutely all! Do you want me to tell it to you?" Lyuba offered.

"You don't have to," Nikita said. "You'd better keep it for yourself, because I'd forget it anyway."

He swept the floor around the stove with a broom, and went home to his father.

After that he called on Lyuba almost every day, except that sometimes he let a day or two go by so that Lyuba would miss him. Whether she missed him or not he didn't know, but on these empty evenings Nikita had to walk for eight or ten miles, around and around the whole town, trying to control himself in solitude, to endure his longing for Lyuba and to keep himself from going to her.

When he did call on her, he was usually busy stoking the little stove and waiting for her to say something to him in the moments when she wasn't reading in her book. Every time Nikita brought her some supper from the restaurant at the furniture workshop; she ate her dinners at her academy, but they served too little there and Lyuba was thinking a lot, studying, and still growing, too, so she didn't get enough nourishment. The first time he was paid Nikita bought a cow's horns in a neighboring village and boiled meat jelly on the little stove all night while Lyuba was busy at her books and her note-books until midnight, when she mended her clothes, darned her stockings and washed the floor until the dawn came, and then took a bath in the courtyard in a tub filled with rainwater before people who might see her had even wakened from their sleep.

Nikita's father was lonely every evening all alone, without his son, but Nikita never said where he was going. "He's a man now, in his own right," the old man thought. "He might have been killed or wounded in the war, so since he's still alive, let him go!"

One day the old man noticed that his son had brought home two white rolls. But he wrapped them up right away in a piece of paper, and didn't offer either of them to his father. Then Nikita put on his army cap, as was his habit, and walked out into the night, taking the two rolls with him.

"Nikita, take me along with you," the father begged him. "I won't say a thing, I'll just look. . . . It must be interesting there, with something happening!"

"Another time, father," Nikita said, embarrassed. "Besides, it's time for you to sleep, you've got to go to work tomorrow."

Nikita didn't find Lyuba that night, she wasn't home. He sat down on the bench by the gate, and began to wait for her. He put the white rolls inside his shirt so that they would keep warm until Lyuba arrived. He sat there patiently until late in the night, watching the stars in the sky and the few people passing by who were hurrying home to their children, listening to the sounds of the town clock striking in the tower, the barking of dogs in the courtyards, and various other quiet, unclear sounds which are not made in the daytime. He could probably have sat there, waiting, until he died.

Lyuba appeared, unheard, out of the darkness in front of Nikita. He stood up, but she told him: "You'd better go home," and she was crying. She walked into her room, and Nikita waited a little longer outside, not understanding, and then walked after her.

"Zhenya's dead," Lyuba said to him in the room. "What will I do now?"

Nikita was silent. The warm rolls were lying against his chest—he didn't have to take them out right then, right then there was nothing that had to be done. Lyuba was lying on the bed in her clothes, her face turned to the wall, and she was crying to herself, soundlessly and almost without stirring.

Nikita stood alone for a long time in the night-filled room, ashamed to disturb someone else's deep sorrow. Lyuba paid him no attention, because the sadness of one's own grief makes people indifferent to all other suffering. Nikita sat down without being asked on the bed at Lyuba's feet, and took the rolls out of his shirt to put them down somewhere, but for the moment he couldn't find anywhere to put them.

"Let me stay with you now!" Nikita said.

"But what will you do?" Lyuba asked, in tears.

Nikita pondered, afraid of making a mistake or of accidentally offending Lyuba.

"I won't do anything," he answered. "We'll just live as usual, so you won't be so worried."

"Let's wait, we've no reason to hurry," Lyuba declared pensively and prudently. "But we've got to think what we can bury Zhenya in—they haven't any coffin. . . ."

"I'll bring it tomorrow," Nikita promised, and he put the rolls down on the bed.

The next day Nikita asked the foreman's permission and started to make a coffin; they were always allowed to make coffins freely, without paying for the lumber. From lack of experience he took a long time making it but then he fashioned the place for the dead girl to lie inside it with special care and neatness; Nikita himself was upset just by thinking about the dead Zhenya and some of his tears fell among the shavings. His father, who was walking by, walked up to Nikita and noticed his trouble.

"What are you so sad about: has your girl died?" the father asked.

"No, her girl friend," he answered.

"Her girl friend?" the father said. "Well, plague take her! . . .

Here, let me even up the side of that coffin, you've made it look bad, it's not right."

When he finished work, Nikita carried the coffin to Lyuba; he didn't know where her dead friend was.

A warm autumn lasted for a long time that year, and people were glad of it. "It's been a bad harvest, so we'll save on firewood," thrifty persons said. Nikita Firsov had ordered ahead of time a woman's coat to be made for Lyuba out of his Red Army overcoat, and it had been ready for quite a while without any need to wear it, thanks to the warm weather. Nikita kept right on going to Lyuba's as he had before, to help her live and in return to get what he needed for the enjoyment of his own heart.

He asked her once how they should go on living—together or apart. And she answered that she would have no chance to feel happy before the spring, because she had to finish her medical academy as quickly as she could, and then they would see. Nikita listened to this long-term promise, he wasn't asking for any greater happiness than what he already had, thanks to Lyuba, and he did not even know if there was anything better, but his heart was shivering from its long endurance and from uncertainty—what did Lyuba need of a poor, unschooled, demobilized man like him? Lyuba sometimes smiled when she looked at him with her bright eyes, which had large, incomprehensible spots in them, and the face around her eyes was filled with goodness.

Once Nikita started to cry, while he was covering Lyuba with a blanket for the night before he went home, but Lyuba only stroked his head and said: "Well, you'll be all right, you musn't worry so while I'm still alive."

Nikita hurried home to his father, to take refuge there, to come to his senses, and to stay away from Lyuba for several days in a row. "I'll read," he decided, "and I'll start to live the way I ought to, and I'll forget Lyuba, I won't remember her or even know her. What has she got that's so special? There are millions of persons on this earth, and better than she is, too! She's not good-looking!"

In the morning he couldn't stand up from the bedding where he slept on the floor. His father, going out to work, felt his head, and said:

"You're burning up. Lie down in bed! You'll be sick for a while, and then you'll get better.... You weren't wounded anywhere in the war?"

"Nowhere," Nikita answered.

Toward evening he lost his memory; at first he saw the ceiling all the time, with two late flies on it about to die, sheltering themselves there for warmth with which to go on living, and then these same things began to fill him with melancholy and revulsion—it was as if the ceiling and the flies had penetrated into his brain, he couldn't drive them out or stop thinking about them in one steadily swelling thought which had already eaten up all the bones in his head. Nikita closed his eyes, but the flies were seething in his brain, and he jumped up from the bed, to drive the flies from the ceiling, but fell back on the pillow; it seemed to him the pillow still smelled of his mother's breath—his mother had slept right here next to his father—Nikita remembered her, and then he lost consciousness.

After four days, Lyuba found out where Nikita Firsov lived and showed up there for the first time. It was in the middle of the day, all the houses where workers lived were empty, the women had gone out to get food, and the children not yet old enough for school were scattered through the courtyards and the clearings. Lyuba sat on Nikita's bed, stroked his forehead, wiped his eyes with the end of her handkerchief, and asked him:

"Well, how about it, where do you hurt?"

"Nowhere," Nikita said.

His high fever had taken him far away from people and from things around him, and he barely saw and recognized Lyuba; afraid to lose her in the darkness of his flickering consciousness, he held on with his hand to the pocket of her coat, made over from his Red Army greatcoat, and he clung to it as an exhausted swimmer, between drowning and being saved, clutches at the shore. His illness was trying all the time to sweep him over the shining, empty horizon—into the open sea where he could rest at last on its slow, heavy waves.

"You have the grippe, probably, and I'll cure you," Lyuba said. "Or maybe it's typhus. But never mind—it's nothing to be frightened of."

She lifted Nikita by the shoulders and leaned his back against the wall. Then quickly and insistently she dressed him in her coat, she found his father's muffler and tied it around the sick man's head, and she stuck his feet into a pair of felt boots which were waiting under the bed for winter to come. With her arms around Nikita, Lyuba told him to move his legs and she led him, shivering, out into the street. A horse cab was waiting there, Lyuba pushed the sick man into it, and they drove off.

"He's not long for this world," the driver said and he turned to his horses, urging them with his reins into a gentle trot.

In her own room Lyuba undressed Nikita, put him to bed, and covered him with the blanket, an old strip of carpet, a decrepit shawl of her mother's—with everything she had that could keep him warm.

"Why stay there at your house?" Lyuba asked with satisfaction, tucking the blanket around Nikita's burning body. "Just why? Your father's off at work, you lie there all day alone, you get no care of any kind, and you just pine for me. . . ."

For a long time Nikita thought and wondered where Lyuba had got the money for the cab. Maybe she had sold her Austrian boots, or her textbook (she would have learned it by heart first, so she wouldn't need it) or else she had given the cab-driver her entire monthly stipend.

At night Nikita lay there in deep trouble: sometimes he

understood where he was, and could see Lyuba who had lit the stove and was cooking food on it, and then he could see only the unknown phantoms of his mind, operating independently of his will in the compressed, feverish tightness of his head.

His fever chills grew steadily worse. From time to time Lyuba felt Nikita's forehead with the palm of her hand, and counted the pulse in his wrist. Late in the night she poured out some warm water for him and then, taking off her outer clothing, lay down under the blanket with the sick man because he was shaking with chills and had to be warmed. Lyuba put her arms around Nikita and drew him to her while he rolled himself into a ball, away from the cold, and pushed his face against her breast in order to sense more closely this other, higher, better life and to forget his own torment, and his own shuddering, empty body. But now Nikita did not want to die—not because of himself, but in order to keep on touching Lyuba, this other life—and so he asked her in a whisper if he would get well or if he would die: for she had studied and must know the answer.

Lyuba hugged Nikita's head in her arms, and answered:

"You'll be well soon.... People die because they get sick all alone, and have nobody to love them, but you're with me now...."

Nikita grew warm, and fell asleep.

After three weeks Nikita was well again. Snow had already fallen outside, everything had suddenly grown quiet, and Nikita went home to spend the winter with his father. He did not want to bother Lyuba until she had finished the academy. Let her mind grow to its full size, for she came from poor people, too. The father was glad at his son's return, even though he had visited him at Lyuba's two days out of three, each time taking some food for his son while for Lyuba he took no present of any kind.

In the daytime Nikita started to work again at the workshop, in the evenings he visited Lyuba, and the winter went well; he knew that she would be his wife in the spring and that a long and happy life would start then. Sometimes Lyuba would poke him, push at him, run away from him around the room, and then—after the playing—Nikita would kiss her carefully on the cheek. Usually Lyuba would not let him touch her without some reason.

"Or else you'll get tired of me, and we've still got a whole life ahead of us!" she said. "I'm not that attractive, it just seems so to you."

On their day off Lyuba and Nikita took walks along the winter roads outside the town, or they walked, half-frozen, along the ice of the sleeping Potudan River—far downstream as it ran in summertime. Nikita would lie on his stomach and look down through the ice to where the quiet flowing of the water could be seen. Lyuba too would settle down next to him and, touching each other, they would watch the flowing of the water and they would talk about how happy the Potudan River was because it was running out to the sea and because this water under the ice would flow past the shores of faraway lands where flowers were now blooming and birds singing. When she had thought a little about this, Lyuba made Nikita stand up from the ice at once; he was now going around in an old quilted coat of his father's, it was too short for him and didn't keep him very warm, so he might catch cold.

They patiently were friends with each other almost all winter long, tormented by anticipation of their imminent future happiness. The Potudan River was also hidden under the ice all winter long, and the winter grain was sleeping under the snow—these natural phenomena calmed Nikita Firsov and even comforted him: his heart was not the only thing lying buried until spring. In February, waking up in the mornings, he would listen—were there new flies buzzing yet? Outdoors he would look at the sky and at the trees in the garden next door: maybe the first birds were already flying in from faraway countries. But the trees, the grass and the eggs of the flies were all still asleep in the depth of their strength, in embryo.

In the middle of February, Lyuba told Nikita that final examinations would begin on the twentieth, because doctors were so badly needed and people could not wait long for them. And by March the examinations would be over, and then the snow could stay and the river could go on running under its ice until July if they wanted to! Happiness would start in their hearts before warmth began in nature around them.

During this time—just before March—Nikita wanted to get out of the town, to make the time go more quickly until he and Lyuba could live together. He volunteered at the furniture workshop to go out with a brigade of carpenters to repair furniture in village Soviets and village schools.

At the same time his father finished making, at his own pace, a big wardrobe as a present for the young people. It was like the one which had been in Lyuba's room when her mother was about to become the bride of Nikita's father. In the old carpenter's eyes life was repeating itself for a second or third time. You could understand this but you couldn't change it, and Nikita's father, sighing deeply, loaded the wardrobe on to a sledge and hauled it to the home of his son's intended bride. The snow was getting warm and melting under the sun, but the old man was still strong and he pulled the sledge with some effort even across the black stretches of bare earth. He was secretly thinking that he himself could easily marry this girl, Lyuba, although he had once been too shy for her mother, but he was somehow still ashamed, and he didn't have enough at home to attract and pamper a young girl like her. And Nikita's father concluded from this that life was far from normal. His son had only just come back from war, and here he was leaving home again, this time for good and all. The old man would have to pick up a beggar off the streets, not for the sake of family life but so that there might be some kind of second being in the house, if only a domesticated hedgehog or a rabbit: it might upset life and dirty everything up, but without it he'd cease to be a man.

When he gave Lyuba the wardrobe, Nikita's father asked her when he would be coming to her wedding.

"Whenever Nikita comes back. I'm ready now," Lyuba said.

That night the father walked fourteen miles to the village where Nikita was fixing desks in a school. Nikita was asleep on the floor in an empty classroom, but the father woke him and told him it was time to go back to the town—he could get married.

"You get going, and I'll finish the desks for you," the father told him.

Nikita put on his cap and right away, without waiting for the dawn, set out on foot for the town. He walked alone through the whole second half of the night through empty country: the wind off the fields was blowing fitfully around him, sometimes in his face, sometimes against his back, and sometimes disappearing entirely into the silence of the ravine next to the road. The ground lay dark along the slopes and in the high fields, the snow had run down into the bottom lands, there was the smell of young water and of rotting grass dead since the autumn. But the autumn was already a forgotten, long-past time—the earth was now poor and free, it would give birth to everything from scratch and only to new things which had never lived before. Nikita wasn't even in a hurry to get to Lyuba; he liked being in that dim light of night on that unthinking, early ground which had forgotten all that had already died on it and knew nothing of what it would give birth to in the warmth of the new summer.

Toward morning Nikita got to Lyuba's house. A light hoar frost covered the familiar roof and the brick foundations—Lyuba was probably sleeping sweetly now in her warm bed, and Nikita walked past her house so as not to wake his bride, not to let her body cool just because of him.

By evening of that day Nikita Firsov and Lyubov Kuznetsova had been registered in the district Soviet as married, and they went back to Lyuba's room, and didn't know what to do. Nikita now felt it on his conscience that complete happiness had arrived for him, that the person he needed most in all the world wanted to live together with him, as if there were some great and priceless goodness hidden inside him. He took Lyuba's hand and held it for a long time; he delighted in the warm feeling of her palm, through it he could feel the distant beating of the heart he loved, and he thought about the mystery he could not understand: why Lyuba was smiling at him, and loved him for reasons he could not guess. He knew precisely, for himself, just why Lyuba was dear to him.

"First of all, let's eat," Lyuba said, and she took her hand away from Nikita.

She had already got something ready: on completing the academy she had been given a bigger stipend both in provisions and in cash.

Nikita shyly started to eat the different tasty dishes his wife had prepared. He could not remember that anyone had ever given him something for nothing, he had never visited people in his whole life just for his own satisfaction, and then been fed by them too.

When they had eaten, Lyuba got up from the table first. She opened her arms to Nikita, and said:

"Well!"

Nikita stood up and embraced her shyly, afraid of hurting something in this special, tender body. Lyuba herself squeezed him hard to help him, but Nikita asked her: "Wait a minute, my heart is hurting badly," and Lyuba released her husband.

Dusk had fallen outside, and Nikita wanted to start the stove, to get some light, but Lyuba said: "We don't have to, I've finished studying, and today's our wedding day." Then Nikita turned down the bed while Lyuba undressed in front of him, feeling no shame before her husband. Nikita walked over to his father's wardrobe and took off his own clothing quickly and then lay down next to Lyuba for the night.

Nikita got up very early the next morning. He cleaned up the room, lit the stove to boil the teakettle, brought in water in a pail from the shed for washing, and ended up not knowing what else to do, while Lyuba went on sleeping. He sat down on a chair, and grieved: now Lyuba would probably tell him to go back to his father for good because, it appeared, one had to know how to take pleasure, and Nikita couldn't torment Lyuba just for the sake of his own happiness, but all his strength was pounding inside his heart, rushing up into his throat, leaving nothing anywhere else.

Lyuba woke up and looked at her husband.

"Don't be downhearted, it's not worth it," she said smiling. "You and I'll fix everything together."

"Let me wash the floor," Nikita asked her, "else it will be dirty here."

"Well, go on and wash it," Lyuba agreed.

"How pitiful and weak he is from his love for me!" Lyuba thought in bed. "How good and dear he is to me! May I always be a girl to him! I can stand it. And maybe some time he'll start loving me less, and then he'll be a strong man."

Nikita was fidgeting with a wet mop on the floor, scrubbing the dirt from the boards, and Lyuba laughed at him from the bed.

"Here I am a married woman!" she told herself with delight, and she stretched out in her nightgown on top of the blanket.

When he had scrubbed the room, Nikita wiped all the furniture with a wet cloth, then he added cold water to the pail of hot water and pulled a washbasin out from under the bed so that Lyuba could wash in it.

After they had drunk tea, Lyuba kissed her husband on the forehead and went off to work at the hospital, telling him that she would be back at three o'clock. Nikita touched the place on his forehead where his wife had kissed him, and stayed by himself. He didn't know why he wasn't going to work today—it seemed to him it was shameful now for him to be alive, and maybe he did not have to. Why did he need to earn money now? He decided somehow to live out the rest of his life, until he wasted away from shame and grief.

Having looked over all the family property in their new home, Nikita found the food he needed to fix a one-dish dinner—a thick beef soup. After this work, he lay face down on the bed and began to count how much time would have to go by before the rivers started to flow again, when he could drown himself in the Potudan.

"I'll wait until the ice breaks up; it won't be long now," he said out loud, to calm himself, and he dozed off.

Lyuba brought a present back with her from work—two earthenware bowls with winter flowers in them: the doctors and the nurses had celebrated her wedding. And she had held herself important and mysterious in front of them, like a real married woman. The younger girls among the nurses and the nurses' aides were envious of her, one earnest worker from the hospital pharmacy asked Lyuba confidentially: was it true or not that love was something fascinating but that getting married for love was truly an entrancing happiness? Lyuba answered her that this was the honest truth, and that this was why people go on living in this world.

The husband and wife talked with each other in the evening. Lyuba said that they might have children, and that they should think about this ahead of time. Nikita promised to begin making some children's furniture in overtime at the workshop: a little table, a chair, and a cradle-bed.

"The revolution is here for good, now it's all right to have children," Nikita said. "There'll never be unhappy children ever again."

"It's all right for you to talk, but I'm the one who'll have to bear them," Lyuba said, pouting.

"Will it hurt?" Nikita asked. "In that case, better not to have children, not to suffer. . . ."

"No, I'll survive it, thanks just the same," Lyuba agreed.

At twilight she fixed the bed, and then, so it wouldn't be too crowded for sleep she extended it with the two chairs for their feet and had them sleep across it. Nikita lay down as he was instructed, was silent, and late in the night he cried in his sleep. But Lyuba didn't fall asleep for a long time, she was listening to his crying, and she carefully wiped Nikita's sleeping face with the end of the sheet, and in the morning, when he woke up, he had no memory of his sadness in the night.

After that their life together went on at its own pace. Lyuba took care of people in the hospital, and Nikita made his furniture. In his free time and on Sundays he worked in the yard and in the house, although Lyuba didn't ask him to do this—she herself no longer knew exactly whose house it was. Once it had belonged to her mother, then it had been taken over as government property but the government had forgotten about the house—no one had ever come to check on its condition or to ask any money as rent. It made no difference to Nikita. He managed to get some green paint, through acquaintances of his father, and he painted the roof and the shutters as soon as spring weather had set in. With the same diligence he gradually fixed up the decrepit old shed in the yard outside the house, repaired the gate and the fence, and prepared to dig a new cellar since the old one had caved in.

The ice was already breaking up in the Potudan River. Nikita walked down to the bank twice, looked at the flowing water, and made up his mind not to die as long as Lyuba could stand him, and whenever she couldn't stand him any longer, he'd manage to end it all. The river wouldn't freeze over quickly. Nikita usually did his work around the house slowly so as not to be sitting in the room, making Lyuba tired of him. And whenever he finished it completely, he would fill the hem of his shirt with clay from the old cellar and walk back into the room. There he would sit on the floor and shape little human figures and other objects out of the clay, with no meaning or likeness to anything—things like hills with animal heads growing out of them, or the root system of a tree in which the root seemed an ordinary root but so tangled and impassable, with each of its branches pierced by another, gnawing at and torturing itself, that looking long at this root made you want to go to sleep. Nikita smiled carelessly and blissfully while he worked with his clay, and Lyuba would sit there on the floor next to him, sewing linen or singing little songs that she had heard at some time, and along with what she was doing she would caress Nikita with one hand, sometimes stroking his head, sometimes tickling him under his arm. Nikita lived through these hours with his heart beating gently, and he did not know if he needed something higher and mightier, or if life in actual fact was nothing very big—just about what he already had. But Lyuba would look at him with her tired eyes full of patient goodness, just as if what was good and happy had become heavy work for her. Then Nikita would knead his clay toys back into the clay from which he had made them, and he would ask his wife if she didn't want him to stoke up the stove, to heat water for tea, or to go out somewhere on an errand. . . .

"You don't have to," Lyuba would say, smiling at him. "I'll do it all myself. . . ."

And Nikita understood that life was indeed something very big, and maybe beyond his strength, that it was not all concentrated in his pounding heart—it was still stronger, more interesting and dearer in another person he could not reach. He picked up the pail and went to get water at the town well where the water was cleaner than in the tanks on the street. Nikita could not drown his grief with anything, with any kind of work, and he was afraid of the approaching night as he had been in childhood. When he had got the water, Nikita went along with the full pail to call on his father.

"What's the matter, didn't you have a wedding?" his father asked. "Did you do it in the Soviet way, secretly...?"

"We'll have it yet," his son promised. "Come on, help me make a little table, with a chair and a cradle-bed. You talk to the foreman tomorrow, so he'll give me the material.... Because we'll be having children, probably."

"Well, why not? That's possible," the father agreed. "But you shouldn't be having children soon: it's not time yet...."

In a week Nikita had made for himself all the children's furniture he needed; he stayed late every evening, and worked hard at it. His father sanded each piece neatly, and painted it.

Lyuba set up the child's furniture in a special corner, decorated her unborn child's table with two earthenware bowls of flowers, and hung a newly embroidered towel over the back of the chair. Lyuba hugged Nikita in thanks for his devotion to her and to her unknown children, she kissed his throat, pressed herself against his chest, and warmed herself next to her beloved, knowing that there was nothing else that could be done. And Nikita dropped the hands with which he had covered his heart and stood there silent in front of her because he did not want to look strong when he was really helpless.

Nikita went to sleep early that night and woke up a little after midnight. He lay there in the quiet for a long time and listened to the sounds of the clock striking in the town—half past twelve, one, half past one, a single peal for each of the three times. In the sky outside the window a vague kind of growing started—it was not yet dawn but only a movement of the darkness, a slow stripping away of empty space, and all the things in the room and the child's furniture, too, began to be visible, but after the dark night they had lived through they looked miserable and exhausted, as if they were calling out for help. Lyuba stirred under the blanket, and she sighed; perhaps she too was not asleep. In any case Nikita kept quiet, and began to listen hard. But Lyuba didn't stir any more, she was breathing evenly again, and it pleased Nikita that Lyuba was lying there next to him, alive, essential to his soul, and not even realizing in her sleep that he, her husband, even existed. As long as she was whole and happy, Nikita needed for his own life only his consciousness of her. He dozed off in peace, comforted by the sleep of someone close and dear to him, and then he opened his eyes again.

Lyuba was crying, carefully, almost inaudibly. She had covered over her head, and was tormenting herself there alone, squeezing her grief to keep it down without a sound. Nikita turned his face to Lyuba and saw how quickly she was breathing and how dispirited she was as she sadly hid under the covers. Nikita was silent. It's not possible to comfort every grief, there is some grief that ends only after the exhaustion of the heart, in long oblivion or in the distraction of the cares of daily living.

By dawn Lyuba had grown quiet. Nikita waited for a while and then lifted the corner of the blanket and looked at his wife's face. She was sleeping quietly, warm, at peace, with dry eyes. . . .

Nikita got up, dressed quietly, and went outside. A pale morning was starting across the world, and a wandering beggar was walking down the street, carrying a full bag. Nikita started to follow this man, so as to have a feeling of going somewhere. The beggar walked out of the town and set off along the high road to the settlement of Kantemirovka where from time immemorial there had been a big bazaar and many prosperous people. It's true, they gave little away to a poor man there, and the beggar could really feed himself only in the far-away villages where poor peasants lived, but still it was fun in Kantemirovka, interesting, one could live at the bazaar just by watching the crowds of people, distracting the spirit for a little while.

The beggar and Nikita got to Kantemirovka about noon. In the outskirts of the town the beggar sat down in a ditch, opened his bag, and he and Nikita ate together, and then inside the town they went off in different directions because the beggar had his own plans and Nikita had none. He came to the bazaar, sat down in the shade next to a merchant's bin with a hinged cover, and stopped thinking about Lyuba, about the cares of life, and about himself.

The watchman at the bazaar had already lived there for twenty-five years and all this time he had lived a rich life with his fat, childless old lady. The merchants and the cooperative stores were always giving him leftovers of meat, they sold him sewing materials at cost and even household necessities like thread, soap, and such products. For a long time he had been a small trader himself, selling broken-up packing cases and hoarding the money in a savings account. His responsibility was to sweep up the trash all through the fair grounds, to wash the blood from the counters in the butchers' row, to clean the public latrines, and at night to patrol the trading sheds and the stores. But he only strolled up and down the bazaar at night in a warm sheepskin coat while he turned the hard work over to beggars and vagabonds who passed the night at the bazaar; his wife almost always emptied the remains of yesterday's meat and cabbage soup into a garbage pail, so the watchman could feed some poor wretch for cleaning the latrines for him.

His wife used to order him not to do the dirty work himself, seeing how gray his beard had grown—he was no longer to be a watchman, but a supervisor. But it was hard to get a beggar or a tramp to work forever in exchange for grub like that; he'd work for a day, eat what was given him, ask for more, then disappear back into the countryside.

Recently the watchman had driven the same man out of the bazaar for several nights in a row. When the watchman shoved him, as he slept, this man would get up and walk away, saying nothing, and then he would sit down or lie down somewhere else behind a bin which was farther away. Once the watchman hunted this homeless man all night long, his blood fairly sparkling with his passionate desire to torment and to subdue this strange, exhausted creature. Twice the watchman threw his stick at him and hit him in the head, but by dawn the vagabond was still hiding from him—probably he had quit the fair grounds completely. In the morning the watchman found him again—he was sleeping on the roof of a cesspool at the latrines, out in the open. The watchman called to the sleeping man, who opened his eyes but did not answer, looked at him and then dozed off again with complete indifference. The watchman thought—this must be a dumb man. He prodded the sleeper's stomach with the end of his stick and gestured with his arm that he should follow him.

In his neat, official apartment—kitchen and one room—the watchman fed the dumb man from an earthenware pot of cold soup, and after he had eaten ordered him to take a broom, a shovel, a scraper and a pail of lime from the shed and to clean the latrines thoroughly. The dumb man looked at the watchman with dull eyes: probably he was deaf, too. . . . But no, he couldn't be, because the dumb man picked up in the shed all the tools and things he needed, just as the watchman had told him. This proved that he could hear.

Nikita did the job accurately, and the watchman came back later to see how it looked; for a start, it was tolerable, so the watchman took Nikita to the place where horses were hitched and told him to pick up all the manure and take it away in a wheel-barrow.

At home the watchman-supervisor instructed his wife that now she was no longer to scrape the leavings from their supper and dinner into the garbage pail but to keep them in a separate crock: let the dumb man have his fill to eat.

"And I suppose you're going to have him sleep in the room, too," the wife asked him.

"That's not the point!" the man declared. "He'll spend the nights outside: for he's not deaf, let him lie there and listen for robbers, and when he hears one, he'll run and tell me. Give him a piece of sacking, he'll find a place and make himself a bed."

Nikita lived for a long time at the bazaar. Having first become unused to talking, he thought, remembered, and worried less and less. It was only rarely that a weight lay on his heart, and he endured this without reflecting about it, and the feeling of grief inside him gradually weakened and disappeared. He was already used to living at the bazaar, and the crowds of people, the noise of voices, all the daily happenings, kept him from remembering about himself and from his own concerns —food, rest, and the desire to see his father. Nikita worked all the time; even at night when he would fall asleep in an empty box somewhere in the empty bazaar, the watchman-supervisor would come up to him and order him just to nap and to listen, not to sleep like the dead. "You've got to," the watchman told him, "only the other day the crooks ripped two boards off a shop and ate fifteen pounds of honey without any bread." And by dawn Nikita was already working, hurrying to get the bazaar clean before the people came; in the daytime he couldn't eat, there was the manure to be shoveled into the communal cart, a new pit to be dug for slops and sewage, or old boxes to be broken up which the watchman got free from the traders and then sold, board by board, to peasants from the country, and then there was still more work to do.

In the middle of the summer they took Nikita to jail on suspicion of having stolen some chandler's goods from the government store at the bazaar, but the investigation cleared him because this dumb, desperately tired man was too indifferent about the charge against him. The investigator could find no evidence of any desire for life or enjoyment or satisfactions of any kind in Nikita's character or in his modest work at the bazaar as the watchman's helper. In jail he didn't even eat up the food that was given to him. The investigator realized that this was a man who did not know the value of either personal or public property, and there was not even any circumstantial evidence against him in the case. "There's no reason to dirty up a prison with a man like that!" the investigator decided.

Nikita stayed in jail for five days, and then went back to the bazaar. The watchman-supervisor was already tired out from having to work without him, so he was overjoyed when the dumb man showed up again. The old man summoned him to his apartment and gave him hot, fresh cabbage soup to eat, breaking all the rules of thrift in his own household. "Let him eat for once—it won't ruin him!" the old watchman-supervisor reassured himself. "And then back to yesterday's cold leftovers, when there are any."

"Go over and clean up the rubbish along the grocers' row," the watchman instructed Nikita when he had eaten up the soup.

Nikita went back to his usual place. By now he was only dimly aware of himself at all, and he thought very little, about anything that happened to come into his mind. By autumn, probably, he would have forgotten entirely what he was. Looking around at the activity of the world he would have ceased to have any understanding of it. Other people might think this man was living but actually he would be there and exist only in forgetfulness, in the poverty of his mind, in his loss of consciousness, as if in some warmth of his own, taking shelter from mortal grief. . . .

Soon after his stay in jail, at the end of summer when the nights were growing longer, Nikita started once to lock the door to the latrines, as required by the rules, when he heard a voice from inside:

"Wait a little, before you lock up! Are you afraid someone's going to steal something out of here?"

Nikita waited for the man. His father walked out of the building, holding an empty sack under his arm.

"Hello, Nikita!" the father said, and he suddenly began to cry, sadly, ashamed of his tears and not wiping them away so as not to admit that he was crying. "We thought you were a dead man long ago. This means you're all right?"

Nikita embraced his thin, drooping father; his heart, which had grown unused to feeling, had now been touched.

Then they walked through the empty bazaar and settled down in the passageway between two big merchants' bins.

"I just came for some barley, it's cheaper here," his father explained. "But I was late, you see, the bazaar is closed. Well, I'll spend the night now, and tomorrow I'll buy it and go back home. And what are you doing here?"

Nikita wanted to answer his father, but his throat dried up and he had forgotten how to talk. He coughed, and whispered:

"I'm all right. Is Lyuba alive?"

"She threw herself in the river," his father said. "But some fishermen saw her right away and pulled her out—she was in the hospital for a while, she got better."

"And she's alive now?" Nikita asked in a low voice.

"So far she hasn't died," his father declared. "Blood runs often from her throat; she probably caught cold when she tried to drown herself. She picked a bad time—the weather had just turned bad and the water was cold. . . ."

The father pulled some bread out of his pocket, gave half of it to his son, and they sat there for a little, chewing their supper. Nikita was silent, and the father spread his sack out on the ground, and got ready to lie down on it.

"Have you got any place to sleep?" the father asked. "If not, you lie on the sack, and I'll lie on the ground. I won't catch cold, I'm too old. . . ."

"But why did Lyuba drown herself?" Nikita whispered.

"What's the matter? Does your throat hurt you?" the father asked. "You'll get over it. . . . She missed you badly, and just wasted away from grief, that's why. . . . For a whole month she just walked up and down the Potudan River, back and forth, along the bank for sixty miles. She thought you'd drowned and would come to the surface, and she wanted to see you. While, it turns out, you were right here all the time. That's bad. . . ."

Nikita thought about Lyuba, and once more his heart filled with grief and with strength.

"You spend the night here alone, father," Nikita said. "I'm going to have a look at Lyuba."

"Go on then," the father agreed. "It's good going now, cooler. And I'll come back tomorrow, then we'll talk things over. . . ."

Going out of the settlement Nikita started to run along the deserted high road. When he got tired, he walked again for a while, then he ran again in the free, light air spread over the dark fields.

It was late at night when Nikita knocked at Lyuba's window and touched the shutters he had painted once with green paint. Now the dark night made them look blue. He pressed his face against the window glass. A pale light was filtered through the room, from the white sheets dropping off the bed, and Nikita could see the child's furniture he had made with his father—it was all there. Then Nikita knocked loudly on the window frame. But Lyuba still did not answer, and she didn't come to the window to see who he was.

Nikita climbed over the gate, went through the shed and

then into the room—the doors were not locked; whoever lived here was not worried about protecting his property from thieves.

Lyuba was lying under the blanket on the bed, her head covered.

"Lyuba!" Nikita called to her in a low voice.

"What?" Lyuba asked from under the blanket.

She wasn't asleep. Maybe she was lying there all alone in terror, or sick, or thought the knock on the window and Nikita's voice were a dream.

Nikita sat on the edge of the bed.

"Lyuba, I've come, it's me," Nikita said.

Lyuba lifted the blanket away from her face.

"Come here to me, quickly," she begged in her old, tender voice, and she held out her arms to Nikita.

Lyuba was afraid this would all go away; she grabbed Nikita by the arms and pulled him to her.

Nikita hugged Lyuba with the force that tries to pull another, beloved person right inside a hungering soul; but he quickly recovered his senses, and he felt ashamed.

"I didn't hurt you?" Nikita asked.

"No, I don't feel anything," Lyuba answered.

He wanted her badly, so she might be comforted, and a savage, miserable strength came to him. But Nikita did not find from loving Lyuba intimately any higher happiness than he had usually known—he felt only that his heart was now in charge of his whole body and could divide his blood with his poor but necessary pleasure.

Lyuba asked Nikita—maybe he could light the little stove for it would still be dark outside for a long time. Let there be a fire inside the room, she wouldn't be sleeping anyway, she wanted to wait for the dawn and look at Nikita.

But there was no more firewood in the shed. So Nikita ripped two boards off the side of the shed, split them into pieces and some kindling, and stoked up the little stove. When the fire was burning well, Nikita opened the little door so the light could shine outside the stove. Lyuba climbed out of bed and sat on the floor, facing Nikita, where there was some light.

"Is it all right with you now, you won't be sorry to live with me?" she asked.

"No, I'm all right," Nikita answered. "I'm already used to being happy with you."

"Build up the fire, I'm chilled to the bone," Lyuba asked him.

She was wearing only her worn-out nightgown, and her thin body was freezing in the cool half-light of early morning at the end of summer.

# HOMECOMING

ALEXEI ALEXEIEVICH IVANOV, a Guards sergeant, left the army on demobilization. In the unit where he had served all through the war they saw him off with regret, with affection and respect, and with music and with wine. His close friends and comrades drove to the railroad station with Ivanov, and after the last farewells left him by himself. But the train was reported to be hours late and then, when those hours had run out, it was still delayed. Finally the cold autumn night began; the station had been destroyed in the war, there was no place to spend the night, and Ivanov hitched a ride back to his unit in a passing car. The next day his colleagues saw him off again. They sang their songs again and hugged him with words of eternal friendship, but this time they poured out their feelings more briefly and the affair involved only a small circle of his friends.

The second time Ivanov went to the station he learned that yesterday's train had not yet arrived and that he might just as well go back to his unit again to spend the night. But it would have been awkward to be seen off a third time and to trouble his comrades, so Ivanov settled down for the tedious wait on the empty asphalt of the station platform.

An undamaged switchman's cabin stood next to the main switch of the station. A woman in a quilted jacket, with a warm shawl around her head, was sitting on a bench by the cabin; she had been sitting there the day before, surrounded by her things, and here she still was, waiting for the train. When he had gone back the day before to sleep at his unit, Ivanov had wondered if he should not invite this lonely woman to go too, she could have spent the night with one of the nurses in a warm cottage, why should she freeze all night, for it was uncertain if she could get warm in the switchman's cabin. But while he was wondering, the automobile had started, and Ivanov forgot all about the woman.

Now she was where she had been the day before, and just as motionless. This constancy and patience showed the fidelity and the immutability of the female heart, at any rate in relation to her baggage and to her home to which this woman was probably returning. Ivanov walked over to her: maybe she too would find it less boring with him than all alone.

The woman turned her face toward Ivanov, and he recognized her. This was a girl everyone called "Masha, the spaceman's daughter" because she had once called herself this, although she was really the daughter of an employee in a public bath. Ivanov had run into her from time to time during the war when he visited an airfield service battalion (BAO) where this Masha, the spaceman's daughter, worked in the restaurant as assistant cook.

At this time of day there was something cheerless and sad about the autumn landscape around them. The train which was supposed to take Ivanov and Masha to their homes was lost somewhere in the gray distance. The only thing that could possibly distract and comfort a human heart was the heart of another human being.

Ivanov started to talk with Masha, and he felt better. Masha was pretty, simplehearted, with goodness in her big worker's hands and in her healthy young body. She was also going home, and wondering how she would manage with a new, civilian life; she had become used to her army friends, used to the fliers who loved her like an older sister, gave her presents of chocolate, and called her "Spacious Masha" because of her size and her big heart which embraced all brothers in one love, as real sisters do, and no one of them separately. And now it was unusual, strange, and a little frightening to Masha to be going home to relatives whom she was no longer used to.

Ivanov and Masha both felt themselves orphaned without the army, but Ivanov could not stay long in any sad or despondent mood. At times like this it seemed to him that someone far away must be making a fool of him, being happy in his place while he went on scowling like a simpleton. So Ivanov always turned back quickly to the business of living, that is, he would turn up some occupation or relaxation, some simple, improvised happiness as he himself called it, and this would pull him out of his depression. He turned to Masha and asked her, like a good comrade, to let him kiss her on the cheek.

"Just a little kiss," Ivanov said, "because the train's so late, and it's so tiresome waiting for it."

"Only because the train is late?" Masha asked, and she looked carefully at Ivanov's face.

The former sergeant looked about thirty-five, the skin on his face had been blown by the wind and burned by the sun until it was dark brown, and his gray eyes looked modestly at Masha, even shyly, and although he spoke directly to her, he talked delicately, and politely. Masha liked his toneless, hoarse voice, like that of an elderly man, and his dark rough face with its look of strength and defenselessness. Ivanov tamped down the fire in his pipe with his thumb, not feeling the burn, and sighed as he waited for permission. Masha drew back a little from Ivanov. He had a strong smell of tobacco, of dry toasted bread, a little bit of wine, and of the clean things which come from fire or can make fire. It was as if Ivanov lived on just tobacco, rusks, beer and wine. He repeated his request.

"I'll be careful, I'll just kiss you lightly, Masha. . . . Just imagine that I'm your uncle."

"I already imagined. . . . I imagined that you were my father, not my uncle."

"That's the way. . . . So you'll let me?"

"Fathers don't ask their daughters," Masha said, laughing.

Later Ivanov told himself that Masha's hair smelled like leaves falling in the woods in autumn, and he would never be able to forget this. . . .

Going a little away from the tracks, Ivanov lit a small fire so he could make an omelet for Masha and himself for supper.

During the night the train came and took Ivanov and Masha on their way to their homes. They traveled together for two days and nights, and on the third day they came to the city where Masha had been born twenty years before. Masha collected her things in the compartment, and asked Ivanov to adjust the duffel bag more comfortably on her back, but Ivanov took the sack on his own shoulder and climbed down from the train with Masha although he was still more than a day's travel from his own home.

Masha was surprised and touched by Ivanov's attention. She felt suddenly scared of being left alone in the town where she had been born and had grown up but which had now become almost a foreign country to her. Masha's mother and father had been driven out by the Germans and had perished no one knew where or how, and now in her home town Masha had only a cousin and two aunts, and she felt no strong attachment to them.

Ivanov fixed up a stopover in the city with the station commandant, and stayed with Masha. He really needed to go on as quickly as he could to his own home where his wife and two children, whom he had not seen for four years, were waiting for him. But Ivanov was putting off the happy, frightening moment of reunion with his family. He didn't know just why he was doing this, perhaps it was simply because he felt like strolling around in freedom for a little while longer.

Masha did not know about Ivanov's family situation and out of some girlish shyness did not ask him about it. She trusted Ivanov out of the goodness of her heart, with no thought of anything else.

Two days later, Ivanov traveled on, to his own home town. Masha went to the railroad station with him. Ivanov kissed her conventionally and promised with affection to remember her forever.

Masha smiled in reply, and said:

"Why remember me forever? It's not necessary, and you'll forget anyway.... I'm not asking anything from you, so forget me...."

"Masha, my dear one ... where were you before? And why didn't I meet you a long, long time ago?"

"Well, before the war I was in school, and a long, long time ago I didn't even exist."

The train pulled in, and they said good-bye. Ivanov went away, and he did not see that Masha cried when she was alone, because she could never forget anyone, neither her girl friends nor her comrades, with whom fate had ever linked her. Ivanov looked out of the train window at the houses in the little town which he would probably never see again in his life, and thought that it was in just such a little house, only in a different town, that his wife Lyuba lived with their children Peter and Nastya and they were expecting him. He had sent his wife a telegram from his unit, saying that he was coming home without delay and that he wanted to hug her and the children as soon as he could.

Lyuba Vassilievna, Ivanov's wife, met all the trains coming from the west for three days in a row. She took leave from her job, did not fulfill her production quota, and did not sleep at night for happiness, listening to how slowly and uncaringly the pendulum swung in the clock on the wall. On the fourth day, Lyuba Vassilievna sent the children Peter and Nastya to the station to meet their father in case he came in the daytime, but she herself went to meet the night train.

Ivanov arrived on the sixth day. His son met him. Peter was now in his twelfth year, and at first the father did not recognize his own child in this serious young fellow who seemed older than his age. The father saw that Peter was an undersized and skinny little boy, but still he had a big head and a broad forehead and his face had a kind of calm, as if he were already used to the worries of the world, and his small brown eyes looked out gloomily and unhappily, as if they could see nothing but disorder anywhere around him. Peter was carefully dressed; his shoes looked worn but still serviceable, his trousers and jacket were old, made over from his father's civilian clothes, but without any rips or tears—they had been darned where this was needed and patched where that was necessary and all of Peter added up to a little man who was not rich but in good working order. The father was surprised, and he sighed.

"You're my father, aren't you?" Peter asked when Ivanov had thrown his arms around him and kissed him, holding him close. "You must be my father."

"Your father . . . How do you do, Peter Alexeievich?"

"How do you do? Why were you so long getting here? We've waited and waited."

"The train, Petrushka, went slowly. . . . How are your mother and Nastya—alive and well?"

"As usual," Peter said. "How many decorations do you have?"

"Two, Peter, and three medals."

"But Mother and I expected—there wouldn't be any empty space on your uniform at all. Mother has two medals, too, they gave them to her for her services to the war effort. . . . Why do you have so little baggage, just one duffel bag?"

"I don't need any more."

"Someone with a trunk, is it hard for him to fight?" the son asked.

"It's hard for him," the father agreed. "With just a bag it's easier. Nobody at war had a trunk."

"And I thought they did have. I would have kept my good things in a trunk. They would all get broken or mussed up in a bag."

He took the duffel bag from his father and carried it home, and the father walked along right behind him.

The mother met them on the porch of the house; she had taken time off from her job again, as if her heart had told her that this was the day her husband would arrive. She went straight home from the factory, so she could go to the station later. She was worried—maybe Semyon Yevseyevich would show up at their house: he liked to come sometimes in day-time, he had the habit of appearing in the middle of the day and sitting there with five-year-old Nastya and with Peter. It was true, Semyon Yevseyevich never showed up empty-handed, he always brought something for the children—candy, or sugar, or a white roll, or a ration coupon for goods in the store. Lyuba Vassilievna had never had any fault to find with Semyon Yevseyevich; during these two years that they had known each other Semyon Yevseyevich had been good to her, and he treated the children like their own father and even more thoughtfully than if he had been their father. But today Lyuba Vassilievna did not want her husband to see Semyon Yevseyevich. She cleaned up the kitchen and the living room, everything in the house must be tidy, with nothing strange left around. And later, tomorrow or the day after tomorrow, she would tell her husband the whole truth herself, just how it had been. Luckily, Semyon Yevseyevich did not show up today.

Ivanov went up to his wife, embraced her, and stood with his arms around her, not letting go, feeling the forgotten but still familiar warmth of a person who is loved.

The little Nastya came out of the house and, seeing her father whom she did not remember, began to pull him away from her mother, tugging against his leg, and then she began to cry. Peter stood silently next to his father and his mother, with his father's duffel bag still on his shoulder, and after waiting a little, he said:

"That's enough for you two, or else Nastya won't stop crying, she doesn't understand."

The father moved away from the mother, and picked Nastya up in his arms. She was crying in terror.

"Nastya!" Peter called to her. "Pull yourself together, I'm talking to you. He's our father, our own father!"

Once inside the house, the father washed his hands and sat down at the table. He stretched out his legs, closed his eyes, and felt a quiet happiness in his heart, and a deep satisfaction. The war was over. His legs had covered thousands of miles during these years, lines of fatigue lay on his face, and pain stabbed his eyes behind their closed eyelids—now they wanted to rest in twilight or in darkness.

While he sat there all his family bustled around the room and in the kitchen, preparing a feast to celebrate his return. Ivanov looked at all the things in his house in order: the clock, the china cupboard, the thermometer on the wall, the chairs, flowers on the windowsill, the Russian kitchen stove . . . they had all lived here a long time without him, and they had missed him. Now he had come back, and he looked at them, getting acquainted with each all over again as with relatives who had been living in grief and poverty during his absence.

He breathed in the house's own solid smell—decaying wood, warmth from the bodies of his children, a wisp of something burning in the stove. The smell was the same as it had been four years before, and it had not weakened nor changed while he had been gone. Ivanov had not found this smell anywhere else, although he had been in several countries and hundreds of dwelling places during the war; the air had smelled different there, it had none of the fragrance of his own house. Ivanov could still remember Masha's smell, and how her hair had smelled; but that was of leaves in the woods, of some unfamiliar, overgrown road, not like a home at all but like all the troubles of life. What was she doing now, and how would she manage as a civilian, Masha, the spaceman's daughter? God be with her. . . .

Ivanov saw that Peter ran the house. It was not just that he worked hard himself, but he gave orders to his mother and to Nastya, what to do and what not to do and how to do it right. Nastya listened obediently to Peter, and she was no longer frightened of her father as a stranger; she had the lively, concentrated face of a child who takes everything in life as true and serious, and a good heart, too, because she didn't resent her brother, Peter.

"Nastya, empty that pot of potato peelings, I need the dish. . . ."

Nastya dutifully emptied the pot and washed it. Meanwhile the mother was hurriedly fixing bread, made without yeast, to put in the oven where Petrushka had already made a fire.

"Beat it, Mother, beat it quicker!" Petrushka ordered. "You can see I have the oven ready. You've got used to dawdling, you Stakhanovite!"

"Right away, Petrushka, right away. I . . ." the mother said obediently. "I'll put in raisins because your father probably hasn't eaten raisins for quite a while. I've been saving them a long time."

"He's eaten them," Petrushka said. "They give raisins to our soldiers, too. Our soldiers—just look how fat they are when they walk around, they must really eat their rations. . . . Nastya, what are you sitting down for? Did you just stop in here to visit? Peel the potatoes, we'll heat them for dinner in the frying pan. You can't feed a family just on cake!"

While the mother was fixing the bread, Peter put a cast-iron pot of cabbage soup into the oven with a big oven tongs, so as not to waste the fire, and he gave orders even to the fire in the stove:

"Why are you burning so unevenly, fidgeting every which way? Burn evenly. Get hot right under the food. Do you think trees grow in the woods for nothing? And you, Nastya, why did you put the kindling in the stove like this, you should have put it in the way I taught you. And you've peeled the potatoes too thick again, instead of thin peels. And why did you cut the meat up with the potatoes? That way some of the nourishment is lost. How many times do I have to tell you? Well, now is the last time, next time you'll get it in the back of the neck!"

"What's the matter with you, Petrushka, picking on Nastya all the time?" the mother said meekly. "What has she done to you? How do you expect her to peel so many potatoes, and to get the peels as thin as a barber could make them, and the meat won't be hurt anyway. Your father has come home, and all you do is lose your temper!"

"I'm not losing my temper, I'm serious. Our father needs to be fed, he's come home from the war, and you're just wasting what we've got. How much food do you suppose we waste in a year just in potato peelings? If we had a pig, we could feed it for a whole year on potato peels alone, and if we sent it to a show, they'd give us a medal. . . . You see how it should be, but you just don't understand!"

Ivanov had not suspected that he was raising such a son. Now he sat there and marveled at his intelligence. But best of

all he liked his little Nastya, whose small hands were busy
with the housework, too, and they were used to it, and skillful.
That meant, she must have learned to work around the house
a long time ago.

"Lyuba," Ivanov asked his wife, "why don't you tell me
anything, about how you've lived all this time without me,
how your health is, what you do at your job...."

Lyuba Vassilievna felt as flustered by her husband now as a
new bride: she had grown unused to him. She even blushed
when her husband spoke to her, and her face took on the timid,
frightened expression, as in her youth, which Ivanov had liked
so much.

"There's not much to tell, Alyosha. We've got along all
right. The children weren't sick much, I've brought them
up.... It's bad that I'm home with them only at night. I work
at the brick factory, on the press, it's a long way to walk from
here...."

"Where do you work?" Ivanov did not understand.

"At the brick factory, where they stamp out the bricks. I had
no training, so at first I did general work around the place but
then they taught me, and put me on the press. Work is fine, only
the children are alone all the time.... You see how they've
grown? They know how to do everything themselves, they've
become grownups." Lyuba Vassilievna was speaking quietly.
"Whether this is good or not, Alyosha, I don't know myself...."

"We'll find that out later, Lyuba. Now we'll just all live together, and afterwards we'll work out what's good and what's
bad...."

"With you here everything will be better, but I just don't
know what's right and what's wrong all by myself, and I was
frightened. Just think now, how to raise our children...."

Ivanov stood up and started to walk around the room.

"Well then, in general everything's been all right, you say,
and you feel good?"

"All right, Alyosha, everything's gone on, we've got through it. Only we missed you terribly, and it was awful to think you'd never come back to us, you could be killed there, like the others. . . ."

She cried as she leaned over the bread, which was already in its iron plate, and her tears dropped onto the dough. She had just brushed the top of one loaf with beaten egg and she rubbed the dough with the palm of her hand, continuing now to grease the holiday dish with her own tears.

Nastya threw her arms around her mother's leg, pressing her face into her skirt, and she looked up sideways at her father with a stern expression.

Her father leaned down to her.

"What's the matter with you? Nastya darling, what's wrong? Are you cross at me?"

He lifted her in his arms, and stroked her head.

"What's wrong, daughter? You've just forgotten me entirely, you were very little when I went away to war. . . ."

Nastya put her head on her father's shoulder and started to cry.

"What's the matter, my little Nastya?"

"Mama's crying, so I'm going to."

Peter, standing in bewilderment in front of the stove, was growing impatient.

"What's the matter with all of you? Your feelings are all upset while the fire's going out in the stove. Shall we stoke it up again, is that it? And who'll give us a ration ticket for more firewood? We've drawn all our ration and burned it, there's hardly any left in the shed, about a dozen logs and one aspen. Come on, Mother, give me the dough, before the heat's all gone."

Petrushka took the cast-iron pot of cabbage soup out of the oven and raked the fire across the hearthstone, while Lyuba Vassilievna, hurrying to please Petrushka, put the bread into the oven, forgetting to rub the second loaf with the beaten egg.

There was something strange and not yet quite understandable to Ivanov about his own house. His wife was just as she had been before, with the same beloved, shy, but now deeply exhausted face, and the children were the same ones that had been born to him except that they had grown during the war years, just as they should have. But something kept Ivanov from feeling the happiness of his return with all his heart—probably he had become too unused to home life and couldn't understand even his own folk, those closest to him, right away. He watched Peter, his grown-up firstborn, heard how he gave orders and directions to his mother and his little sister, observed his serious, worried face, and felt ashamed to realize that his father's feeling for this little boy, his attraction to him as a son, was just inadequate. Ivanov felt even more ashamed of his indifference to Petrushka because he sensed that the boy needed love and care more than the others—he was pitiful just to look at now. Ivanov did not know in any detail the life his family had lived without him, and he could not clearly understand why Petrushka had developed as he had.

Sitting with his family around the table, Ivanov realized what he had to do. He must get to work as quickly as he could, find a job in order to earn some money, and help his wife bring up the children properly—then gradually everything would get better, and Petrushka would be running around with other children, or sitting over his books, and not giving orders at the stove with the iron prong in his hand.

At the table Petrushka ate less than any of the others, but he brushed up the crumbs and put them into his mouth.

"What's the matter with you, Petrushka?" his father said to him. "You eat up the crumbs, but you haven't finished your piece. . . . Eat! Then Mother will cut you some more."

"It can all be eaten," Petrushka said, frowning. "But I've had enough."

"He's afraid that if he really begins to eat a lot, then Nastya will notice it and will eat a lot, too," Lyuba Vassilievna said simply, "and he grudges it to her."

"And you don't grudge anything," Petrushka said calmly. "All I want is that there should be more left for you."

The father and mother glanced at each other and shivered at the words of their son.

"And why aren't you eating?" her father asked Nastya. "Looking at Petrushka, aren't you? . . . Now eat the way you ought to, or you won't get to be a big girl."

"I was born big," Nastya said.

She ate a small piece, but another, bigger piece she pushed aside, and she covered it with her napkin.

"Why are you doing that?" her mother asked her. "Do you want me to put some butter on it?"

"I don't want any more, I'm already full."

"Come on, eat now. Why did you move that piece away?"

"Because Uncle Semyon's coming. I left this for him. It isn't yours, it's what I didn't eat myself. I'll put it under a pillow, or it will get cold." Nastya got up from her chair, and took the bread, wrapped up in her napkin, over to the bed and placed it under a pillow.

The mother remembered that when she had baked a loaf on the first of May she too had covered it with pillows so it would not get cold before Semyon Yevseyevich came.

"And just who's this Uncle Semyon?" Ivanov asked his wife.

Lyuba Vassilievna did not know how to answer, and she said:

"I don't know exactly who he is. . . . He comes to see the children, the Germans killed his wife and his children, he is used to our children now and he comes to play with them."

"What kind of play?" Ivanov asked in surprise. "And why do they play here with you? How old is he?"

Petrushka looked quickly at his mother and father; the mother didn't answer her husband's question but just looked at

Nastya with sad eyes, and the father smiled unpleasantly, got up from the table, and lit a cigarette.

"Where are the toys you and this Uncle Semyon play with?" the father asked Petrushka.

Nastya got up from the table, dragged a chair up to the chest of drawers, took out a little book, and brought it to her father.

"They're book toys," Nastya told him. "Uncle Semyon reads them out loud to me: look at Mishka here, he's a toy but he's in a book. . . ."

Ivanov took in his hand the book toys his daughter gave him: about a bear named Mishka, about a toy cannon, about a little house where an old woman named Domna lived and spun flax with her granddaughter.

Petrushka remembered that it was time to close the damper in the stovepipe to keep the warmth inside the house. As he closed it, he told his father:

"He's older than you are—Semyon Yevseyevich. He's been good to us, let him be. . . ."

Looking out of the window, Petrushka noticed that the clouds drifting across the sky were not the kind to be expected in September.

"Look at those clouds," he said. "They're like lead, it must be because they're full of snow. Are we going to have winter by morning? Because if so, we've got things to do—the potatoes are all still in the ground, nothing is fixed up for storing them yet. . . . What a situation!"

Ivanov looked at his son, heard his words, and felt shy in front of him. He wanted to ask his wife in more detail just who was this Semyon Yevseyevich who had been coming to see his family for two years now, and just who it was he came to see— Nastya or his good-looking wife, but Petrushka was distracting Lyuba Vassilievna with household problems.

"Give me the bread cards for tomorrow, Mother, and the coupons to be clipped to them. And give me the kerosene coupons, too—tomorrow's the last day, and we've got to get our charcoal, too, but you lost the sack for it. They'll give it out only in our container, so look for the sack now, or sew up a new one out of old rags, we can't get along without a sack! And Nastya shouldn't let anyone come in our courtyard to-morrow to get water, or they'll draw a lot out of the well. Winter will be here, the water level always drops lower then, and we won't have enough rope to drop the bucket all the way down. You won't have to eat snow but we'll have to have fire-wood to melt it. . . ."

While he was saying this, Petrushka was sweeping the floor beside the stove and at the same time straightening up the kitchen utensils. Then he took the pot of cabbage soup out of the oven.

"You've eaten the bread, now eat the cabbage soup," he instructed them all. "And you, Father, tomorrow morning you've got to go to the District Council and the Military Commissary, to get on their lists right away, so we'll get ration tickets for you sooner."

"I'll go," the father agreed obediently.

"Don't forget, be sure to go, or else you'll oversleep in the morning and forget all about it."

"No, I won't forget," the father promised.

The family ate its first dinner together after the war, cab-bage soup with meat in it, in silence, and even Petrushka sat there quietly. It was as if the mother and the father and the children were all afraid of destroying by some accidental word the quiet happiness of the family sitting all together.

Then Ivanov asked his wife: "How are you off, Lyuba, for clothes? You're probably short of them?"

"We've got along with our old ones, and now we'll manage to get some new clothes," Lyuba Vassilievna said smiling. "I made things over for the children, what they had, and your suit, two pairs of your trousers, and I altered all your linen for them. We didn't have any extra money, you know, and the children had to have clothes."

"You did just right," Ivanov said, "to give the children everything we had."

"I gave them everything, and I sold the overcoat you bought for me. I wear a quilted jacket now instead."

"Her jacket's too short; when she wears it, she can catch cold," Petrushka spoke up. "I'm going to be a stoker in the public bath, and I'll get paid, and then I'll get her a good coat. They sell them at the market. I went and priced them, some of them look all right. . . ."

"We'll manage without you, without your wages," the father said.

After dinner Nastya put on a big pair of glasses and sat at the window repairing her mother's mittens which she wore over her gloves at work. It had already grown cold, autumn was in the courtyard. Petrushka looked at his sister and scolded her.

"What are you up to? Why are you in Uncle Semyon's glasses?"

"I'm looking through the glasses, I'm not in them."

"And so what? I can see! You'll spoil your eyesight and go blind, and then you'll be an invalid the rest of your life, on a pension. Take those glasses off right away, I'm telling you! And stop darning those mittens, Mother will do them herself, or I'll do them as soon as I get time. Take your notebook and write out the alphabet, you've forgotten when you did it last!"

"Is Nastya studying already, really?" the father asked.

"Not yet," the mother answered, she was still too little, but Peter ordered his sister to keep busy every day, he had bought her a notebook, and she was writing out the letters. Peter was also teaching her arithmetic, making little piles of pumpkin seeds with her and then counting them, while Lyuba Vassilievna herself was teaching her the alphabet.

Nastya put the mittens down and took a notebook and a

penholder with a pen in it out of a drawer in the chest. Content that everything was being done properly, Petrushka put on his mother's jacket and went out to the courtyard to split wood for the next day; he usually brought the split wood into the house every night and piled it next to the stove so that it would dry out there, and burn both hotter and more economically.

That evening Lyuba Vassilievna got supper ready early. She wanted the children to get to sleep quickly so she could sit alone with her husband and talk with him. But the children were not sleepy after supper; Nastya, lying on the wooden couch, watched her father for a long time from under her blanket, while Petrushka, on top of the stove where he always slept in winter and in summer turned and tossed, coughed, whispered something, and didn't settle down at all. It was already late in the night before Nastya closed her tired eyes and Petrushka started snoring on the stove.

Petrushka always slept lightly and on his guard: he was afraid something might happen in the night without his hearing it—a fire, or robbers breaking in, or his mother might forget to turn the key in the lock and the door would blow open and the house lose all its warmth. Tonight Petrushka was wakened by the troubled voices of his parents talking in the room next to the kitchen. What time it was—midnight or almost morning—he did not know, but his mother and father were not sleeping.

"Alyosha, don't make so much noise, the children will wake up," the mother was saying softly. "You mustn't swear at him, he's a good man, and he loved your children. . . ."

"We don't need his love," the father said. "I love my own children. . . . Just think, he fell in love with somebody else's children! I sent you an allotment from my pay, and you were working yourself—what did you need him for, this Semyon Yevseyevich? Maybe your blood was still a little hot, no? Ah, Lyuba, Lyuba! I thought of you quite differently. It means, you've made a fool out of me. . . ."

The father was silent, and then he struck a match, to light his pipe.

"What are you saying, Alyosha, what are you saying!" the mother said loudly. "I've brought the children up, they were hardly sick at all, and I've fed them. . . ."

"Well, and what of it!" the father said. "Others left as many as four children behind, and they didn't live badly, and the children grew up no worse than ours. But look at what kind of man you've let Petrushka grow into—he makes decisions like a grandfather but he's probably forgotten how to read."

Petrushka sighed on top of the stove, and he went on snoring carefully so he could go on listening. "All right," he thought, "so I'm a grandfather, but it was all right for you with your meals all fixed for you. . . ."

"But he's been learning what's hard and what's important in life," the mother said. "And he's not behind in reading and writing."

"Just who is he, anyway, this Semyon of yours? You could at least try to fool me by talking about him," the father said angrily.

"He's a good man."

"You love him, don't you?"

"Alyosha, I'm the mother of two children. . . ."

"Well, go on, give me a straight answer!"

"I love you, Alyosha. I'm a mother, and it was a long time ago that I was a woman, and only with you, I've already forgotten when that was."

The father was silent, smoking his pipe in the darkness.

"I missed you, Alyosha. . . . It's true, the children were here, but they were no substitute for you, and I kept on waiting for you through those long, terrible years. I didn't want to wake up in the mornings."

"What does he do for a trade? Where does he work?"

"He works in the materials supply division at our factory."

"Of course. A swindler."

"He's not a swindler. I don't know. . . . His whole family was killed in Mogilyev, he had three children and his daughter was already married."

"That didn't matter, he just took another family instead, one already prepared . . . and the old lady not so old, pretty good-looking too, so life was nice and cozy for him again."

The mother made no answer. It was quiet, but soon Petrushka heard his mother crying.

"He used to talk to the children about you, Alyosha," the mother said, and Petrushka could tell from the voice that her eyes were full of big tears. "He used to tell them how you were fighting there for us, and suffering. . . . They would ask him: but why? and he would tell them: because you are a good man. . . ."

The father laughed, and knocked the embers out of his pipe.

"So that's the kind he is, your Semyon! Never saw me in his life, but gives me his blessing. That's a character for you!"

"He never saw you. He made it all up on purpose, so the children wouldn't forget you, so they'd love their father."

"But just why, why did he need to do that? So that he could get you quicker? Just tell me, why did he do it?"

"Maybe he just had a good heart, Alyosha, that's why. Why not?"

"You're stupid, Lyuba. Forgive me, please. Everything has to be paid for."

"But Semyon Yevseyevich always brought something to the children, every time he'd bring them candy, or white flour, or sugar, and just the other day he brought Nastya some felt boots but they didn't fit—they were too small. And he didn't ask anything from us for himself. We didn't need anything either, Alyosha, and we'd have got along without it, we're used to it, but he'd say he felt better inside himself when he was worrying about other people, then he didn't grieve so much for his own family, all murdered. You'll see him—this isn't the way you think it is. . . ."

"This is all some kind of nonsense," the father said. "Don't try to fool me. . . . I'm tired of it, Lyuba, but I still want to live. . . ."

"Live with us, Alyosha."

"I'm to live with you, and you'd live with Semyon?"

"No, I won't, Alyosha. He won't come here ever again, I'll tell him not to come any more."

"So. That means there really was something between you, since you now say there won't be any longer. Ah, what a woman you are, Lyuba! All you women are the same."

"And just what are you?" the mother asked, offended. "What does that mean—we're all the same? I'm not. . . . I've worked day and night, we've been making fire-resistant bricks for the lining of locomotive fireboxes. I've got so thin in the face people don't recognize me, even beggars don't ask me for alms. . . . It's been hard for me, too, with the children home alone. I'd come home with the house not heated, nothing cooked, all dark, with the children unhappy, they couldn't learn right off to take care of the house themselves, the way they do now. Petrushka was little, too. And that's when Semyon Yevseyevich started to come to see us. He'd come, and sit with the children, because he lived all alone. 'May I come and visit you,' he asks me, 'and get warm in your house?' I tell him that it's cold here, too, and our firewood is green and he answers me: 'Never mind, it's my spirit that's chilled, just let me sit next to your children and you won't have to light a fire for me.' I said: 'All right, come in for a while. With you here, it won't be so frightening for the children.' Then I got used to him, too, and we all felt better when he showed up. I'd look at him, and remember you, that we had you. . . . It was so evil and sad here without you, let somebody come by, then it won't be so lonely, and the time will go quicker. What good was time to us, when you weren't here?"

"And then, then what happened?" the father asked hurriedly.

"Then nothing happened. And now you've come, Alyosha."

"Well then, it's all right, if that's the way it was," the father said. "It's time to sleep."

But the mother interrupted the father: "Let's wait before we sleep. Let's talk a little, I'm so happy with you back."

"They can't settle down any which way," Petrushka thought on top of the stove. "They've made up, and that's good; Mother has to get up early to go to work, but she's still up. She hasn't cheered up yet, but at least she's stopped crying."

"Did this Semyon love you?" the father asked.

"Wait. I'm going to tuck in Nastya, or she'll throw the blanket off in her sleep, and freeze."

The mother put a blanket on Nastya, and then walked into the kitchen and stood next to the stove to hear if Petrushka was sleeping. Petrushka understood this, and went on carefully snoring. Then his mother went back again, and he heard her voice:

"He probably loved me. He looked at me tenderly, I noticed that, but what was I—am I any good even now? Things weren't easy for him, Alyosha, and he had to have somebody to love."

"You might as well have kissed him, once your problem got so complicated," the father said good-naturedly.

"Well, what do you think! He did kiss me twice, although I didn't want to."

"Why did he do it then, if you didn't want to?"

"I don't know. He said he just forgot, and then he remembered his wife, and I look a little like his wife."

"And does he look like me?"

"No, he's not like you. Nobody's like you, you're the only one, Alyosha."

"I'm the one, you say. But that's where counting starts— one, then comes two. . . ."

"And he only kissed me on the cheek, not on the lips."

"It doesn't make any difference—where."

"Yes, it does make a difference, Alyosha. What can you understand about how we lived?"

"What do you mean? I've fought all through the war, I've seen death a lot closer than you have. . . ."

"You were fighting, and here I was helpless without you, my hands were shaking with grief, but I had to go on working cheerfully, to feed the children, to help the government against the Fascist enemies."

The mother was talking quietly, but she was sick at heart, and Petrushka felt sorry for her: he knew that she had learned how to repair shoes, for himself and Nastya, so as not to pay the shoemaker, and he knew that she had repaired electric stoves for their neighbors in return for potatoes.

"But I just couldn't go on living, and missing you," the mother said. "If I could have, I'd have died. I know I would have died, but I had the children. . . . I just had to feel something else, Alyosha, some kind of gladness, just to relax. One man said he loved me, and he treated me just as tenderly as you did once. . . ."

"Who was that, your Semyon again?" the father asked.

"No, another man. He was working as a teacher for the district committee of our union, he had been evacuated. . . ."

"The hell with him, whoever he was! So it turned out that he comforted you too, did he?"

Petrushka had known nothing of this instructor, and he was surprised that he hadn't known about him. "Well, our mother's a pretty sharp one, too," he whispered to himself.

The mother answered the father: "I didn't get anything from him, no happiness at all, and afterwards everything was still worse. My heart reached out toward him because it was dying, but when he was close to me, really close, I didn't care at all. I was thinking at that moment about all my household problems, and I was sorry that I had let him be close to me.

I realized that I could feel peaceful only with you, really happy, and that I'd be able to relax only when you'd be close to me again. There was just nowhere for me to go without you, I couldn't save myself even for the children. Live with us, Alyosha, things will be good for us!"

Petrushka heard how his father got up from the bed without speaking, lit his pipe, and sat down at the table.

"How many times were you with him, when you were close to him?" the father asked.

"Only once," the mother said. "It never happened again. How many times should I have been?"

"As many as you liked, it was your business," the father declared. "Only why did you say that you were the mother of our children, and had been a woman only with me, and that a long time ago . . . ?"

"It's the truth, Alyosha."

"What do you mean? What's the truth? You admit you were a woman with him?"

"No, I wasn't a woman with him. I wanted to be, but I couldn't. . . . I felt I'd be lost without you. I needed someone to be with me, but I was just worn out, my heart had grown dark, I couldn't love my own children any longer, and for them, you know it yourself, I'd endure anything, for them I'd give the bones out of my body!"

"Wait a minute!" the father said. "You say yourself that you made a mistake with this new Semyon of yours, you didn't get any happiness from him, but just the same you say you didn't fall and weren't ruined, you stayed safe and whole? Is that it?"

"I wasn't done for," the mother whispered. "I go on living."

"It just means you're lying to me about this, too. Where is the truth, for you?"

"I don't know," she whispered. "I don't know anything very much."

"All right. To make up for it, I know a lot. I've lived through more than you have," the father declared. "You're a bitch, and that's all there is to it."

The mother was silent. The father could be heard breathing fast and hard.

"Here I am home," he said. "The war's over, but you've wounded me, in the heart. Well, what of it? You can live now with both of them, your Semyon and your Yevseiev. You've had your fun, and you've made a fool out of me, but I'm a human being, too, and not just some toy. . . ."

In the dark the father started to put on his clothes and his shoes. Then he lit the kerosene lamp, sat down at the table, and put his watch on his wrist.

"Four o'clock," he said, talking to himself. "Still dark. It's the truth, what they all say, there's lots of women but not a single wife."

Everything grew quiet in the house. Nastya was breathing evenly in her sleep on the wooden couch. Petrushka burrowed into his pillow on the warm stove and forgot that he was supposed to snore.

"Alyosha!" the mother said in a gentle voice. "Alyosha, forgive me!"

Petrushka heard his father start to groan, and then the sound of breaking glass. Through cracks in the curtain, he could see the room grow darker where his mother and father were sitting, but the lamp was still burning. "He's broken the lampshade," Petrushka guessed, "and there's no glass to be had anywhere."

"You've cut your hand," the mother said. "You're bleeding. Take that towel from the cupboard."

"Shut up!" the father yelled at her. "I don't even want to hear your voice. Wake up the children, wake them up right away! Wake them up, I tell you! I'll explain to them what kind of mother they have! Let them know about it."

Nastya gave a little shriek of fright in her sleep, and woke up. "Mama!" she called. "Can I get in bed with you?"

Nastya loved to get into bed with her mother at night, and get warm under the blanket.

Petrushka sat up on the stove, swung his legs over the side, and said to them all:

"It's time to sleep! Why did you wake me up? It's not daylight yet, everything's dark outside. Why are you making such a racket, and burning the lamp?"

"Sleep, Nastya, sleep, it's still early, I'll come to you in a minute," the mother said. "And you, Petrushka, don't get up, and don't say anything more."

"And what are you talking for? What does Father need?" Petrushka said.

"Just what business is it of yours what I need?" the father answered. "What a sergeant you are!"

"And why did you break the glass in the lamp? What are you frightening Mother for? She's so thin because she eats her potatoes without any meat, and gives the meat to Nastya."

"Do you know what your mother was doing here, what she was busy at?" the father screamed in a complaining voice, like a little boy's.

"Alyosha!" Lyuba Vassilievna said sharply, and she turned toward her husband.

"I know, I know it all!" Petrushka said. "Mother was crying for you, waiting for you, and now you've come and she's crying again. It's you who don't know!"

"You don't understand anything about it!" the father said angrily. "What a sprout we've raised in you!"

"I do too understand it all, completely," Petrushka answered from the stove. "It's you who don't understand. We've got things to do, we've got to live, and you're cursing here like some kind of madman. . . ."

Petrushka stopped talking, lay back on his pillow and unexpectedly, quietly, began to cry.

"You've become the boss in this house," the father said. "Well, it's all the same now, you can live as master here...."

Wiping his tears, Petrushka answered his father:

"Well, what kind of a father are you? What do you think you're saying? And you're a grownup, and were in the war.... Look, tomorrow, you go to the wounded soldiers' cooperative, that's where Uncle Khariton works at the counter, he cuts the bread, and doesn't cheat anybody. He was in the war, too, and then came back. Go and ask him, he tells everything, and laughs about it, I've heard him myself. He has a wife, Anyuta, she learned to drive a truck and she delivers the bread now, but she's very good, she doesn't steal any of it. She made friends, too, and went out with them, they used to stand her treats. And she made friends with a man with a medal, only he has no arms, and he was the head man in the store where they sell manufactured goods...."

"What are you talking about? You'd better go back to sleep, it will be light soon," the mother said.

"But you two wouldn't let me sleep.... It won't be light yet for a long time. This man with no arms became friends with Anyuta and they started to live all right. And Khariton was off at the war. Then Khariton came back, and he started to swear at Anyuta. He cursed her all day, and at night he drank wine and stuffed himself with food while Anyuta just cried, and didn't eat a thing. He swore and he swore, then he got tired of it, and he told her: 'What if you did have one fellow, and without any arms, too, you're just a stupid old woman, while I managed without you to have Glashka and Aproska and Maruska, and there was a name-sake of yours, another Anyuta, and then there was a Magdalinka thrown in, too.' And he laughed and laughed, and Aunt Anyuta laughed, too, and then she started to praise him: 'Khariton's still a good man, there's no better anywhere, he killed the Fascists, and there was no way for him to get away from all those girls.' Uncle Khariton still tells us all about it at the store while he's handing out the bread, piece by piece. And now they're living together peacefully, as fine as can be. But Uncle Khariton goes right on laughing, and he tells us: 'I was fooling Anyuta. I didn't have any of those girls. There wasn't any Glashka, or any Anyuta, or any Aproska, and there wasn't any Magdalinka thrown in, because a soldier is the son of his fatherland, he hasn't got time to be fooling around, his heart works only against the enemy. I was just frightening Anyuta on purpose.' Lie down and go to sleep, Father, and turn out the lamp, the flame's smoking without a lamp-shade. . . ."

Ivanov had listened with amazement to the story Petrushka told. "What a son of a bitch!" the father thought. "I was afraid he was just about to tell about my Masha. . . ."

Petrushka was starting to snore; this time he had really fallen asleep.

He woke up when it had already become fully light, and he was frightened that he had slept so long, with nothing done in the house since dawn.

Nastya was alone in the house. She was sitting on the floor turning the pages of a picturebook her mother had bought her a long time ago. She looked at it every day, because she had no other real book, and she traced the letters with her finger, as if she were reading.

"What are you messing with the book for all morning long? Put it back where it belongs!" Petrushka told his sister. "Where's Mother? Has she gone to work?"

"To work," Nastya said in a low voice, and she closed the book.

"And where did Father go off to?" Petrushka looked around the house, in the kitchen and in the main room. "Did he take his bag with him?"

"He took his bag," Nastya said.

"What did he say to you?"

"He didn't say anything, he just kissed my mouth and my eyes."

"So, so," Petrushka said, and he pondered for a moment. "Get up off the floor," he ordered his sister. "Let me wash you cleaner and get you dressed, you and I are going out together...."

At this moment, their father was sitting in the station. He had already drunk two hundred grams of vodka and had eaten a morning meal with a coupon issued for travelers. During the night he had made up his mind definitely to go back to the town where he had left Masha, to see her again, and maybe never to go away from her. It was too bad that he was much older than the spaceman's daughter, whose hair smelled of outdoors. But there it would become clear how things might work out, there was no good in guessing about it in advance. Still Ivanov hoped that Masha would be at least a little pleased when she saw him, and this would be enough: it would mean there was someone close to him again, and someone fine, cheerful, with a good heart. And there he'd see how things stood.

Soon the train came which would take Ivanov back in the direction from which he had come just the day before. He took his bag and walked out on the platform. "Masha won't be expecting me," Ivanov thought. "She told me to forget her anyway, and that we'd never see each other again, but here I am going back to her for good."

He climbed on to the platform of the last car in the train, and stayed there so he could see for the last time, when the train pulled out, the little town where he had lived until the war, where his children had been born. He wanted to look once more at the house he was leaving; he would be able to see it from the train because the street on which he lived ran straight from a level crossing which the train would go through.

The train started off, moving quietly past the station

switch-points into the empty autumn fields. Ivanov held on to the railing of the car and watched from the platform the little houses, the buildings, the barns, the fire tower of what had been his native town. From a distance he could recognize two high chimneys: one was the soap factory and the other the brick factory. Lyuba was working there right now, at the press which shaped the bricks: let her live now as she liked, and he would live the way the he wanted to. Maybe he could have forgiven her, but what would that have meant? Anyway, his heart had grown hard against her, and there was no forgiveness in it for a person who had kissed and lived with someone else just so the time of war and of separation from her husband would not go by so tediously, all by herself. And the fact that Lyuba had been close to her Semyon or her Yevseiev, just because her life had been hard, because need and grief had got her down, this was only proof of her real feelings. All love springs from need and grief; if a person didn't need anything and didn't grieve he would never love anyone.

Ivanov was getting ready to leave the platform, to go into the car and lie down and sleep, no longer wanting to see for the last time the house he had lived in and where he had left his children: there was no reason to punish himself to no good end. He looked ahead to see how far away the level crossing was, and he saw it at once. Here the railroad tracks crossed a country dirt road leading into the town; wisps of hay and straw were lying on this dirt road where they had fallen from farm wagons, together with willow twigs and horse droppings. Usually, except for two market days each week, this road was empty; it was not often that a peasant drove into town with a load of hay or went back to his village. Today was no exception; the country road was deserted. But from the town, out of the street the country road ran into, two children were running. One was bigger, the other smaller, and the big one was pulling the other by the hand because the little one could not keep up no matter how great the effort, no matter how hard the little legs pumped up and down. Then the bigger one started to drag the other behind him. At the last house, they stopped and looked toward the station, probably deciding whether to go on or if it was already too late. Then they looked at the passenger train going through the level crossing, and started to run along the road straight toward the train, as if they were trying to catch up with it.

The car on which Ivanov was standing was almost at the crossing. Ivanov had picked up his bag to go into the car and lie down to sleep on an upper seat where the other passengers would not disturb him, but would those two children manage to make it before the last car had gone by? Ivanov leaned out of the platform, and looked back.

The two children, still holding hands, were running along the road toward the crossing. Suddenly both fell, then stood up, and started running again. The bigger one raised his free hand and, with his face turned in the direction of the train, beckoned toward himself, as if he were summoning someone to come back to him. And then they both fell down again. Ivanov noticed that the bigger child had one foot in a boot and the other in an overshoe; this was why he was falling down so often.

Ivanov closed his eyes, not wanting to see and feel the hurt of the falling, exhausted children, and he realized how hot his chest had grown, just as if the heart languishing inside it, after beating uselessly all his life, had suddenly broken out into a kind of freedom, filling his whole being with warmth and with trembling. He was now aware of all that he had known before, but much more precisely and more realistically. Before, he had felt life through a barrier of pride and self-interest, and now suddenly he had touched its naked heart.

Once more he looked from the steps of his car at the children disappearing in the distance. Now he knew they were his children, Petrushka and Nastya. They must have seen him when his car went past the crossing, and Petrushka was calling him home, to his mother, yet he had looked at them indifferently, thinking about something else, and had not recognized his own children.

Now Petrushka and Nastya were running far behind the train along the sandy path beside the rails. Petrushka was holding on to Nastya's hand as he had before, and dragging her behind him when her running couldn't keep up with his.

Ivanov dropped his bag from the car onto the ground, and then lowered himself to the bottom step and dropped off on to the sandy little road along which his children were running toward him.

## THE THIRD SON

AN OLD WOMAN died in a provincial town. Her husband, a seventy-year-old worker living on a pension, went to the telegraph office and sent off six telegrams to various districts of the country, all with the same wording: "Your mother has died come Father."

The elderly clerk in the telegraph office counted the money for a long time, figured it wrong, and wrote out the receipts and stamped them with shaking hands. The old man looked gently at her through the wooden window out of his reddened eyes, and thought absentmindedly about something, trying to distract his heart from its grief. It seemed to him the elderly clerk had a broken heart, too, and a soul that was permanently confused—maybe she was a widow, or a wife abandoned in ill will.

So here she was, working slowly, getting the change mixed up, her memory and her attention wandering; even for ordinary, uncomplicated work a person needs to have happiness inside him.

The old father went back home after the telegrams had

been sent; he sat down on the bench next to the long table, at the cold feet of his dead wife, and he smoked, and whispered to himself a few melancholy words, looked after the lonely gray bird hopping on the little perch in its cage, sometimes quietly cried a little, and then calmed down, wound up his pocket watch, looked at the window beyond which the weather was changing back and forth—first leaves would fall with flakes of wet, tired snow, then it would rain, then the late sun would shine, as cold as a star—and the old man was waiting for his sons.

The oldest son arrived by airplane the next day. The other five sons had arrived by the end of two more days.

One of them, the third in age, came with his daughter, a little girl of six who had never before seen her grandfather.

On the fourth day their mother was still lying on the table, but her body did not smell of death, so neat and tidy was it from her illness and from her dry exhaustion; having given abundant, healthy life to her sons, the old woman had kept for herself only her small, spare body, and she had tried to save it for a long time, no matter how wretched it was, so she could love her children and be proud of them until she died.

The big men—ranging in age from twenty to forty—stood around the coffin on the table without talking. There were six of them, and the seventh was the father, smaller than the youngest of his sons and weaker, too. He held his granddaughter in his arms, her eyes blinking in terror at the sight of this strange, dead old woman, who barely looked at her out of unblinking white eyes all but closed under their eyelids.

The sons silently wept their occasional, controlled tears, twisting their faces to endure their grief in silence. The father was no longer crying, he had cried himself out before the others, and now he was looking at his half-dozen powerful sons with concealed emotion, and with inappropriate joy. Two of them were sailors—ship captains—one was a Moscow actor, another

—the one with the daughter—was a physicist, and a Communist, while the youngest son was studying to be an agronomist, and the oldest was working as foreman of a department in an airplane factory and wore a ribbon on his chest awarded him for his achievement as a worker. All six of them and their father stood quietly around their dead mother and mourned her wordlessly, hiding from each other their despair, their memories of their childhood, of the vanished happiness of that love which had welled up without interruption and freely in their mother's heart and which had always found them—across thousands of miles. They had felt this constantly and instinctively, and been made stronger for feeling it and bolder in achieving success in their lives. Now their mother had been transformed into a corpse, she could no longer love anyone, and she lay there like any indifferent, strange, old woman.

Each of her sons felt lonely now, and frightened, as if a lamp had been burning somewhere on the windowsill of an old house in a dark field, and it had lit up the night and the flying beetles and the blue grass, the swarms of midges in the air—the whole world of childhood around that old house abandoned by those who had been born in it; the doors had never been locked in that house, so that anyone who left it could come back, but no one had returned. And now it was as if the light had suddenly gone out in that window in the night, and reality had been transformed into remembrance.

When she was dying, the old woman had instructed her husband to have a priest celebrate a requiem for the dead over her while her body was still lying in the house, but then to take her out and bury her in her grave without a priest, so as not to offend her sons and so that they could walk behind her coffin. The old woman did not believe in God as much as she wanted her husband, whom she had loved all her life, to mourn her more deeply and to grieve for her to the sound of prayer-singing and in the light of the wax candles above her lifeless face; she didn't want to part from life without a celebration and without leaving some memory of herself behind. After their children's arrival, the old man looked for a long time for some kind of priest and finally in the evening brought back with him a man, also elderly, dressed in ordinary, nonclerical clothes, pink-faced with the flush of vegetarian, Lenten eating, and with lively eyes in which some sort of small thoughts, for some special purpose, were glistening. The priest arrived holding an army officer's map case against his thigh; he carried his spiritual requirements in it: incense, thin candles, a book, the vestment to hang around his neck, and a small censer hanging on a chain. He set up the candles quickly around the coffin and lit them, blew on the incense burning in the censer, and without any warning started to mutter, as he walked, what he read from the book. The sons who were in the room stood up; they felt uncomfortable and somehow a little ashamed. They stood there in a file in front of the coffin without moving, their eyes cast down. The old priest sang and muttered there in front of them without hurrying, almost ironically, watching these sons of the dead woman out of small, understanding eyes. Partly he was a little afraid of them, partly he respected them, and it was clear that he was not far from starting up a conversation with them, even from expressing his own enthusiasm for the building of socialism. But the sons were silent, no one—not even the old husband—crossed himself; this was an honor guard around a coffin and not participation in any divine service.

When the priest had finished his requiem, he quickly packed up his things, blew out the candles burning around the coffin, and put all his property back in the officer's map case. The father put some money in his hand, and the priest, without delaying, made his way through the ranks of the six big men without looking at them, and meekly disappeared outside the door. Actually, he would have stayed in this house for the funeral repast with pleasure, he would have talked about the perspectives of war and revolution, and been comforted for a long time by this meeting with representatives of the new world which he secretly admired but which he couldn't make his way into; when he was alone he used to dream of sometime accomplishing some kind of heroic feat so he could burst into the brilliant future together with this new generation—to this end he had even submitted a petition to the local airfield, asking that he be taken up to a great height and dropped by parachute without an oxygen mask, but they had given him no answer.

In the evening the father fixed up six beds in the second room of the house, and he put his little granddaughter beside him in his own bed, where the dead old woman had slept for forty years. The bed was in the same big room where the coffin was, and the sons went off into the other room. The father stood in the door until his sons had undressed and lain down, and then he closed the door and lay down to sleep next to his granddaughter, after having put out all the lights. The granddaughter was already asleep, alone in the big bed, her head under the blanket.

The old man stood over her in the dim nighttime light: the falling snow outside picked up the faint glow of the sky and with it lighted the darkness inside the room through the window. The old man walked up to the open coffin, kissed his wife's hands, her forehead, and her lips, and told her: "Now you rest." He lay down carefully next to his granddaughter and closed his eyes, so his heart might forget everything. He drowsed off, and suddenly woke up again. A light was shining underneath the door to the room where his sons were sleeping—they had turned on the electric light again, and laughter and noisy talking could be heard.

The little girl began to toss and turn from the noise; maybe she wasn't sleeping but only afraid to take her head out from under the blanket, afraid of the night and of the dead old woman.

The oldest son was talking about hollow metal propellers with enthusiasm and with the pleasure of deep conviction; his voice had a satisfied and powerful sound, and one could imagine his healthy teeth, which had been taken care of in good time, and his full red throat. The sailors were telling stories of foreign ports, and giggling because their father had given them old blankets they had used to cover themselves in childhood and adolescence. White pieces of coarse calico had been sewed on to the tops and bottoms of these blankets with the words "head" and "feet," so the blankets could be spread correctly, without covering your face with the dirty, sweaty part where your feet had been. Then one of the sailors started to wrestle with the actor, and they rolled on the floor as they had when they were boys and all lived together. The youngest son egged them on, promising to take them both on with just his left hand. It was clear that the brothers all liked each other and were glad at this meeting. They had not been together for many years now, and no one knew when they might meet again in the future. Perhaps only at their father's funeral? While they were wrestling, the two brothers tipped over a chair, and for a minute they were all still, but then, apparently remembering that their mother was dead and could hear nothing, they continued what they had been doing. Soon the oldest son asked the actor to sing something in a low voice: he must know the good new Moscow songs. But the actor said it was hard for him to start cold like that. "Cover me up with something," the actor insisted. They covered his head with something, and he started to sing from under the covering, so he wouldn't feel embarrassed. While he was singing, the youngest son did something which made another brother fall off the bed onto still a third who was lying on the floor. They all laughed, and they told the youngest one to lift his brother up again with just his left hand. The youngest son answered his brothers in a low voice and two of them burst out laughing—so loudly that the little girl stuck her head out from under the blanket in the dark room and called out.

"Grandfather! Oh, grandfather! Are you asleep?"

"No, I'm not asleep, I'm all right," the old man said, and he coughed shyly.

The little girl gave way, and sobbed. The old man patted her face: it was all wet.

"What are you crying for?" the old man whispered.

"I'm sorry for grandmother," the little girl answered. "All the rest of us are alive, and laughing, and she's the only one who died."

The old man said nothing. First he puffed a little through his nose, then he coughed a little. The little girl grew frightened, and she raised herself up to see her grandfather better and to find out why he wasn't sleeping. She looked at his face, and she asked him:

"And why are you crying, too? I've stopped."

The grandfather patted her head, and answered in a whisper:

"It's nothing. . . . I'm not crying, it's just sweat."

The little girl sat down near the head of the bed.

"Do you miss the old woman?" she said. "Better don't cry: you're old, and you'll die soon, then you won't cry anyhow."

"I won't," the old man answered quietly.

Silence suddenly fell in the other, noisy room. One of the sons had said something just before this. Then they all were quiet. One son said something again in a low voice. The old man recognized his third son by his voice, the physics scholar, the father of the little girl. His voice had not been heard before this; he had said nothing and had not been laughing. He quieted all his brothers somehow, and they even stopped talking to each other.

Soon the door opened, and the third son appeared, dressed for daytime. He walked up to his mother's coffin and leaned over her dim face in which there was no more feeling left for anybody.

Everything was quiet in the late night. No one was walking

or driving on the street outside. The five brothers did not stir in the other room. The old man and his granddaughter kept watching his son and her father, so attentively that they didn't breathe.

The third son suddenly straightened up, put out his arm in the darkness and reached for the edge of the coffin, but he could not hold on to it and only shoved it a little to one side on the table, as he fell to the floor. His head hit the floorboards, but the son did not make a sound—only his daughter screamed.

The five brothers in their underclothes ran in to him and carried him back to their room, to bring him around and to calm him. After a little while, when the third son had recovered consciousness, all the others were dressed in their suits or their uniforms, even though it was only two o'clock in the morning. One by one they covertly scattered through the rooms and the yard outside, through the night around the house where they had lived their childhood, and they wept there, whispering words and sorrowing, just as if their mother was standing over each of them, listening to him, and grieving that she had died and forced her children to mourn for her; if she could have, she would have gone on living forever, so that nobody should suffer on her account, or waste because of her the heart and the body to which she had given birth. . . . But the mother had not been able to stand living for very long.

In the morning the six sons lifted the coffin on to their shoulders and carried it off to bury it, while the old man took his granddaughter by the hand and followed after them; now he had already grown used to sorrowing for the old lady and he was satisfied and proud that he, too, would be buried by these six powerful men, no worse than this.

## APHRODITE

WAS HIS APHRODITE still alive? Nazar Fomin was no longer asking this question, with doubt and with hope, of people and of institutions—they had already answered him that there was no trace of his Aphrodite anywhere—but of nature, of the sky, the stars and the horizon, and of lifeless things. He believed some kind of oblique sign or cryptic signal would show him if his Aphrodite was still breathing, or if the breath within her had grown cold. He walked out of the dugout into the field, stopped in front of a small blue flower, looked at it for a long time, and finally asked it: "Well? You can see more down there, you're connected to the whole earth, while I walk around up here all by myself—is Aphrodite alive or not?" The little flower was moved neither by his grief nor by his question, it stayed silent and went on living in its own way, the wind went on blowing indifferently over the grass just as it had already blown, perhaps, over Aphrodite's grave or across her living, smiling face. Fomin looked into the distance, at the clear shining light of a cloud floating above the horizon, and he thought that maybe up there, from that height, it might be possible to see where Aphrodite was. He believed in a general bookkeeping in nature, in which could be measured the sadness of loss as well as the satisfaction of saving what one values, and through the general connectedness of all the living and dead things in this world, he wanted to find some faint, secret news of the fate of his wife Aphrodite, of her life or of her death.

At the start of the war Aphrodite had disappeared among the people fleeing toward the east from the Germans. Nazar Ivanovich Fomin himself was already in the army at that time and could not help his beloved in any way to save herself. Aphrodite was a young woman, easy to live with, not one to get lost without trace or to die of hunger or need among her own people. Some misfortune, of course, was possible along the roads so far away, or death by accident. But neither in nature nor among people could a word be heard or a trembling felt which answered a man's open, expectant heart with sad news, so Aphrodite should still be living on this earth.

Fomin gave himself up to memories, reliving his past at the slow pace of happiness which has been lived through and fixed in the mind for good. In his memory he could see a little town, its lime-chalked walls blinding white in the sunshine, the tiled roofs of its houses, its orchards growing in gladness under a blue sky. Toward midday Fomin used to walk for lunch to a cafe not far from the fireproofing construction enterprise where he was works superintendent. A gramophone played in the cafe. Fomin would go up to the counter, ask for sausages and cabbage, a so-called "flier" (salted peas to be thrown into the mouth), and also take a mug of beer. The woman serving the beer poured it into the mug, and Fomin would watch the stream of beer, interested chiefly in seeing that it was poured accurately, without filling the mug with empty foam; in this daily struggle with the foam on his beer he never looked care-

fully at the face of the woman serving him, and did not remember her when he walked out of the cafe. But one time the
woman sighed deeply and desperately at the wrong moment,
and Fomin stared at her as she stood behind the counter. She
looked at him, too; the foam overflowed the mug, and she
forgot what she was doing, paying no attention to the beer.
"Stop!" Fomin said to her and for the first time he noticed
that she was young, with a clear face, and dark, shining eyes,
strangely combining thoughtfulness with laughter in their expression, and with thick black hair growing with a wild sort of
strength on her head. Fomin turned his glance away from her,
but his feeling had already been attracted by this woman, and
the feeling was quite independent of his intelligence and of
his peace of spirit, cutting right across them both, leading the
man toward his own happiness. He looked at the foam, and did
not mind its spilling uselessly across the marble surface of the
counter. Later on, he called Natalya Vladimirovna his Aphrodite, because her image had appeared rising above the foam, although not of ocean waters but of another liquid.

And so Nazar Ivanovich lived with his Aphrodite for twenty
years, as man and wife, not counting one interruption of two
and a half years, and then the war had separated them; and now
here he was hopelessly asking the plants and all the good creatures of the earth about her fate, and even looking at the movement of clouds and of stars in the sky with the same question.
The information bureau concerned with evacuees had been
searching for Natalya Vladimirovna Fomin zealously and for a
long time, but so far they had not found her. There was no one
closer to Nazar Fomin than Aphrodite; all his life he had grown
used to talking with her, because this helped him to think and
built up his confidence in whatever task he was carrying out.
And now, at war, separated from Aphrodite for four years, Nazar
Ivanovich Fomin used up all his free time in writing her long
letters, which he mailed to the information bureau for evacuees

in Buguruslan, with a request that they be forwarded to her as soon as she was found. During the war a great many such letters had probably piled up at the information bureau some of them would be delivered some day, others never and would turn to dust unread. Nazar Ivanovich wrote his wife calmly and in detail, still believing in her existence and in his future reunion with her, but so far he had never received an answer from Aphrodite. The Red Army soldiers and officers under Fomin's command checked the mail with great care, so that no letter might be lost which was addressed to their commander because he was practically the only man in the regiment who never received a letter either from his wife or from his relatives.

Now the happy years of peace had long gone by. They could not have lasted forever, for even happiness must change if it is to be preserved. In war Nazar Ivanovich Fomin had found another happiness for himself, different from what his peacetime work had given him but related to it; after the war he hoped to find a higher kind of life than anything he had yet experienced, either as a worker or as a soldier.

Our front-line units recaptured the southern city in which Fomin had lived and worked before the war. Fomin's regiment was withdrawn into the reserve, held out of action because it was not needed. It made itself comfortable around the city, in the rear, so it could advance later on the long march to the west. Nazar Ivanovich wrote a letter to Aphrodite on his first day of rest, and then went on leave in what was the city he loved best in all the Russian land. The town had been shattered by artillery shelling, consumed by the flames of big fires, and its solid buildings had been reduced to dust by the enemy. Fomin was already used to seeing wheat fields trampled down by big machines, the earth cut with trenches, settlements where people lived torn apart by high explosives: this was the ploughing of war, in which the land is planted with what should never grow again upon it—the corpses of scoundrels, and with what was born for good and active living but preserved only in everlasting memories—the flesh of our soldiers, watching in death over our enemies in the earth.

Fomin walked through a fruit orchard to the place where Aphrodite's cafe had once been. It was December. The naked fruit trees had grown cold for the winter and quiet in sorrowful sleep, and their spreading branches which had held fruit in the autumn had now been ripped by bullets and hung down help-lessly in the ribbons of wood that survived, with only an occa-sional twig left whole and healthy. Many of the trees had been chopped down by the Germans for material with which to build defenses.

The building where the cafe had been more than twenty years before, and which had later become a dwelling house, now lay shattered into broken bricks and rubbish, murdered and dead, blown into space by the wind. Fomin could still re-member the look of the building, but soon, after a little time, this would be effaced in him, and he would forget it too. Wasn't it the same somewhere in the faraway, wild fields where Aphrodite's big, beloved body was lying cold, gnawed at by carrion-eating animals, melting into water and air, the wind drying and blowing it away, so that all the substance of Aphro-dite's life might be spread evenly across the world, without trace, so that she herself would be forgotten as a person?

He walked on to the outskirts of the city where he had lived as a child. The desertedness cooled his spirit. A late wind was fluttering through the ruins of the silenced homes. He saw the place where he had lived and played as a youth. The old wooden building had burned down to its foundation, tiles crumbled by great heat lay on the scorched earth on top of his childhood home. A poplar in the courtyard, under which the little Nazar had slept in summertime, had been cut down, and it lay there next to its stump, dead, its bark rotting.

Fomin stood for a long time next to this tree of his child-hood. His numbed heart suddenly seemed to lose all feeling, so as not to take any more grief into itself. But Fomin picked up some of the tiles which were still whole and put them in a neat little pile, as if he were getting material ready for future building, or collecting seed with which to plant all of Russia once again. This tile and all the others around it had been made in the kiln which Fomin had established here in the old days of peace and which he had managed for years.

Fomin walked out into the steppe; there, about a mile from the city, he had once upon a time built his first dam. He had been a happy builder then, but now the meadow of his youth was sad and empty, ripped up by the war and bar-ren; unfamiliar little blades of grass could be seen in places through the thin, melting snow, indifferent to man, bowing humbly under the wind. . . . The earth dam had been shattered in the middle, the reservoir had dried up, and the fish in it had died.

Fomin went back to the city. He found Shevchenko Street and the house where he had lived after his return from Rostov, when he had finished the polytechnic institute. The house was no longer there, but a bench remained. It had formerly stood under the windows of his apartment; he used to sit on this bench in the evenings, at first alone and then with Aphrodite, and in this house that was now destroyed they had lived to-gether in one room, with windows facing on the street. His fa-ther, a foundry worker, had suddenly died while Fomin was still studying in Rostov, and his mother had married again and gone away to settle in Kazan. The young Nazar Fomin had been left then to live by himself, but the whole sunlit world, filled with attractive people, that seductive world of youth and eternal unsolved mysteries, a world not yet constructed, poor, but filled with the hope and with the will of the Bolshevik workers, this world was waiting for young people, and their fa-

miliar, native land, made hungry and naked by the miseries of
the first world war, lay there in front of them.

Fomin sat down on the bench where he had passed so many
quiet summer evenings talking and making love with Aphrodite. Now there was an empty, shattered world in front of him,
and his best friend, perhaps, was no longer on this earth. Everything had now to be done from scratch, in order to go on with
what had been planned a quarter of a century ago.

Probably Nazar Fomin's life would have worked out quite
differently if belief in the idea of the working class had not inspired him in those bygone days of his youth. It is possible he
might have lived more quietly, but cheerlessly and fruitlessly;
he might have worked out his own individual destiny, but he
would not have known that invincible necessity which came
when, trusting his people with nothing but his heart, he felt
and understood the meaning and sense of his own existence.
But when he presses close to the people who gave him birth,
and through them to nature and to the world, to past time and
to future hope—then there is opened to his spirit that secret
spring where a man must drink to win strength without limit
for what he does, and the power of really believing that his
own life is important.

Soviet Russia was then only starting to work out its own
fate. The people had set off on a great road with no returning,
into that historical future where no one had marched before:
it wanted to find the fulfillment of all its hopes, to achieve
through work both deeds of lasting value and the dignity of human life, and to share these with other peoples. . . . Fomin had
once seen a simple vision on the Sea of Azov when he was a
boy. He was on the shore, and the single sail of a fishing boat
was moving in the distance on a blue sea under a shining light-
gold cloud; the boat moved farther and farther away, its white
sail reflecting the sun with its gentle light, and the boat was
still visible for a long time to the people on the shore; then it

disappeared entirely over the enchanted horizon. Nazar had felt a melancholy happiness then, just as if someone he loved had called to him from the shining distance of sky and water when he could not follow him. And Soviet Russia seemed to him just like that boat disappearing into the distance, sailing off into the world and into time. He also remembered a midday hour of a forgotten day. Nazar had been walking through fields, moving down into a ravine where wonderful wild grass was growing; the sun called out to everyone from high in the sky, and plants and beasts moved up to answer it from the darkness of the earth—they were all of different colors, each of them different, not resembling each other: each took shape and came to life on the earth as best it could, just so it could come for this, take breath and celebrate, and play its part in the general assembly of all existence, succeed in loving all living things and then once more part forever from them. The young Nazar Fomin felt at that moment the great, dumb, and universal grief which only man can understand, express, and overcome, and this is precisely what man is for. Nazar was happy then about what he owed to mankind; he knew in advance that he would pay it because the working class and the Bolsheviks had taken on themselves all the obligations and all the burdens of humanity, and by heroic labor and by the power of an accurate understanding of their meaning on this earth the working people would carry out their assignment, and the dark destiny of mankind would have the truth break over it. This was how Nazar Fomin thought in his youth. He felt things then more than he knew them, he could not yet express the idea of all the people in clear language, but he was content with just the happy certainty that the dusk which had covered the world and shadowed the hearts of men was not an eternal darkness but only the dark which comes before the dawn.

Nazar Fomin's contemporaries, Young Communists and Bolsheviks, were inspired by the same idea of creating a new world; just like Nazar, they were convinced that they had been challenged by Lenin to take part in a worldwide triumph of humanity. It was in order that a time of true living should begin at last on this earth, in order to fulfill all the hopes which people had earned by their centuries of hard work and of sacrifice, the hopes they had saved up through long trials and much patient thinking. . . .

When he had finished the special institute in Rostov, Nazar Fomin returned to his birthplace, to this same town where he was now sitting all alone. Nazar had become a technical builder, and started his lifework. He took everything that was material, rough, and ordinary so close to his heart that it became something spiritual for him, and sustained his passion for his work. Now he no longer remembered: had he realized then or not that everything that is truly spiritual comes only from the living needs of human beings? But with his own hands he accomplished this transformation of the material into the spiritual, and he believed in the truth of the revolution because he had accomplished this and seen its effect on the destiny of his people.

At first Nazar Fomin had been in charge of rural production of fireproof materials throughout the district; this was not considered a big responsibility. But he was excited by this work and he cherished it, not just as a public service but as the very meaning of his existence, and he looked with passionate eyes at the first baked tiles prepared in his village kiln. He stroked the first tile, sniffed it, and carried it back to the room where he was living so that he could look at it again in the evening and in the morning, to make sure it really was completely good and solid, fit to last for long years in place of the straw on the roofs of village houses and thus to save the peasants' homes from fire. Then he studied the fire statistics of his district in the rural reports and figured out that if straw thatch could be replaced by tiles, this economy alone would save the

peasants enough from fire damage to build, for example, an arte-
sian well with abundant clean water in every village in three
years' time, or even more; and then in the next three or four
years, out of the same funds saved from fire by the tiled roofs,
enough to construct a local electric power station with a mill
for hulling grain and another for grinding it. With these ideas
Nazar Fomin could stare at a tile for a long time without growing bored, thinking about how it could be made stronger and
cheaper. Tiles had become both feeling and experience for him,
they had replaced books and friends; later on he understood
that no object could really replace human beings, but when he
was young just thinking about man was enough for him.

There are times when people live on hopes and expectations of a change in their destiny; there are other times when
only the memory of the past can comfort the living generation;
and there are lucky times when the historical development
of the world coincides in people with the beating of their own
hearts. Nazar Fomin was a man of his people's lucky times,
and at the beginning, like many of his contemporaries and
those who thought as he did, he believed it was the beginning
of an epoch of quiet happiness, of peace, of brotherhood, and of
blessedness, all of which would gradually spread across the entire world. For all of this to happen it would be enough just to
work hard and to build: this was how the young man Fomin
thought at that time.

And Nazar Fomin found spiritual peace for himself in his
love for his wife Aphrodite and his faithfulness to her; with
these he conquered all the troubled passions inside himself which pulled him toward the dark sides of the world of
sensations where a man could only squander his life to no
purpose, even if with some delight, and he devoted all his
energy to his work and to the service of the idea which had become his heart's desire—not what wasted a man but what
regenerated him again and again, in which his real delight

was found, not furious and incapacitating but gentle, like quiet goodness.

Nazar Fomin was preoccupied then, like his whole generation, with the spirituality of a world which had existed until that time only in misery, in disconnection, and without any general, clear meaning.

At the beginning of his work, Fomin made tiles for fire-resistant roofing; then his responsibilities were increased, and he soon was elected vice president of the village Soviet, but the real significance of his job was to be the chief engineer of all construction in the settlement and the district around it. At that time this town was only a settlement, the center of a small rural district.

Fomin built dams in the dry steppe for watering the cattle, he dug wells in the villages and reinforced them with concrete tiles, and he paved roads all through the district with a kind of local stone, in order to use all the means available to overcome the poverty of the economy and to bring a unified peasant spirit to the whole people.

But even then he was already thinking about something more important and one idea dominated his dreams, giving hopes to his happiness. For two years Fomin worked on his plan before the district executive committee trusted him to start it. This plan was for the construction of an electric power station in the district with the gradual extension of a power network over the entire region, so as to give the people light with which to read books, machine power for lightening their labor, and warmth in wintertime for heating their houses and their stables. With the realization of this simple dream, the whole tenor of life of the population would be transformed, and man would then feel true freedom from poverty and grief, from the burden of heavy work which exhausts him to his very bones, and from all the hopelessness which leaves him no satisfaction in his life. . . .

Reflections of these memories were moving now across the face of Colonel Fomin as he sat there among the ruins of his town that had been destroyed, the town he had built once upon a time together with his comrades. The memories showed on his face first in a smile, then in grief, in the quiet recollection of what had happened a long time ago.

He had built the power station. A dance had been organized in the hall of the district political education club to celebrate the completion of what was for that time a powerful generator, and Aphrodite had danced at that ball under the radiance of the new electric lights, with an orchestra of three accordions, and she had been even happier than Nazar himself, because her husband's project had succeeded.

But it had been hard for Fomin to complete the construction. Too little money was available from the district budget, so it was necessary to explain the usefulness of electricity to the whole population of the district so the people themselves would invest in the station and in the power network their own labor and their wealth beyond what had already been accumulated for the purpose. Because of this Fomin organized thirty-four peasant associations for electricity and he joined them all up in a district union. This cost him a lot of courage, a lot of anxiety, and a lot of unquiet work. He remembered one peasant orphan girl, Yevdokia Remeiko; her parents had left her a small dowry, and she invested it all in her association and then went to work harder and more eagerly than most, as an assistant carpenter on the construction of the station. By now Yevdokia Remeiko would be a grown woman, if she was still alive, but if she had been still young, she would probably be serving in the Red Army, or fighting in a partisan detachment.

Fomin could remember a lot of the other people who had worked with him then—peasant men and women, people who lived in the settlement, old people and young ones. In all sincerity and candor they were building a new world on this earth with all the skills they had: their hidden, inhibited abilities burst forth then and started to develop in beneficial, intelligent labor; their spirits and their understanding of life blossomed and grew as plants grow out of the ground when stones are lifted from on top of them. The station had not yet been completely built and equipped when Fomin could already see with satisfaction that its builders—peasants working as volunteers over and above their work in the fields—had become so much more profound in doing this and had developed such interest in each other and in their relations to the working class, making turbines for generating the electricity, that the wretched loneliness of their hearts had disappeared, and their individual peasant-farmer indifference to the whole strange world around them and their terror in front of it also began to leave them. It is true that in the secret thinking of every man there is a desire to go out of his own courtyard, out of his own loneliness, to see and to live through all that is worldwide, but it is necessary to find a path which is not beyond a man's powers and which is open to everyone. An old peasant named Yeremeyev expressed his tangled ideas about this at that time to Fomin:

"You see, Nazar Ivanovich, we don't feel that Soviet power is giving us any easy life: go on, it tells us, be glad, and be responsible yourself for good and evil, it says, you're not any longer just a bystander on this earth. And what kind of life did we have before! When you're in your mother's womb you don't remember who you are, then you come outside and grief and hardship drive you, you live in a hut like in some dungeon where you can't even see the light, and then you die and lie there quiet in your grave and forget that you even existed. We've been in tight places everywhere, Nazar Ivanovich—a womb, a prison cell, a coffin, with nothing but blankness all around us. And everybody hindering everybody else! While now everybody comes to help—that's where Soviet power and cooperation have brought us!"

Where was that old man Yeremeyev now? Maybe he was still alive somewhere, although it wasn't likely, a lot of time had gone by. . . .

The power station did not work long; seven days after it began to operate it burned to the ground. Nazar Fomin was miles away when this happened; he had gone out to look at the dam near Dybrovka's farmstead, which had been washed away by the autumn floods, and to estimate the work needed to rebuild it. They had sent him an urgent message about the fire, and Fomin had gone back immediately.

Just outside the settlement, where the new adobe building of the power station had been yesterday, there was nothing now. Everything had been reduced to ashes. Nothing was left but the dead frames of the machinery—the motor and the generator. But the heat had made all the copper parts run out of the body of the motor; the ball bearings and the fittings had melted like streams of tears and then hardened and grown cold on the building's foundations; the coils had gone up in smoke and all the copper had boiled down to nothing.

Nazar Fomin stood next to his dead machinery staring up at him out of the blind holes of its burned-out vital parts, and he wept. A rainy wind was dolefully ruffling the sheets of metal on the floor which had been curled up by the heat of the fire. Fomin looked into the sky at this melancholy moment of his life; dark autumn clouds were scudding across it, driven by heavy bad weather; there was no interest to be seen there, no sympathy for man, because nature, despite its bigness, is all the same, knowing nothing except itself. Only what had been consumed in the fire had been different; here had been a world created by people in sympathy with each other, here in a small way a hope for a higher life was being realized, for a future end to all the pain with which nature oppresses even itself. This was a hope, perhaps, which existed in all creation only in the consciousness of men, and not of all men but only those who first in sacrifice, in work, and in revolution have struggled through to an understanding of their destiny. How small this blessed force still is, inside the enormous world, and how urgent it is to preserve it!

A sad time started for Nazar Fomin. Investigatory authorities informed him that the fire had started not by accident or because of carelessness, but had been set by a criminal. Fomin could not understand this at first—how was it possible that something good for everybody could provoke hatred, and become the reason for a crime? He went to see the man who had set fire to the station. The criminal looked to him like any ordinary man, but he did not regret his act. In what he said Fomin could feel an unslaked hatred; before his arrest the criminal had fed his spirit with it. Now Fomin could no longer remember clearly his face or his words, but he still remembered the man's unhidden malice toward him, the chief engineer of this people's building which had been destroyed, and his explanation of what he had done as an act absolutely essential to satisfy his own mind and his own conscience. Fomin had listened quietly to the criminal then, and realized that it would be impossible with words to make him change his mind and that this could be done only with deeds, except that he would never allow the deeds to be accomplished, he would constantly sabotage and destroy what he had not helped to build.

Fomin was seeing a creature whom he had thought not to exist on this earth, or at best to be living in a helpless, harmless condition since the revolution. In actual fact this creature was living a real life and even had its own intelligence, in the truth of which it believed. And then Fomin's belief in an imminent heaven on earth was shattered by doubt; the whole picture in his mind's eye of a shining future seemed to fade back toward the misty horizon, and under his feet was only that drab, hard, impassable earth along which there was still a

239

long way to go before reaching the radiant world which had seemed so close and so attainable.

The peasants, the builders, and the investors in the power station held a meeting. They listened to Fomin, and they were quietly thoughtful, not hiding their general grief. Then Yevdokia Remeiko stood up and said shyly that they must collect the funds again and rebuild the burned-down station; in a year, or a year and a half, Remeiko said, they could do it with their own hands, and maybe a good deal faster. "What's the matter with you, girl?" some cheerful peasant, nobody knew who, answered her from his seat, "you've burned up one dowry in the fire, and now you're throwing in another, so you'll never get married before you're in your coffin, and you'll just wither away with the old folks."

When they had considered the problem, how much they could get from state insurance funds for the fire, how much the government would lend them, how much was left to be covered by voluntary labor, the investors took on the task of building the station from the beginning for a second time. "The electricity's gone off," a craftsman at making barrels named Yevtukhov said, "but we want to live without being turned off! So we empower you, Nazar Ivanovich, in a categorical sense to build it to the same plan and scale as it was before!" With both big things and little things, Yevtukhov loved to recommend that they be done in a categorical sense; he himself lived in a categorical and revolutionary style, and he had invented a completely spherical box. And now it was as if a warm light had shone on Nazar Fomin's darkened spirit. Not knowing what to do or to say, he went up to Yevdokia Remeiko and, shy in front of all the people, wanted to kiss her cheek, but he managed to kiss only the dark hair above her ear. This is how it had been then, and the living feeling of happiness, the smell of the Remeiko girl's hair, and her shy look had all stayed intact in Fomin's memory.

Once more Nazar Fomin built an electric power station on the same site, and it was twice as powerful as the one which had been burned. Two years went into this work. During this time Aphrodite left Nazar Fomin; she fell in love with another man, an engineer who had come from Moscow to install a radio transmitter, and she married him. Fomin had a great many friends among the peasants and the working people, but without his beloved Aphrodite he felt himself an orphan, and his heart trembled with loneliness. He had always thought before this that his faithful Aphrodite was a goddess, but now she was pitiable in her wanting, in her need to satisfy her new love, in her pull toward happiness and enjoyment, which were stronger than her will, stronger than her faithfulness and her pride in relation to someone who had always loved her and no one else but her. But even after his divorce from Aphrodite, Nazar Fomin could not lose the habit of loving her just as before; he did not want to struggle against the feeling which was now turning into suffering—life had taken his wife from him, and she had gone away, but it isn't essential to possess a person closely and to be happy only next to her—it is sometimes enough to feel a beloved person as a permanent dweller in one's heart; it's true that this is harder and more demanding than close, satisfying possession, because unrequited love lives only on its own true strength, feeding on nothing in return. But were Fomin and the other people of his country making the world over for a better fate simply in order to hold power over people, or to use them later like their property? Fomin still remembered that a strange idea had come to him then, which he could not explain. He felt that in his divorce from Aphrodite an evil power had again blocked his road to life; in its original cause this was perhaps the same force which had caused the fire in the power station. He realized the difference between the two events, he saw their incongruity, but they had destroyed his life with equal brutality, and it was one and the same man who had withstood them. It was possible that he had been to blame with Aphrodite, for sometimes it happens that evil is done without being intended, unwillingly and unnoticed, and even when a man is straining every nerve to do good to someone else. This must be because every heart is different from every other: one heart, recipient of what is good, applies it entirely to its own needs, with none of the goodness left over for another; a different kind of heart is capable of working over even what is evil, and of turning it into what is good and strong, for itself and for others, too.

After losing Aphrodite, Fomin realized that general blessedness and enjoyment of life, as he had expected them hitherto, were false dreams and that it was not in these that a man's truth consisted and his real felicity. As he conquered his own suffering, endured what might have crushed him, and raised again what had been destroyed, Fomin unexpectedly felt a kind of free happiness which was independent both of scoundrels and of sheer chance. He understood his former naiveté, all his nature started to grow harder, ripening in misery, and began to learn how to overcome the mountain of stone which blocked the road of his life; and then the world in front of him, which had seemed to him clear and attainable until now, spread itself out in a faraway mysterious haze, not because it was really dark there, or sad, or strange, but because it actually was enormously larger in all directions and could not be surveyed all at once, either inside a man's heart or in simple space. And this new conception satisfied Fomin more than the miserable blessedness for whose sake alone, he used to think, people lived.

But at this time he found himself, together with the rest of his generation, just at the start of the new road to life of the whole Soviet Russian people. All that Nazar Fomin had lived through up to this time was only an introduction to his hard destiny, an initial testing of a young man and of his preparation for the urgent historical task his people had undertaken. In actuality, there is something base and insecure in striving for one's own happiness; a man begins to be a man only with the paying of his debt to those who brought him to life in this world, and it is here that his highest satisfaction lies, the true, eternal happiness which no misery, no grief, no despair, can ever destroy. But at that moment Fomin could not hide his grief over his misfortune, and if there had not been people around him who loved him as someone who thought as they did, perhaps he might have lost his courage completely, and not survived. "Calm down," one of his closest comrades told him with the sadness of understanding, "calm yourself! What else did you expect? Who has guaranteed us happiness and truth? We've got to make them ourselves, because our party is giving meaning to life for all the world. Our party—it's humanity's honor guard, and you're a guardsman. The party is not bringing up happy cattle, but heroes for a great time of war and revolution. . . . Problems will keep right on growing in front of us, and we'll be climbing up such high mountains—from their tops you'll see all the horizon right up to the very ends of the earth. What are you whining and being bored about? Live with us— what's wrong with you? You think all warmth comes from the stove at home, or from a wife, don't you? You're an intelligent man, you know we've got no need for weak creatures who take care of themselves. A different kind of times have started."

It was the first time Fomin had heard that phrase "honor guard." His life went on. Aphrodite, Nazar Fomin's wife, hurt by the infidelities of her second husband, met Nazar one day and told him that life was sad for her, and that she missed him, that she had understood life wrongly when she had tried to find nothing but joy in it, without knowing either debts or obligations. Nazar Fomin listened to Aphrodite silently; jealousy and hurt pride were still inside him, held down and almost mute but still alive, like creatures that never die. But his joy at seeing Aphrodite's face, the nearness of her heart, beating its way toward him, killed the wretched sadness in him, and after two and a half years of separation, he kissed Aphrodite's hand which was being held out to him.

New years of life followed. Circumstances often made Fomin their victim, leading him to the very edge of destruction, but his spirit could no longer grow weak in hopelessness or in dejection. He lived, thought, and worked as if he constantly felt some great hand leading him gently and firmly forward, to the destiny of heroes. And the hand which led him strongly forward was the same big hand that warmed him, and its warmth penetrated inside him to his very heart.

"Good-bye, Aphrodite!" Nazar Fomin said out loud.

Wherever she was now, alive or dead, her footprints were still on the ground here in this deserted town, and the ashes held things she had at some time touched with her hands, printing the warmth of her fingers on them—everywhere around him there still existed unnoticed signs of her life, which are never completely destroyed, no matter how deeply the world is changed. Fomin's feeling for Aphrodite was humble enough to be satisfied even by the fact that she had breathed here once upon a time, and the air of her birthplace still held the diffused warmth of her mouth and the weak fragrance of her body that had disappeared—for there is no destruction in the whole world that leaves no trace behind it.

"Good-bye, Aphrodite! I can feel you now only in my memories, but I still want to see you, alive and whole!"

Fomin stood up from the bench, looked at the town which had settled into its own ruins and could be easily seen from one end to the other, bowed to it, and walked back to his regiment. His heart, schooled now in patience, would be able to stand, perhaps, even eternal separation, and could preserve its faithfulness and its feeling of affection until the end of his existence. He kept quietly inside himself the pride of a soldier who can perform any labor or human deed; he rejoiced when he triumphed over an enemy, and whenever despair in his heart turned into hope, and hope into success and victory.

His orderly lit the candle in a saucer on the wooden kitchen table. Fomin took off his greatcoat and sat down to write a letter to Aphrodite: "Dear Natasha, trust me, and don't forget me, just as I remember you. Trust me, that everything will work out as it ought to, and we'll live again together. You and I will still have these wonderful children we're sure to have. They wear my heart out in my yearning for you. . . ."

## THE FIERCE AND
## BEAUTIFUL WORLD

1

ALEXANDER VASSILIEVICH MALTSEV was considered to be the best locomotive engineer at the Tolubeyev station.

He was thirty years old, but he already had the rating of a first-class engineer and he had been driving express trains for a long time. When the first high-powered passenger locomotive of the "JS" (Joseph Stalin) series arrived at our station, it was Maltsev who was assigned to it, which was completely reasonable and right. His assistant was an elderly worker from the station repair shops named Fedor Petrovich Drabanov, but he soon passed his own examination as an engineer and went off to work on another locomotive and I was assigned to work in his place as an assistant on Maltsev's crew. I had been an assistant before that, but only on older, less powerful engines.

I was pleased at the assignment. Just looking at that "JS" locomotive, the only one then in our division, filled me with enthusiasm: I could look at it for a long time and a specially moving kind of happiness welled up in me, just as wonderful as what I felt when I first read Pushkin when I was a child. Besides, I wanted to work under a first-class engineer in order to learn from him the art of driving heavy, high-speed trains.

Alexander Vassilievich was quiet and indifferent about my assignment to his crew; it was clearly all the same to him who worked as his assistant.

Before each trip I always checked every detail of the engine, testing all its maintenance and auxiliary mechanisms until I could relax, confident that the engine was ready for the trip. Alexander Vassilievich would watch me work, following each step, but then he would check the machinery after me with his own hands as if he didn't trust me.

This happened repeatedly and I was already getting used to having him mix into my responsibilities all the time, even though it disappointed me. But usually I forgot about my disappointment as soon as we started off. Turning away from the instruments which recorded the condition of the locomotive and from watching the left side of the train and the tracks ahead of us, I would watch Maltsev. He drove the train with the bold self-confidence of a great expert, with the concentration of an inspired artist, absorbing everything around him and thus achieving mastery over it. Alexander Vassilievich's eyes looked straight in front of him, empty and abstracted, but I knew that through them he was watching the tracks in front and all of nature rushing toward us—even a swallow, swept upward by the edge of the wind made by the train, would catch his glance for an instant, and in that instant his head would turn after the swallow: What happened to him behind us, where had he flown?

We were never late through our own fault; on the contrary, they held us up often at way stations which were not scheduled stops because we were ahead of the timetable and they could get us back into the schedule only by delaying us.

Usually we worked without talking. Occasionally Alexander Vassilievich would rap the boiler with his wrench, without even turning toward me, wanting to direct my attention to something that wasn't quite right in the way the engine was working, or preparing me for some sudden change, so I would be ready for it. I always understood these unspoken instructions of my senior comrade and I carried them out diligently, but he still treated me as impersonally as if I had been a fireman or an oiler, and at all our stops he always tested the pressure gauges and the tightness of the bolts in the connecting rods, and he would check the axle-boxes on the driving wheels, and everything else. If I had just examined and oiled some moving part, Maltsev would examine and oil it again, right after me, as if he didn't consider my work efficient.

"I just checked that crosshead, Alexander Vassilievich," I told him once when he started to examine the block between a piston rod and a connecting rod just after I had done the same thing.

"And I want to do it myself," Maltsev answered, smiling, and there was a kind of sadness in his smile which startled me.

I later understood the meaning of this sadness and the reason for his always holding himself aloof from us. He felt a superiority over us because he understood the locomotive better than we did and because he didn't believe that I or anybody else could learn the secret of his skill, the secret of seeing at the same time the swallow flying by and the signal ahead, being aware at the same moment in time of the track, the whole train, and the power of the locomotive. Maltsev realized of course that we could outdo even him in our zeal, but he couldn't imagine that we could love the engine more than he did or drive the train better—anything better, he thought, would be impossible. And this was why Maltsev was sad with us; he was lonesome with his talent, as if he lived all by himself, not knowing how to express it to us so we could understand.

And it's true, we couldn't have understood his skill. I asked him once to let me drive the engine by myself; Alexander Vassilievich let me have his place for forty kilometers, and sat in the assistant's place. I drove the train, and after twenty kilometers I was already four minutes late, and at the end of the longer climbs we were doing no better than thirty kilometers an hour. Maltsev took the engine back again from me; he took the grades at a speed of fifty kilometers an hour, and the engine didn't sway on the curves as it did with me, and he quickly made up the time that I had lost.

## 2

I worked as Maltsev's assistant for about a year, from August to July, and on July 5 Maltsev made his last trip as the engineer of an express train. . . .

We had picked up a train of forty passenger cars which was four hours late when we took it on. The train dispatcher came out to the engine and especially asked Alexander Vassilievich to make up as much of this time as he could, cutting it down to three hours if possible, for otherwise it would be hard for him to send a train of empty cars out on the next track. Maltsev promised him to make up the time, and we started off.

It was eight o'clock in the evening, but the summer day was still hanging on and the sun was shining with a kind of triumphal, morning-time power. Alexander Vassilievich asked me to keep the steam pressure in the boiler constant at only half an atmosphere below maximum.

In a half hour we pulled out into the steppe, on a quiet, soft stretch of land. Maltsev raised the speed to ninety kilometers and didn't let it fall below this; on the contrary, he raised it to a hundred on the level and on small grades. On the grades I forced the firebox up to its maximum and made the fireman shovel coal by hand to help out the stoking machine, because my steam pressure was falling.

Maltsev drove the locomotive on, throttle wide open. We were now headed straight for a big stormcloud which had appeared above the horizon. From our side the cloud was lighted up by the sun, but its interior was being ripped by severe, angry bolts of lightning, and we could see how the shafts of lightning plunged vertically down onto the quiet distant earth and we were racing madly toward that distant ground as if hurrying to its defense. It was clear that the sight appealed to Alexander Vassilievich; he leaned far out of his window as he stared ahead, and his eyes which were used to smoke and flame and distance were glittering now with excitement. He realized that the work and the power of our locomotive were comparable with the might of the storm, and perhaps this idea made him feel proud.

Soon we saw a whirlwind of dust moving toward us across the steppe. This meant the storm was carrying the thundercloud straight at us. The air grew dark around us: the dry earth and the sand of the steppes whistled and crackled against the steel body of the locomotive, there was no visibility at all, and I started the generator to give us light and switched on the headlight on the front of the locomotive. Breathing was made hard by the burning whirlwind of dust forcing its way into the cabin and doubled in strength by the motion of the train toward it, and also by the gases from the firebox and by the early twilight surrounding us. The locomotive plunged on with a howl into the confused, stifling darkness, along the crack of light made by the front headlight. Our speed went down to sixty kilometers an hour; we were working and staring in front of us as if in a dream.

Suddenly a big drop of water hit the windshield and dried

251

up at once, consumed by the hot wind. Then an instantaneous flash of blue light blazed past my eyelashes and seemed to move through me to my shuddering heart itself. I grabbed at the injector stopcock, but the pain in my heart had already stopped, and I looked at once toward Maltsev—he was looking in front and driving the engine, with nothing changed in his face.

"What was that?" I asked the fireman.

"Lightning," he said. "It wanted to get us, and it didn't miss by much."

Maltsev heard what we were saying.

"What lightning?" he asked, quite loud.

"What we had just now," the fireman said.

"I didn't see it," Maltsev said, and he turned his face again toward the tracks in front of us.

I was also wondering if this had really been lightning.

"But where's the thunder?" I asked.

"We've gone right through it," the fireman explained. "Thunder always comes afterwards. While it was striking, while the air was shaking loose, we'd already run past it. Probably the passengers heard it, they're behind us."

We went on through the downpour but were soon past it, and we came out onto the hushed and darkened steppe over which peaceful clouds were now resting motionless, their work done.

It had grown quite dark all around us, the quiet night had begun. We could sense the smell of the wet earth, the fragrance of the grass and the grain refreshed by the rain and the storm, and we plunged on, making up time.

I noticed that Maltsev was driving the engine worse than usual; it swayed on the curves, and the speed went up to a hundred and more kilometers an hour, and then would drop to forty. I decided that Alexander Vassilievich was probably dead tired, and so I said nothing to him even though it was very hard for me to keep the firebox and the boiler running properly when the engineer was driving as he was. But we were supposed to stop in half an hour, to take on water, and Alexander Vassilievich could get something to eat there, and rest a little. We had already made up forty minutes, and by the end of our run we'd make up at least an hour.

But still I was worried by Maltsev's tiredness and I started to stare forward myself, at the tracks and the signals. On my side, on the left, an electric light was hanging on a cord, lighting up the driving shaft machinery. I could see quite clearly the heavy, accurate working of the left-hand driving shaft, but then the light above it flickered and began to burn dimly, like a single candle. I turned around in the cabin. There, too, the lights were now burning at quarter strength, hardly illuminating the instruments. It was curious that Alexander Vassilievich had not signaled to me with his wrench, to point out what was wrong. It was obvious that the generator was not producing the required number of revolutions, and the tension had fallen. I started to adjust the generator, beyond the steam pipeline, and I was busy at this for quite a while, but the tension did not increase.

At this moment a foggy cloud of reddish light moved across the dials of the instruments and the ceiling of the cabin. I looked outside.

Ahead of us in the darkness—it was impossible to tell whether near or far away—a red beam of light was oscillating across our tracks. I didn't understand what this was, but I knew what had to be done.

"Alexander Vassilievich!" I shouted and I gave three whistles to stop the train.

We could hear torpedoes exploding under our wheels. I rushed across the cabin to Maltsev, he turned his face toward me and looked at me with quiet, empty eyes. The needle on the dial of the speedometer showed a speed of sixty kilometers an hour.

"Maltsev!" I screamed. "We're going over torpedoes!" And I reached out my hand toward the controls.

"Get away!" Maltsev exclaimed, and his eyes began to shine, reflecting the light of the flickering lamps hanging over the speedometer.

He immediately pulled the brakes on full and put the engine in reverse.

I was pressed up against the boiler, and I could hear the wheels of the engine grinding hard against the rails.

"Maltsev!" I said. "We've got to open the stopcocks of the cylinders, or we'll blow up the engine."

"Not necessary. It won't blow up," Maltsev answered.

We stopped. I started water running into the boiler through the injector, and looked outside. In front of us, about ten meters away, an engine was standing on our tracks, its tender toward us. A man was standing on this tender with a long poker in his hands which had been heated red-hot at its end, and he had been waving this in his effort to stop our express train. This engine had been pushing a freight train which was now stopped at this point between two stations.

It meant that while I had been working on the generator and not looking in front of us we had gone through a yellow signal and then a red one and probably more than one warning signal given us by trackwalkers. But why hadn't Maltsev noticed all these signals?

"Kostya!" Maltsev called to me.

I walked over to him.

"Kostya! What's this, in front of us?"

I told him.

"Kostya . . . From here on you drive the engine. I'm blind."

The next day I took the train back on the return trip to our station and turned the locomotive in to the repair shops because the rims of our wheels had been slightly damaged in two places. Having reported on what happened to the head of the station, I led Maltsev by his hand to the place where he lived; Maltsev himself was in deep depression and had not gone to see the head of the station.

We hadn't got to the house where Maltsev lived on a street grown over with grass when he asked me to leave him by himself.

"I can't do that," I answered. "Alexander Vassilievich, you're a blind man."

He looked at me with clear, thoughtful eyes.

"Now I can see. Go on home.... I can see everything. There's my wife who's come out to meet me."

At the gate of the house where he lived a woman really was standing and waiting for him, Alexander Vassilievich's wife, and her uncovered black hair was shining in the sun.

"And has she got something on her head or not?" I asked him.

"Nothing," Maltsev answered. "Now who's blind, you or I?"

"Well, once you can see, go on and look," I decided, and I walked away from him.

3

Maltsev was arrested, and an investigation started. I was summoned as a witness, and asked what I thought about the happenings on that express train. I answered what I thought—that Maltsev was not guilty.

"He was blinded by a very close explosion, by the bolt of lightning," I told the investigator. "He was shocked, and the nerves which control sight were damaged. I don't know how to say this precisely."

"I understand you," the investigator said, "you're talking very precisely. This is all possible, but not very likely. Because Maltsev himself gave evidence that he never saw the lightning."

"But I saw it, and the fireman saw it, too."

"That means, the lightning struck closer to you than to Maltsev," the investigator reasoned. "Why weren't you and the fireman shocked, why weren't you blinded, while the engineer Maltsev suffered damage to his optical nerve and was blinded? What do you think?"

I felt as if I were in a blind alley, and then I thought it over.

"Maltsev couldn't see the lightning," I said.

The investigator listened to me in surprise.

"He couldn't see it. He was blinded instantaneously, by the electromagnetic wave that always precedes the flash of lightning. The flash of lightning is the result of an explosion, and not the reason for the lightning. Maltsev was already blind when the lightning produced its flash, and a blind man cannot see light."

"Interesting!" the investigator said, smiling. "I would close Maltsev's case if he were still blind. But you know yourself, he can see now just as well as you or I."

"He can see," I confirmed this.

"Was he blind," the investigator went on, "when he drove his express train at enormous speed almost into the rear end of a freight train?"

"He was," I stated.

The investigator looked at me attentively.

"Why didn't he turn over the control of the locomotive to you, or at the very least instruct you to stop the train?"

"I don't know," I said.

"So you see," the investigator said. "A grown-up, responsible man driving the locomotive of an express train, taking hundreds of people to certain death, avoids catastrophe only by accident, and then excuses himself on the grounds that he was blind. What's this all about?"

"But he would have been killed himself," I told him.

"Probably. But I'm more interested in the lives of hundreds

of other people than in the life of one man. Maybe he had some reason to kill himself."

"He had no reason," I said.

The investigator had grown indifferent; he was already bored with me as a stupid fool.

"You know everything except what's most important," he said with deliberation. "You can go."

I went straight from the police station to Maltsev's house.

"Alexander Vassilievich," I said to him, "why didn't you ask me for help when you were blind?"

"But I saw," he answered. "What did I need you for?"

"What did you see?"

"Everything: the tracks, the signals, the wheat growing in the steppe, the pulling of the right-hand driving wheels—I saw it all."

I was puzzled.

"Then how did it happen to you the way it did? You went through all the warnings, you were driving straight into the rear end of another train. . . ."

The man who had been a first-class engineer thought sadly for a moment, and then answered me as if he were talking to himself:

"I'm used to seeing light, and I thought that I was seeing it, but what I saw was only in my head, in my imagination. I really was blind, only I didn't know it. . . . I didn't even believe the torpedoes, although I could hear them: I thought I was hearing wrong. And when you blew the stop whistle and yelled at me, I saw green lights in front of us. I didn't guess what had happened right away."

Now I understood Maltsev, but I couldn't think why he had not told this to the investigator—about how he had gone on seeing the world in his imagination for a long time, and believing in its being real, after he was already blind. So I asked Alexander Vassilievich about this.

"But I did tell him," Maltsev answered.

"And what did he say?"

"That, he said, was your imagination; maybe you're imagining something right now, I just don't know. I've got to establish the facts, he said, and not your imagination or the state of your nerves. Your imagination—whether it was that or not—I can't check, it was only inside your own head, this is all your words, but the catastrophe, which almost happened—that's something real."

"He's right," I said.

"Right. I know it myself," the engineer agreed. "But I'm right, too, and not guilty. What's going to happen now?"

I did not know how to answer him.


4


They put Maltsev in prison. I went on working as an assistant but with another engineer, a careful old man who would start to brake a full kilometer before the yellow light so that when we got up to it the signal would have turned to green and the old man could start to drag the train along again. It wasn't real work, and I was lonesome for Maltsev.

That winter I went to the district town to visit my brother who was a student, living in a university dormitory. He told me in one of our talks that in the physics laboratory at the university they had a Tesla induction coil with which to make artificial lightning. An idea came to me then that was not clear even to myself.

When I got home I thought out my guesses about the Tesla coil and decided that my idea was correct. I wrote a letter to the investigator who had been working on the Maltsev case with a request for an experiment on the prisoner Maltsev to test his susceptibility to the action of electrical charges. In the event that susceptibility of Maltsev's psyche should be proved, or of his organs of sight to the action of sudden, close electrical charges, then his whole case should be reviewed. I told the investigator where the Tesla equipment could be found, and how the experiment could be carried out on a human being.

For a long time the investigator did not answer me, but then he notified me that the district prosecutor had agreed to carry out the experiment I suggested in the university physics laboratory.

Several days later the investigator served me with a subpoena. I went to see him in great excitement, convinced in advance that Maltsev's case would have a happy ending.

The investigator greeted me but then was silent for a long time, reading some kind of paper with sad eyes. My hope disappeared.

"You've done your friend a bad turn," the investigator told me.

"How? The sentence stays as it was?"

"No, we've released Maltsev. The order's already been given, maybe he's home by now."

"I thank you." I stood up in front of the investigator.

"But we won't be thanking you. You gave very bad advice. Maltsev is blind again. . . ."

I sat down again, exhausted. My heart felt as if it were burning. I wanted a drink badly.

"The experts tested Maltsev with the Tesla induction coil without any preparation by us, in the complete dark as to what it was all about," the investigator told me. "The current was turned on, the lightning was produced, and a sharp blow was heard. Maltsev went through it calmly, but now he can't see light—this has been proved objectively by experts in judicial medicine."

The investigator drank a glass of water, and went on:

"Now he can see the world again only in his imagination. . . . You're his comrade, help him."

"Maybe his sight will come back to him again," I spoke my hope, "as it did before, after the locomotive. . . ."

The investigator thought for a moment.

"Hardly. That was a first shock, this one is a second. He's been hurt right at the spot where the wound was before."

And no longer controlling himself, the investigator stood up and began to pace up and down the room in great agitation.

"I'm to blame in this. . . . Why did I listen to you, and insist on this experiment, like a fool? I put a man in great danger, and he lost."

"You're not to blame, you didn't risk a thing," I comforted the investigator. "Which is better—to be a free blind man or to see everything inside a prison when you're innocent?"

"I didn't realize that I would have to prove a man's innocence by hurting him so badly," the investigator said. "It's too high a price."

"You're an investigator," I explained to him. "You've got to know everything about a man, even what he doesn't know about himself."

"I understand that, you're right," the investigator said in a low voice.

"Don't be disturbed about this, comrade investigator. Things inside a man were operating here, and you were only looking for things on the outside. But you were at least able to realize your own inadequacy, and you acted toward Maltsev like a good man. I respect you for this."

"I respect you, too," the investigator acknowledged. "You know something? We could make a good assistant investigator out of you."

"Thanks, but I'm already busy. I'm assistant engineer on express train locomotives."

I walked out. I wasn't Maltsev's friend, and he had always

treated me without any care or attention. But I wanted to defend him against the misfortune he had suffered, and I was bitter at the fatal powers that can accidentally and indifferently destroy a man; I felt some secret, elusive calculation of these forces in the fact that they had destroyed Maltsev, and not—let's say—me. I knew there was no such calculation in nature, in our human, mathematical sense, but I saw how facts do occur that prove the existence of hostile circumstances which are destructive of human life, and I saw how these terrible forces shatter the lives of selected, outstanding people. I decided not to surrender to them, because I could sense inside myself something which could not exist in the external forces of nature and in our destiny, I felt the special distinction of being a man. And I was in bitter despair, and I made up my mind to stand up against this, although I did not know how it would have to be done.

5

The next summer I passed my examination to qualify as a locomotive engineer, and started to go out on my own in an "SU" engine working on local passenger lines. Almost every time I hitched my engine to a train standing at the station platform, I saw Maltsev sitting there on a painted bench. With his arm leaning on a cane held between his legs he turned his passionate, sensitive face with its sunken, unseeing eyes in the direction of the locomotive and greedily breathed in the smell of burning and of lubricating oil while he listened carefully to the rhythmic working of the steam pump. I had no way of comforting him, and I went on, and he stayed there.

The summer went by. I worked on my engine, and I often saw Alexander Vassilievich, not only on the station platform but also on the street where he used to walk slowly, feeling his way with his cane. His cheeks were sunken, and he had aged a good deal; he had enough to live on—he was given a pension, his wife was working, and they had no children, but grief and his drab destiny were consuming Alexander Vassilievich, and his body was growing thin from his unceasing sorrow. I talked with him sometimes, but I could see that it was boring for him to chat about trifles and to try to satisfy himself with my polite comforting, and I could see that a blind man, too, is still a completely competent and full-fledged man.

"Go away!" he would say when he heard me saying well intentioned things.

But I was an angry man, too, and once when he told me to leave him alone, as he usually did, I told him:

"Tomorrow I'm taking a train out at ten thirty. If you'll sit there quietly, I'll take you along in the engine."

Maltsev agreed: "All right. I'll behave. Let me hold something in my hand, though, give me the reverse lever. I won't turn it."

"You certainly won't turn it," I told him. "If you do, I'll give you a piece of coal to hold instead, and I'll never take you out in the engine again."

The blind man said nothing more; he was so eager to climb into an engine again that he humbled himself in front of me.

The next day I invited him to exchange his painted bench for a seat in the cabin of my engine, and I went to meet him and to help him climb up into the train.

When we started to move, I put Alexander Vassilievich in my own driver's seat, I placed one of his hands on the reverse lever and the other on the brake and then I put my own hands on top of his. I drove with my own hands, as I had to, but his hands were working too. Maltsev sat there silently, and he listened to me, enjoying the motion of the train, the wind in his face, and the work. He was concentrating so hard that he forgot his blind man's sorrow, and a gentle kind of happiness lit up the helpless face of this man for whom just to feel an engine was pure bliss.

On the return trip we traveled the same way: Maltsev sat in the driver's seat, while I stood up, leaning over him and holding my hands over his. Maltsev had already become so used to working in this way that I had only to exert the slightest pressure on his hand and he would sense exactly what I wanted. This man who had formerly been the complete master of his engine was trying to overcome his loss of sight and to feel the world around him by other means, so he could work, and justify his being alive.

On some of the quiet, straight runs, I walked away from Maltsev altogether, and looked out from the assistant's place.

We were already on the approach to Tolubeyev, our regular run was finishing satisfactorily, and we were arriving on time. But on the very last section a yellow signal light flashed against us. I did not reduce speed ahead of time, and drove up to the signal under full steam. Maltsev was sitting there quietly, holding his left hand on the reverse lever: I was watching my teacher with a secret hope. . . .

"Cut down the steam!" Maltsev said to me.

I said nothing, my heart was pounding inside me.

Then Maltsev stood up from his seat, put his hand on the steam valve, and closed it.

"I see a yellow light," he said, and he pulled the brake lever toward him.

"But maybe you're just imagining, again, that you see the light?" I said to Maltsev.

He turned his face toward me, and began to cry. I walked over to him, and kissed him.

"Go on, and drive the engine all the way now, Alexander Vassilievich: now you can see all the lights there are!"

He drove the train into Tolubeyev without my help. After

work was over, I walked home with Maltsev, and we sat there together all evening and all night.

I was as frightened of leaving him alone as if he were my own son, without any protection against all the sudden, hostile forces loose in our fierce and beautiful world.

## ABOUT THE TYPE

The text of this book has been set in Trump Mediaeval. Designed by Georg Trump for the Weber foundry in the late 1950s, this typeface is a modern rethinking of the Garalde Oldstyle types (often associated with Claude Garamond) that have long been popular with printers and book designers.

Trump Mediaeval is a trademark of
Linotype-Hell AG and/or its subsidiaries

Printed and bound by R. R. Donnelley & Sons,
Harrisonburg, Virginia

Book design by Red Canoe, Deer Lodge, Tennessee
Caroline Kavanagh
Deb Koch

# TITLES IN SERIES